Praise for

"I'm in love with a grieving misfit driving around with a donkey-shaped piñata in an old van held together by duct tape. Her name is Penny Rush. . . . The great miracle of McKenzie's writing . . . is how she manages to transform misery into gentle humor. . . . The irresistible sound of *The Dog of the North* is Penny's voice, composed of mingled strains of good cheer and naked lament. . . . Darkly hilarious."

—Ron Charles, *The Washington Post*

"'I was used to being the object of anger,' the down-on-her-luck narrator of this vibrant picaresque says. In her midthirties, she flees a dead-end job and a failing marriage, embarking on a journey that leads to a confrontation with childhood trauma. En route, she contends with her possibly homicidal grandmother; lives in a van owned by her grandmother's ailing accountant; searches for her mother and stepfather, who disappeared years earlier; eludes her abusive biological father; and kindles a promising new romance. 'I seemed to be trapped in a continual reckoning between present and past,' she notes. McKenzie parlays that reckoning into a vibrant novel that combines slapstick comedy with poignancy."

—*The New Yorker*

"The plot gallops along. . . . As the caper wanes, McKenzie allows Penny a modicum of closure. This is the sweet, yet cautionary note the book ends on. The past is a sinkhole, it seems to say. It'll swallow you, if you're not careful, and your Land Cruiser, too."

—Erin Somers, *The New York Times Book Review*

"Gloriously entertaining. *The Dog of the North* addresses all sorts of sadness, but it is mainly an exuberant comedy of human behavior at its nuttiest. It is so engaging that I read it in great gulps, immersed in the sheer eccentricity of her world."   —Kate Saunders, *The Times*

"[A] delightful narrative . . . Sadly, no matter how many times you try to pause so it won't be over, it still ends—with a decent outcome for its protagonist, thank heaven, because by that time you will be fully in love with Penny. McKenzie has created a wonderful addition to the crew of damaged characters beloved by readers, so very endearing and real."
          —*Kirkus Reviews* (starred review)

"Endearing and quirky . . . With the anxious and well-meaning Penny at the helm, McKenzie brings sincerity to the otherwise zany proceedings. This whirlwind tale has heart to spare."   —*Publishers Weekly*

"Zany and fun . . . Penny is always sharp, ready for the other shoe to drop, and lovable. This spinning, upside-down roller coaster of a novel is a delightful portrait of the definitive chaos of love and family and per-fect for fans of Carl Hiaasen and George Saunders."   —*Booklist*

"For readers who like their books odd, haunting, strange, and surpris-ing . . . Through Penny's eyes, we see the beauty in the seemingly bro-ken, in the flawed stories we tell ourselves—and what happens when those stories delightfully shatter."   —Freya Sachs, *BookPage*

"The pleasure in reading Penny's story, then, comes not from seeing what her travails reveal about America, but from discovering what they reveal about her. McKenzie is excellent at meticulously unveiling why Penny thinks and acts the way she does and what led her to her current circumstances. . . . Like Holden Caulfield in *The Catcher in the Rye*,

Penny is a seriously wounded narrator, deeply reticent about her pain, if not in outright denial." —Reed Jackson, *Spectrum Culture*

"Sometimes the modern world seems like an inescapable hellscape. Then I remember that Elizabeth McKenzie is writing novels, and I feel better again. *The Dog of the North* is exactly as much fun as *The Big Lebowski* or one of Charles Portis's comic jaunts, filled with dialogue so fun you'll want to say it aloud and a blissful parade of American eccentrics. Trust me—there's a guy who tries to invent something called Steak in a Trout™." —Ed Park, author of *Same Bed Different Dreams*

"What a wonderfully weird yet deeply familiar world Elizabeth McKenzie has sketched in *The Dog of the North*! These pages are full of the absurdly funny alongside the absurdly tragic—hairpieces, talking fish, disappeared parents, a scalpel-happy grandmother, gastrointestinal disasters—the strangeness is not mere quirk. McKenzie's brilliance lies in her deadpan gaze and cool wit, which shows us how inherently odd reality itself is. Families are odd. Homes are odd. California is odd. Dogs and hair and steak and trout are odd. Look up from this book and feel understood in your own inexplicable oddity. A joy, a pleasure, and an addictive read with an ultimately hopeful core that recalls Haruki Murakami, Sayaka Murata, Richard Brautigan, and Miranda July." —Sanjena Sathian, author of *Gold Diggers*

"Even funnier, even more romantic than McKenzie's wonderful last, *The Portable Veblen*, this is a screwball comedy worthy of a Preston Sturges screenplay. You will be surprised, delighted, and grateful to be aboard *The Dog of the North* with the admirable Penny Rush as she faces every challenge her wild and crazy family can throw at her. A book that lifts the spirits." —Karen Joy Fowler, author of *Booth*

PENGUIN BOOKS

THE DOG OF THE NORTH

Elizabeth McKenzie is the author of the novel *The Portable Veblen*, which was longlisted for the National Book Award and shortlisted for the Baileys Women's Prize; a collection, *Stop That Girl*, shortlisted for The Story Prize; and the novel *MacGregor Tells the World*, a *Chicago Tribune*, *San Francisco Chronicle*, and *Library Journal* Best Book of the Year. Her work has appeared in *The New Yorker*, *The Atlantic*, and *The Best American Nonrequired Reading*, and was recorded for NPR's *Selected Shorts*.

Also by Elizabeth McKenzie

The Portable Veblen
MacGregor Tells the World
Stop That Girl

The Dog
of the North

Elizabeth McKenzie

PENGUIN BOOKS

PENGUIN BOOKS
An imprint of Penguin Random House LLC
penguinrandomhouse.com

First published in the United States of America by Penguin Press,
an imprint of Penguin Random House LLC, 2023
Published in Penguin Books 2024

ISBN 9780593300718 (paperback)

THE LIBRARY OF CONGRESS HAS CATALOGED THE HARDCOVER EDITION AS FOLLOWS:

Names: McKenzie, Elizabeth, 1958– author.
Title: The dog of the north : a novel / Elizabeth McKenzie.
Description: New York : Penguin Press, 2023.
Identifiers: LCCN 2022027971 (print) | LCCN 2022027972 (ebook) |
ISBN 9780593300695 (hardcover) | ISBN 9780593300701 (ebook)
Subjects: LCGFT: Novels.
Classification: LCC PS3613.C556 D64 2023 (print) | LCC PS3613.C556 (ebook) |
DDC 813/.6—dc23/eng/20220613
LC record available at https://lccn.loc.gov/2022027971
LC ebook record available at https://lccn.loc.gov/2022027972

Printed in the United States of America
1st Printing

DESIGNED BY MEIGHAN CAVANAUGH

For C.E.R.

"For a while I went berserk and wished
it would never end . . ."

Part 1

1

My plan was to catch the ten o'clock train from Salinas to Santa Barbara, seeing as I had no car and a few problems to deal with there. It is never convenient to be without a car in California, but I was pretty sure I would be able to borrow my grandfather's Honda station wagon once I arrived. And Burt Lampey would pick me up. Though I had to leave suddenly, the timing was good, as I'd been living in a motel for the past three weeks and was looking for a good excuse to quit my job. You might say the Santa Barbara crises had been timed perfectly for my circumstances. Extricating myself from Santa Cruz, the site of my most recent failures, was very welcome, actually a relief. So I took a bus to Watsonville, transferring to another that would take me through Castroville to the station, and, seeing as how chaotic things had been recently, the thought of being a passenger with nothing to do for the day but sit still while in motion was something to look forward to.

Even so, I was on edge. After all, I'd be facing two unpleasant situations through which great anger was sure to be directed at me. I was used to being the object of anger, especially recently, but that didn't make it any easier.

Adding to my general unease were thoughts of what I was leaving behind. In the past twenty-four hours I'd abruptly left my job, burning a bridge that I was happy to cross for the last time, and I'd confronted my husband, Sherman: *I know all about Bebe Sinatra and the cocaine.*

True, I took the cowardly way and wrote emails, but they were masterpieces of obfuscation. In no way did they reveal the depth of my disgust at what precipitated this rupture. They were the whimper rather than the bang at the end of my world, but I could not move forward if I were to permit myself the full brunt of my feelings.

As the bus neared Salinas, I started to breathe evenly. A hair glinted on my sleeve; I pulled it off and let it fly out the slightly opened window into the fields of brussels sprouts and artichokes flanking the highway. A rotten smell, like that from the neglected vegetable bin at the bottom of my last refrigerator, was blowing in. Despite the fact that I was finished with Sherman, I wondered where he was and what he was doing, and if I'd always wonder, no matter how humiliating the final days of our time together. For instance, last month, pouring Sherman's dirty clothes into the washer, I discovered a slightly worn pink thong. "Yuck, what's this?" I said.

"Oh. I found a bag of stuff at a bus stop. Thought maybe you might like it."

Repulsed, I held up the abbreviated scrap. "But the back part went up somebody else's buttock crevice."

"Can't you just say crack like everybody else?" Sherman said with disgust, peeling back yet another layer of his true feelings toward me.

"Sure. Whose crack was it anyway?" Nothing but anguish would compel me to say a thing like that.

Eventually I boarded the train and settled in. Just after the Zephyr left the station, the train door whooshed open, ushering in a cloud of patchouli oil and the sound of jingling metal objects. A woman came up the aisle and purposefully took the seat across from me. Small brass bells and coins had been sewn onto her billowy patchwork skirt. She then made eye contact and asked if I'd like to have my palm read for twenty dollars.

Twenty dollars was a lot to me, but there I was, heading off into a great unknown. Once I dealt with the issues in Santa Barbara, my future was up for grabs. I was like the strand of hair blowing out the window, uprooted, alone. If ever there was a time I might want my palm read, this was it. So I agreed to it and she took my right hand and began to study the fleshy side, tracing her finger along some of the lines. At last she said, "I can see that in your past lives you experienced many episodes of aggression. Here"—she pointed to a place where two creases intersected—"I can see that you were once beheaded, and also strangled." She looked up to gauge my reaction. Because I'm accustomed to disguising my feelings, she saw no reason not to press on. "And you are easily taken advantage of."

I can't quote the rest of her findings, as I was immediately consumed by the information already imparted. For a moment I wondered if she was mocking me for accepting her services, yet I wasn't willing to rule out that she had provided me with a valuable insight.

The main problem was that the people sitting in front of me were talking loudly enough that I could hear them, and I'm unable to listen to two things at once, and quickly realized I'd much rather listen to them than this bleak history of bodily injury. I gave her the twenty and told her that would be enough.

The people in front of me were discussing everyday matters, but it was somehow pleasant to listen to them. They needed to replace their garbage disposal because their teenage son had fed avocado pits into it. They'd go to a favorite restaurant in L.A. that evening. They had a meeting with someone tomorrow about a tax issue, but didn't seem worried about it. Every now and then I heard them laugh.

I suddenly realized I was being transported to the backseat of our family car with my parents talking up front. Car trips always brought out the best in my mother, a geologist by profession, whereas at home she was often restless and moody. So, while I had some of my best memories of them from the times spent with my sister in the backseat, any pleasure I took was quickly obliterated by the cruel irony that on a long drive, some years later, they disappeared off the face of the earth.

My parents had already taken the step of vacating the northern hemisphere. They were creating a new life for themselves in Australia ostensibly because they liked the climate and the geomorphology, enjoyed the adventure, and got good returns on the exchange rate. But it's also possible to say that they went to denounce the American Dream and avoid the various unpleasant people who had damaged their lives. We, my sister and I, had taken their emigration in stride. In fact, my sister had joined them. But then they had to take it a step further and vanish altogether. My father, also known as my stepfather, also known as Hugh, was as detail-oriented and protective as a spouse could be. They were two people who would leave nothing to chance, who had planned every day of that trip, who provided us with an itinerary before leaving, complete with phone numbers and addresses of their stops along the way. The last known witness to see them alive, at a petrol station in Mount Isa, saw nothing to arouse his concern. Just a middle-aged couple filling up and checking the air pressure in their tires. My sister and I did not know for several days that they had failed to show up at their next destination. Nor was their car ever recovered. Search-and-rescue teams scoured the area for weeks and found nothing.

Though nearly five years had passed, I hadn't really been able to accept or even think about it.

In the late afternoon, I stood outside the Santa Barbara train station with my bag, waiting for Burt Lampey. He'd offered to pick me up and put me up for the night, and we were to have dinner to discuss the plan we'd execute the following day vis-à-vis my grandmother, Dr. Pincer. I had never met Burt in person but had spoken with him a number of times by now. As Pincer's accountant, he had become one of the few people she trusted. Little did Pincer know that Burt called me secretly every time he saw her to keep me updated on her condition.

The day was still bright and warm. As a child I'd spent weeks at a time here with my grandparents and, despite how things had turned out, still had fond feelings for the place. I'd visited over the years too many times to count, though never before by train. I paced in front of the station, scanning the parking lot and beyond, hoping Burt hadn't forgotten. Finally, an old, sea-green van entered the lot and pulled up before me. It had a number of gashes and dents on the body and looked slightly sinister. The man driving leaned over and rolled down the passenger window and called out, "Penny?"

It was Burt. Over the phone, his voice had filled me with confidence.

He threw it in park and jumped out. As he rounded the dented front end, I felt an unexpected jolt of terror. It was a jolt I experienced from time to time when I realized I was about to be thrown into an extended conversation with someone who might notice something about me they didn't like.

Burt reached for my hand. He was a large man with a significant mane of brown hair and a friendly face. He was wearing baggy green shorts, a white T-shirt with the name of a local brewery on it, and high-top white Nikes with black socks.

"How was the trip?" he asked.

I decided not to mention my encounter with the palm reader. I didn't want him to form the idea that I was someone who regularly squandered money. In fact, I was very careful with money, having so little of it. The palm reader had been a whimsical extravagance to celebrate my escape from Santa Cruz, and a good reminder that whimsical extravagances were mostly disappointing.

"Good," I said, in my typically conversationally stunted fashion. "I haven't taken a train in years," I struggled to add, hating small talk but knowing that this kind of comment was considered normal.

"Hop in," he said, holding open the passenger door.

He revealed with that gesture the seat I was to take, gamely held together with duct tape. Once I was in, he slammed the door so hard my eardrums buckled. Between us rumbled a large hump under a blue quilted vinyl cover. The engine, Burt said. I looked in the back, making out a tangle of objects—a hose, a bicycle, boxes, suitcases, an old ironing board, a musty, donkey-shaped piñata, a tire.

"Forgive my mess," Burt said, when he took his seat at the wheel. "I'm kind of between things."

I didn't know anything about Burt's personal life, so I said, "Oh, I see. That makes sense."

"Wouldn't want to do anything radical until your grandmother's squared away."

Radical? I wasn't sure what he meant, nor why my grandmother had anything to do with it.

We started down State Street in the squeaking van. I couldn't help thinking of my childhood days in Santa Barbara when we'd come watch the yearly fiesta and State Street was closed off and beautiful white horses paraded past, bearing pretty ladies with flowers in their hair. And the white rumps of the horses flashed in the sun. My grandmother and grandfather were still married then, but likely already hated each other. At the time I didn't realize such a thing was possible. The fiesta evaporated as we pulled into the parking lot of a modern office building, where Burt found a space.

"Here?"

"This is it. Hop on out."

I grabbed my bag and followed him into the building. At the center of the lobby stood an open flight of stairs made of cement slabs mounted on steel supports, under which a garden of ferns and other struggling houseplants had been assigned to simulate a grotto. I followed him to the second floor, down a hall to a door bearing his plaque: BURTON LAMPEY, CPA.

As he unlocked the door and pushed it open, I came to the sudden and horrible realization that this was where he was living. I sputtered, "Oh my god, Burt, no! I'm really imposing. I can stay in a motel."

"No imposition at all," Burt said.

The air in his office was stuffy and ripe, a blend of masculine aromas. It looked like a dorm room—sleeping bag on the couch, pile of pizza boxes on the desk, plastic laundry basket filled with beer bottles, shirts on hangers hooked onto the bookcase, a stick of deodorant and a bottle of mouthwash on a shelf.

"The couch is all yours," he said generously. But how could I sleep in the same room with Burt Lampey? I began to panic. He was a trusted friend of the family, wasn't he? Certainly he wouldn't try to molest me in my sleep. But how could I relax? Did the window open, was there any fresh air?

"But what about you?" I managed to say.

"Back here," he said, pointing behind his desk. "I'll be on the floor and loving it."

I craned my neck and saw that he'd planned ahead with another sleeping bag and pillow.

"No reason to hang out here, let's go get something to eat!" he said.

With that, it seemed to be decided. I currently had a total of just under eight hundred fifty dollars from selling my 1987 Chevette, with nothing in savings because Sherman's business had proved to be an insatiable money pit. Anything I could avoid paying for, the better.

We walked down State Street to Burt's favorite Mexican restaurant and were lucky enough to be seated in a spacious booth. My spirits picked up. The restaurant was popular and festive and the smells emanating from nearby tables made me feel ravenous. Before I could say anything, Burt ordered a pitcher of margaritas. I supposed there was no reason to stop him.

"Well, we finally meet," Burt said. "How long's this been going on, a couple years now?"

"I can't tell you how much we appreciate how helpful you've been to her," I said.

"I'm a sucker for stubborn old mules," he said.

I nodded and laughed, wanting him to know that it was perfectly fine to call my grandmother an old mule.

"She's never turned on you?" I asked, recalling the ill-fated trip I'd taken with her a few years back.

"Only once," Burt said with a note of pride. It seemed he'd picked up Pincer to take her to lunch, but just after they drove off, she claimed to have left behind a letter she needed to mail and demanded he turn around and go back. Burt said he had another appointment after their lunch and there wasn't time, that he would grab the letter when he brought her home. At that point, she said if he didn't stop the car she'd report him for kidnapping. He tried to calm her down, but she kept on. She told him she'd never liked him, never liked the way he dressed, never liked the way he looked. She accused him of embezzling and said he was one of the ugliest men alive. She said she only ever put up with him because he was too stupid to know he was being used.

"She said my accounting skills were nothing to write home about and that she could do it in her sleep if she had to. And that not only was I professionally inept and unattractive, but the most boring man she'd ever met! She reamed me. I'd never experienced anything like it, even from my wife."

"How did you manage to stay friends?" I wondered.

"Next time I saw her, it was like nothing happened. I feel sorry for the old bat," Burt said. "Anyway, I don't know if one day will be enough to make a dent over there. I still think she's going to have to be forcibly removed and the place cleaned out with a bulldozer," Burt asserted.

I knew I'd never want to forcibly remove her. "But her house means everything to her."

"Bottom line, get the gun," Burt said. "That's the biggie. Until we have the gun, nobody can do anything in there."

I nodded grimly. The urgency of the situation stemmed from a recent incident involving Meals on Wheels. On Pincer's behalf I'd applied for their services, but the day they showed up, she threatened to shoot if they didn't vacate the premises immediately. Someone had seen her wielding an object that looked like a bazooka. That led to a complaint to the police, which led to Adult Protective Services, which led to the involvement of a woman by the name of Ruth Perry, who warned me there would be swift consequences if we didn't disarm her and provide for her needs immediately.

Now the pitcher came, along with our glasses rimmed with salt. Burt poured, and soon we were clinking the glasses together and saying cheers, with the camaraderie of soldiers on the eve of battle. The margarita was great. I was glad Burt had recognized the necessity of it. He'd also ordered nachos and guacamole as a starter and was digging into both with gusto.

Under the influence, Burt began to rhapsodize about my grandmother. "She's a great lady, whatever you say at the end of the day," he said. "A great lady. I've learned a lot from her. She's one of the world's great people," he said, to my surprise.

"What do you like about her?"

"The woman is an original thinker. She has her own opinions and she doesn't suffer fools. She's not afraid to speak her mind. And she's as strong as an ox, let me tell you. You should see her jump into the Dog."

This demanded clarification.

"My van. Dog of the North. All I got at the end of the marriage."

"Really, that's all you got?"

"What can I say, the woman's greedy. When she was greedy for me, I liked it."

"How old are you, Burt?" I asked, disinhibited by the delicious drink.

"Guess."

"Sixty-five?"

"Hey, ouch! I'm fifty-seven! Shit."

"I'm really bad at ages!" I apologized.

"Even with this head of hair? Which is a toupee, by the way. A very expensive one."

I hadn't suspected, though it was true his hair was unusually dense and mink-like.

"You're lucky you're meeting me this month," he said. "Next month you'd tell me I look ninety."

"What happens next month?"

"My brother gets it. We switch off."

Was he telling me he and his brother shared a hairpiece? How could that be? I hated it when I wasn't sure what someone was saying, and always took it to be my fault, an auditory processing problem. So I said, "Cool," hoping that was the right response. "But isn't it inconvenient—when you don't have it?"

"Of course it is. But there are such things as hats."

"There sure are," I said, still not sure I understood him correctly.

"How about you? How old are you? I'm going to guess thirty," Burt said.

I shrugged. "You're very gallant. Thirty-five."

"A great age. Boy, how things change. When we were married, Jenny and I used to drive up north in the Dog and spend a few weeks every summer camping in Washington and British Columbia. We were planning to retire in Washington State on one of those islands in the San Juans. All my life I thought how great it would be to have a few feet of beachfront and a kayak. Throw in a Panama hat and a cocktail and we'd be set. Well, I thought about it so much, sometimes it feels like I really did have it."

I asked why he called it the Dog of the North; he said his ex had named it in honor of a beloved novel with a similar name. Literary references aside, he said, the name combined two of his favorites, trips north and dogs.

Soon we were served hot plates smothered with enchiladas, rice, and beans. Burt ate lustily. It was sad to ponder his shattered dreams for his marriage and future, especially since I had so many of those myself.

"Have another!" Burt said, refilling my salted glass. "So, enough about me. Your grandmother tells me you're separating from your husband, and she's very disappointed."

"I know," I said. "Sherman was always very nice to her, but she doesn't know what he's really like."

"How could she know? We discover things about our spouses that nobody else ever will. Marriage is one long striptease of the soul."

"Right," I said, taking a large gulp of my drink. "Exactly. That is so true."

"It'll be a cold day in hell before I marry again," Burt said.

"I would think twice for sure," I said.

We clinked glasses again.

"You know what I found out about my wife?" Burt said, gulping down some beans.

"What?"

"That she couldn't stand having sex with me. She announced that when we went to a marriage counselor. Was the first I'd heard about it."

"I can see how that would wreck things," I said.

"I had plenty of girlfriends before I met her. They didn't seem to mind."

I couldn't fail to notice the erotic undertone of the comment. I was completely unable to say anything in return, and Burt, like a male bird who had successfully flashed his plumage, sat back and radiated some form of conquest simply for having crowed about himself. But whether or not that conquest was of me or of the memory of the plenty of girlfriends who didn't mind him, it was impossible to determine.

Burt's physical appearance was reasonably attractive. He had broad shoulders and large features. He would look better bald than bewigged, I thought. He appeared to be clean. His hands were large and his fingernails trimmed. Reluctantly I imagined what it would be like to come over to his side of the table and make out with him in the booth, which in turn led me to wonder exactly how elastic my desires had, or should, become.

"So what went wrong with yours?" he was asking.

Not my favorite topic, but the margarita was making me feel relaxed and insouciant.

"Well." Disturbing memories flashed through my mind and I started laughing in reverse proportion to any humor in it. "Ha ha ha. Ha ha ha!" Then my stomach clenched and tears popped from the corners of my eyes. Burt leaned in closer. "Sorry," I said, taking the kind of long, slow breath I'd been taught for moments like these. I stammered through a brief outline of the past few years—Sherman's gradual disillusionment with academia while working on his PhD, his abrupt purchase of a mobile knife-sharpening business, the growing frequency of his nights away from home before I caught on. "And it all got worse after my parents disappeared. Like, instead of trying to help me through it, he was mad."

"Wicked," Burt said. "Human psychology is nuts."

Fortunately, this seemed to satisfy his curiosity, and the conversation moved on. Burt told me that he had a daughter, but that she lived in Montreal and he rarely got to see her. The person he was closest to, he said, was his brother, who lived in San Francisco and was an attorney. To offer something in return, I told him that I still had a biological father named Gaspard who presented problems.

"Just what you need, more problems!" Burt said, suddenly clutching his midsection. "I honor your effort. Maybe we should head back and get rested for the big day."

I pulled out my wallet but Burt said, "No way, Penny, it's on me."

"No no no!" I protested weakly.

"Please."

"Well, okay. Thank you."

By the time he paid the bill, we'd reviewed the plan for the next day. I had a cleaning team scheduled to arrive about an hour after Burt and Pincer's departure from the house. I'd search for the gun while directing their efforts, which were to be aimed at decluttering, dusting, vacuuming, sterilizing, and whatever else was necessary in light of the horrible state of affairs there. Burt had created an itinerary that would keep Pincer away for at least seven to eight hours. It was anyone's guess how she'd react when they returned, but this was the chance we had to take.

Burt wobbled when he rose to his feet. Was he drunk? I did not want to go back to the office of a drunken man. Coming out of the restaurant, he headed off the wrong way.

"Burt, it's this way, isn't it?"

He pivoted; we shuffled down the sidewalk for a few minutes. I could hear him breathing heavily from his mouth.

"I'm sorry, Penny, could you excuse me a second?" We'd come to a gas station on the corner, and he took off abruptly for the mini-mart, disappearing inside.

I waited by a clump of star jasmine growing by the sidewalk. The scent of the flowers mingled with the smell of gasoline and motors, reminding me of my grandfather Arlo, whom I'd see right after dealing with Pincer and who was one of my favorite people. He used to have a war-era jeep that he'd tune and fix whenever necessary, and while tinkering with it, he'd hand me a greasy part to put aside, telling me what it was and what it did. Everything he told me seemed special. Now I had four messages on my phone from his wife, Doris, complaining about the people who were coming into the house to help since he'd had a fall.

Minutes passed. When it seemed like Burt had been in the mini-mart forever, I walked past the pumps and went inside. There, before me, sitting on the floor next to a rack of potato chips, was Burt. An attendant with a mop was working on the men's room, which had been blocked by a sandwich board saying it was out of commission. The whole store smelled like a sewer.

"You okay?" I asked, kneeling beside him.

"Really, just fine," Burt said robotically.

"Can you stand up?"

"Of course I can," Burt said, still sitting on the linoleum. Looking at Burt from above, I could now see that his hair was a wig, by way of its unnatural density obscuring any sign of a scalp. Further, it was askew, as if he'd taken it off in the bathroom and hastily thrown it back on.

The store manager was a short man with black hair and large arms that dangled like game fish on a gambrel. He motioned for me to follow him outside.

"You with that gentleman?"

I nodded.

"He's not a well man," the manager said.

"What happened?"

"He just flooded the bathroom with the foulest crap I've ever seen in my life, and that's saying something. Definitely not normal. You need to get him to a doctor right away."

"Oh wow," I said. "So sorry."

"I can't even describe it."

"Well, thanks for letting me know."

"It was not the normal color."

"Okay! Sorry."

I followed him back into the mini-mart, where Burt was still on the floor. I purchased several bottles of water, some Imodium, and some saltines. Then I helped Burt up and walked with him out to the sidewalk.

"Burt, I'm going to call a taxi, okay?"

"I don't need a taxi," Burt said. "I'm fine."

"The gas station manager said he thinks you might be really sick. You sure?"

"The gas station manager said that? What the hell does he know, pardon the expression?"

"I guess he saw something that worried him," I said.

"I see a lot of things that worry me, but I try to keep my nose out of other people's business," Burt said. "Jeez. I ate a little too much. Forgive me!"

"Okay, sure," I said. "I got some supplies if you need them."

"What kind of supplies?"

"Crackers, Imodium, that kind of thing."

"Shit."

We waddled back to his office building. He took the stairs slowly, huffing volubly. By the time we entered his office he was almost out of breath.

"Burt, are you sure I can't take you to a doctor?" I asked again.

"I'm gonna lie down and get some rest. Just a little indigestion. Seriously, nothing to worry about," Burt said, falling to his knees behind the desk.

"Well, if you need anything during the night, I'm here," I said.

"Good to know. Thanks."

"Hope you feel better in the morning," I said.

I won't spend an inordinate amount of time describing that night on the couch in Burt Lampey's office, but it would be an omission not to mention it. Almost immediately after Burt hit the floor, he began to erupt. First, and by no means that unusual, came the jagged breathing, with the sound of an industrial-sized siphon on the intake, the motorized exhalations on the out. I was accustomed to snoring. Sherman, with his barrel chest, his habits of smoking and overeating, had been a heavy night breather. Snoring could be seen as beautiful, I recalled, having read an advice column once in which a woman wrote that now that her husband was dead, she would give anything to hear his dear snore again. But I wasn't sure one could call what Burt was doing snoring. It seemed as if his body were struggling for its very survival, as if every breath were a battle. I could hear his body twitching around, the myoclonic jerks of his surrendering muscles. More than once a limb struck the desk and made it shake. The air of the room seemed rent by his every breath. This, combined with his episode at the gas station, made me wonder if Burt was truly all right. A belch rang out that should have awakened him, but on he slept. Then came a number of sphincter-popping blasts, and I burrowed down in the bag. I felt more miserable than I had in some time.

Worse, it was one of those mummy bags that narrow to nothing where the feet go. The feeling of having my feet tethered, like an animal about to be hung on a hook, was enough to send me into a silent panic. I considered climbing out of the bag and using it for a cover, but it was slippery and would probably slide off during the night, leaving me exposed.

Eventually I dared to stick my head out to see if the atmosphere had cleared. Obviously I would not stay there the following night. I even considered taking the sleeping bag down to the indoor garden at the base of the stairs and curling up among the plants.

Burt's hellish descent into slumber seemed to have come to an end, and a steady growl replaced the explosive and desperate snorts and gasps. But instead of feeling relief, I realized that I was as depressed now as I had been in Santa Cruz, and that this ache would follow me wherever I was, at least for the time being, and that Sherman had merely been the tool with which my inner depths had been plumbed, exposing all my limitations and vulnerabilities. I knew I had clung to Sherman well past the expiration date, making things far worse than they might have been had we ended things sooner.

. . .

I awoke in the night in a sweat.

My god, where was I? My body was encased in a rancid-smelling sleeve perched on a brick-hard slab. I felt unbearably itchy. Strange little lights, green and red, were blinking in the blackness. All at once I heard a rustling sound, whereupon I detected a ghostly quadruped moving through the room. I let out a piercing scream.

"Penny, it's me!" Burt cried out. "Gotta use the john. Sorry to wake you."

With that, the door of his office flew open, the brilliant light from the hallway blinding me for a second before I was able to see Burt scurrying away, hunched over in his undershirt and shorts.

I looked at my phone. Three-thirty a.m. I dreaded having to listen to Burt fall asleep again, yet couldn't persuade myself to leave and face the unknown. I burrowed down in the bag and turned over, and when Burt finally returned, clumsily slamming the door and stumbling to his nest by his desk, I didn't answer when he said good night.

2

For the rest of the night, sleep was out of the question. I was assaulted from within and without. Burt's innards burbled like the steamy, sulfurous geysers I'd once seen at Yellowstone. And I was nervous about the day ahead, remembering the last time I tried to help Pincer and what came of it.

A few years back, Pincer had been working up a scheme to return to her hometown of Tyler, Texas, where her beloved dad had once been mayor, where her mother had been poet laureate, where the family had been respected as among the original European settlers dating back to the Republic of Texas. Growing up in California, I did not fully appreciate, nor understand, *the pride of the Texans*. For *the pride of the Texans* ran deep. Pincer still carried the accent. Her house was filled with the furniture of the ancestors, each heavy piece with a story. Her great-grandfather owned thousands of acres. Her grandfather was a historian and surveyor. They'd had a ranch called Seven Springs in the rolling hills outside of town. Who knew they'd find oil there one day and fill it with derricks? Who knew they'd frack and cause the springs to disappear forever into the earth?

To aid her return, Pincer leaned on a distant cousin named Frances and began a series of pilgrimages to Tyler to pick out a house using the services of another distant cousin named Tom, who happened to be a real estate agent. In no time he managed to sell her a large new house in an upscale development. This house came with all the latest amenities, including a Jacuzzi bath. Impulsively, Pincer had movers take a truckload of items there that had once been shipped to her in Santa Barbara, things originally from the family house in Tyler. Back to Tyler the big old Eastlake-style antiques went. But shortly after this decisive move, she had a falling-out with Cousin Frances. She called me and said she'd discovered that Frances was a duplicitous and evil woman, never to be trusted. She asked repeatedly if Sherman and I would be interested in moving to Tyler and living with her. When that didn't materialize, Pincer asked for my help packing up and bringing the stuff back to Santa Barbara.

It seemed a reasonable request. She and I flew to Tyler via Dallas. We arrived one spring evening at the grandiose house, where I was confronted by all the poignant evidence of her failed plan. I could plainly see the new life she had imagined for herself with samples of her handsome furniture on display in the large rooms. No rats! No clutter! New friends! A legacy sinecure! Half-unpacked boxes of china sat in the kitchen. Wardrobe boxes stood in the bedroom, bulging with Pincer's excess finery. Minks! Fancy party dresses! It hurt just to look at it.

Clean, spongy Berber carpet ran throughout the house. That night we opened a box of linens and created nests for ourselves to sleep in. I was glad to be there helping her. I felt a painful kind of love for her and all her delusions. Pincer was generally so off-base that she was practically a paragon of how not to live a life, and that made me love her more.

The next morning I woke early and started to pack. I was wrapping some dishes in newsprint in the kitchen when I looked up and saw Pincer staring at me from the doorway. "What on earth do you think you're doing?" she asked.

"Packing the dishes," I said.

"You'll not get away with this," she said.

"With what?"

The doorbell rang at that moment, to my relief.

It was her cousin Tom, the real estate agent, and a dead ringer for LBJ! We'd called him ahead of the trip to let him know she was ready to sell, but she now seemed to have no recollection of it.

"I don't know what the hell you two are up to," she said, after he'd come in carrying his briefcase and contracts ready to sign.

Still woefully unaware of the new state of mind taking hold of Pincer, Tom and I laughed and made small talk. Tom confirmed that it was a great time to sell. This was a hot neighborhood in a hot market. I remarked that there really wasn't much to do. The movers would come tomorrow.

"I take it you two have been communicating behind my back?" Pincer said.

"We wouldn't talk behind your back," joked Tom. "Would we, now, Penny? Louise, I have all the paperwork here," he said. "We can go over everything and I can show you comps and what I'm thinking for pricing."

Pincer began to bellow, calling Tom a goddamned son of a bitch, a conniving criminal, a disgrace to humanity, and a number of other things. I patted her shoulder, tried to calm her down, but Pincer gave me a shove that nearly sent me to the floor.

I was starting to understand that something was going terribly wrong.

Pincer was then eighty-two years old. She had large gnarled knuckles because she had arthritis. She'd had a stent put in her heart. But she'd never broken a bone. Her body was stout and solid. Her skin was fresh and made her look younger than her years. She'd been a rose queen of Tyler in her youth, a Texas beauty, a horse-woman at the University of Texas. Her eyes were still brilliant blue. She'd been a doctor, a pediatrician. She'd conducted research in Japan on radiation victims in Nagasaki. She was knowledgeable and articulate on many subjects, especially history, anthropology, and economics.

Tom backed toward the door, holding up his hands in surrender. "No problem, Louise. If now's not the time, let's wait. I'm happy to help anytime you need me." As he was about to turn and leave, he made the mistake of saying to me, "I'll be in touch."

This was the last straw. Pincer grabbed her phone and called 911, reporting Tom as an intruder; I had no choice but to run out to warn him.

"Sorry about this!" I called out.

He stood by his car shaking his head. "That woman's a bull hippopotamus!"

A police car showed up almost at once. When the officer approached us, Tom nodded and said, "Hey, Grady."

"Hey, Tom."

Tom gave Grady a quick rundown on the situation.

"Here they are, Officer!" Pincer yelled from the front door. "They're stealing me blind! They're here to take everything I have. I'm not going anywhere, and nobody's going to make me!"

"But we planned this together!" I called back.

Pincer slammed the door. Tom and Grady chatted in hushed tones, finally concluding they would back off for now. Tom told me to call later and check in, and after they drove away I took a seat on the front steps. Every few minutes I could hear her storming around inside, muttering to herself or some imagined foe. Though I knew Pincer eventually had fights with everybody, I had been shocked it had finally happened with me.

After about an hour, Pincer cracked the front door. I looked up and beheld a disheveled wreck. Her hair was sticking out in every direction, her eyes and nose red, her blouse untucked, her stretch pants atwist.

"What are you doing out there," she said, in a scratchy whisper.

"Just thinking," I said.

"What are we having for dinner?" she said.

We went to her favorite cafeteria. Pincer chose fried chicken, creamed spinach, grits, cornbread, and a piece of pecan pie. I had chicken-fried steak, collard greens, macaroni and cheese, and cherry pie. She regained her equilibrium talking about various men who'd been in love with her, before, during, and after her long and horrible marriage to my grandfather. One young man from UC Santa Barbara, half her age, had wanted to marry her. Those were the days!

Well, maybe we wouldn't finalize the sale of the house on this trip, I thought. It could be done later by phone. That was three years ago, and the house was still sitting there unoccupied because the topic sent Pincer into a hellspace. Same with her living conditions here in Santa Barbara. It seemed that, deep down, she trusted no one. How had that happened, how does someone come to trust no one?

At seven, Burt's alarm went off. When he failed to silence it, I called out: "Burt? Are you okay?"

His voice croaked from behind the desk. "Good morning, Penny. Moving slow." At last he shut the thing off.

"Bad night," I sympathized.

"Not the best."

"You feeling better?"

"Need some coffee."

"Want to go to that really good donut place?"

"Let's do that," Burt said.

I'd slept in my clothes, so I sat up and let the sleeping bag fall around my legs. It looked so benign now. There was a window behind Burt's desk that I was aching to throw open all the way. Through the blinds I could see a few cheerful clouds hanging over the mountains. I told Burt I'd wait outside so he could get ready in peace.

"Here, take these," he said, handing me his keys.

The building was coming alive with people clutching their coffees, opening their office doors. I clattered down the stairs and found Burt's banged-up Econoline in the parking lot, piebald with rust spots and Bondo. I wondered why he had such a horrible-looking vehicle and how my grandmother felt going around in it. Not that I believed a car defined a person; in fact, I admired people who didn't care what their car looked like. I only hoped Burt felt well enough to endure a day with her. And I really hoped I'd sleep better that night and was dreaming about a bed with clean sheets and a good lamp and a good book. Finally, I saw Burt advancing toward me across the parking lot. He looked awful.

"Donuts, you say," Burt said.

"If that sounds good to you. I never eat them anywhere except here." I looked at my watch—only seven-thirty. My need to start the day with these particular donuts was powerful, no matter what shape Burt was in.

He spoke not a word as he drove to the donut place, and my stomach knotted with dread. I wondered if he had regrets about the plan and resented me. I was always prepared to imagine that the person I was hanging around with had suddenly become enraged at me, but I had nevertheless failed to develop techniques for making things better. My instinct was to get away from them as fast as possible. Therefore, I bolted in and took some time filling a big pink donut box that surely couldn't fail to cheer up anybody on earth. When I returned to the van, Burt was draped over the steering wheel.

"Burt? Got you an apple fritter! Burt?"

"Thanks, Penny," Burt said, drawing himself up. I handed him his coffee first, and he basically poured it down his throat.

"You sure you're okay with the plan?"

"Sure thing," he said, starting the engine. "I just feel a little punk. But she'll do all the talking. That's how it is. I listen, she blabs."

"Okay. But we could reschedule. Really."

"Let's get it over with," Burt said.

We went west, crossing over the freeway to the country-like area where Pincer lived. There the lots were large and some people had horses. I remembered how my mother used to call these people "the horsey set" as an insult. But what could be better than having a horse? My mother had a lot of surprising criticisms to sprinkle around. We passed a lake and a golf course, reminding me of her hatred of golfers. Other stretches were overgrown with palms and pines and hedges of Cape honeysuckle. Nothing to object to there. Pincer lived on a short dead-end road, her driveway guarded with a tall iron gate. Burt had the key to the lock. Just short of the driveway, he stopped to let me out. "God help us," he said.

I laughed, despite the fact that Burt looked miserable. "Tonight's dinner's on me for sure."

"Not. Ready to think. About dinner. Yet," Burt said, belching sonorously.

As Burt proceeded to the gate, I pushed myself into the thick brush flanking the fence, where I would remain until Burt drove out with Pincer in the car. It seemed ridiculous to be hiding in the bushes outside my grandmother's house, but we'd honestly failed to come up with a better idea. The sound of birds and insects all around was pleasant, at least. I could smell the scent of pine sap. When I shifted my weight, the dry leaves beneath my feet crunched in a satisfying manner. I'd thought to wear long sleeves to prevent scratching, but various twigs were gouging my scalp, since I hadn't thought of a hat. Pressing farther in, but still avoiding the spiky centers of the agaves poking at me through the fence, I could see the lower reaches of Pincer's yard. In the twenty-five years since my grandfather moved out, she'd let everything grow wild. From where I stood, the house was fully hidden.

A wasp landed on my hand. I flicked it off and tucked my hands into my armpits, but not before checking my watch—still an hour before the cleaning crew would pull in. Once again I rehearsed:

Tear through the bedroom, find the gun, start clearing all surfaces and consolidating piles to allow for the cleanup, do some laundry, collect garbage in bags to take away in Burt's van later . . .

As my wait continued, I realized that Burt and I had not come up with a Plan B should something go wrong. Was something going wrong? Pincer was usually impatient, and I'd imagined her springing into Burt's van instantaneously upon his arrival. A range of possibilities began to present itself. She couldn't find her dark glasses. A phone call had delayed her. She'd asked Burt to help with something in the house.

Just then I heard somebody coming down the road—through the leaves I made out a young girl walking a low-lying hound. I wondered how visible I was and if I should step out and show myself, as I didn't want to frighten her. On the other hand, Burt and Pincer might come down the driveway at that very moment. As the girl drew closer, the hound began to pull on its leash toward me, sniffing wildly. All at once I saw a shock of recognition rip through its sausage-like body, and it began to bark and snarl, hurling itself at the shrubbery where I stood, its clenched snout thrusting closer with every lunge.

"I can see you," the girl said.

I stepped out onto the road.

"Casper! Quiet!" she said, and Casper was yanked back just as a sharp pain went through my hand. I looked down in time to see the slender black abdomen of a wasp curling into my flesh. With my other hand I struck it to the ground, where I stomped on it repeatedly until there was nothing left.

"It stung me," I cried.

"Why were you hiding?" she asked, not unreasonably.

She was likely around twelve years old, and wore long unfashionable pea-green shorts, a baggy T-shirt, short white socks, and old-fashioned blue Keds much like the ones I used to wear at that age.

"Kind of strange, I know," I said. "You see, I'm planning a surprise for my grandmother who lives here." I was keeping my ears peeled for the sound of the van coming down the driveway.

"Are you related to Dr. Pincer?" she asked.

I nodded. "You know her?"

"Not really," she said, "but everybody talks about her. I didn't know she had any family."

"She's getting older now, so we're trying to help," I said, blowing cool air on my sting.

"What's the surprise?" she asked.

"Well, we're going to clean up the house for her today while she's out."

"Oh. I thought you meant like a party and cake."

Casper had accepted me now, and was friskily licking his midsection.

"Well, nice to meet you," I said. "I'd better go back into my hiding spot before she sees me."

"I live over there, three houses from here," she said. "Everybody thinks she's weird, but she talked to me once and she wasn't that weird. She said, 'You're a girl and you can do anything and don't let any man stand in your way!' I thought that was pretty cool. Bye!"

This was exactly what my grandmother would say to me when I was young.

Though I'd stepped back into the brush, it wasn't long before I recognized the need to investigate. Too much time had elapsed. Out I came again. My ears were alert as I ran through the gate, cleaving to the shrubs on the side, holding my hand close like an injured paw. The house was situated so that the first thing one saw was the garage door, peeling paint in sheets the size of platters. Around the garage was a brick path that skirted Pincer's home medical office. I could hear nothing, and the silence was ominous. Surely Burt would have come for me if something was wrong, wouldn't he?

Squatting beneath the medical office windows, I finally detected some stirrings. With caution I rose and peered in.

In the foreground was a cluttered space crammed with boxes and tools and stacks of linens. Beyond was the old examination room. I squinted to make sure of what I was seeing. It appeared that Burt Lampey was stretched out on the examination table in nothing but his underwear. Pincer was leaning over his nearly naked body holding a silver instrument.

"Grandmother! Hello! It's me! Let me in!"

Pincer turned and recognized me through the window. "Penny? Get in here!" she called, and I waded through the bushes to the door. Inside, I pushed past the boxes and other clutter to get into the room.

"What are you doing to him?" I cried, now standing at her side. Burt appeared to be unconscious. His pale torso was surprisingly hairy.

"Checking his vitals. Good thing I got him on the table before he passed out. Blood pressure's plunged, abdomen's distended, so I suspect a hemorrhage of some kind and I've called for an ambulance."

My grandmother spoke with authority. She was wearing a teal-green blouse with a bejeweled pin at the collar, a soft gray sweater, and a plaid wool skirt. She had her stethoscope around her neck and I could see her big knuckles through her latex gloves.

"I thought you were coming later in the week," Pincer said. "I would've been out today if Burt hadn't collapsed."

"Well, lucky me."

"We had a big day planned. But the minute he walked in I could see he was in extremis. You know I still have my medical license, don't you?"

"Yes, you've mentioned," I said.

The wail of a siren approached. Pincer said, "Go and show them the way."

I went back down the brick path just as the ambulance shot through the gate. Three EMTs jumped out, and I brought them around.

I imagine I was in something like a state of shock. It was obvious I should have insisted we go to the ER the night before. It was also something of a shock to witness Pincer orchestrating her comeback.

She took center stage and explained her credentials, providing Burt's stats. Two of the EMTs lifted Burt onto a gurney, and as they carried him down the path I told them to watch out for his toupee and said it was expensive. One of them, a large guy who happened to be bald, simply reached over and yanked it off, exposing Burt's bare scalp. "You keep it," he said. "Safer that way." They already had Burt's clothes in a plastic bag along with his wallet and phone.

I walked over to the van and placed the hair on the passenger seat. When I turned around, I was surprised to see Pincer being helped into the back of the ambulance.

"Follow us to the hospital," she commanded. "I'm going along to make sure they know what they're doing."

I forced myself to nod. The back door of the ambulance closed and I watched the vehicle roll down the driveway.

It took me a moment to gather my thoughts. I felt terrible about Burt, almost as if it were my fault. My god, I'd tried to stuff an apple fritter into a man who was hemorrhaging. What kind of person does that? On the other hand, I didn't need to show up at the hospital at the same time they did. Burt would want me to go inside and find the gun, as we'd planned. I knew he would! So that's what I would do first.

Pincer had locked up the house, but I had a spare key. Very little had changed since my last visit. In the kitchen, the counters were stacked with jars and containers filled with brown goopy liquid. Something crunched under my shoe. It was a small glass cylinder like a perfume sample; tiny wet shards fanned out on the floor. Bending down, I saw a label marked *Live Polio Vaccine*, meaning there was now live poliovirus on the kitchen floor. But it's possible to say that wasn't the worst thing in the room. Inside the refrigerator were objects in which the contents and their containers had fully merged under furry coats of orange, green, black, and blue mold.

Meanwhile, the living room looked as if there'd been a carnival and nobody cleaned up. Crumpled potato chip bags, Popsicle sticks, and boxes from crackers and other foodstuffs that had been shredded into pieces were scattered from corner to corner. A large round grayish thing sat on the carpet that may or may not have been a cabbage. A trail of feathers disappeared under the old divan.

Focus, find the gun! I dashed down the hallway to the bedroom and beheld the tangle of boxes and papers that surrounded Pincer's bed. I'm afraid to report that the stench there was worse than expected. Rat droppings littered the bedside table. I opened the top drawer; inside was a circular nest of tissue at the center of which were three live pink infant rats, eyes sealed, nosing up toward the light. I shrieked.

Whenever I visited, Pincer generally kept me out of her sleeping quarters. Now I had free rein. An impersonal approach was required for this task, and I began to shove and yank and open and close anything I thought might yield the firearm, without any thought to Pincer's objections. At last, in the bottom drawer of one of her bureaus, tucked under some ancient yellowed nightclothes, I found what could be the item in question. My god. It was a stout silver device that looked like an undersized rocket launcher. It was marked on the side with the words: *The Scintillator.* Could this be the weapon in question? What did it do, scramble your molecular structure? It had a simple gauge on one end and the barrel was sealed off with a metal cap; the Meals on Wheels volunteers had said it resembled a bazooka. From a distance it could look threatening, no doubt. I bundled it up in one of the old nightgowns, tying it into a knot. And then I heard a knock.

I'd forgotten to call off the cleaning service.

I seized the bundle and rushed down the hall. Standing before me when I opened the door was a group of six women holding their cleaning caddies, vacuums, and mops. The crew manager introduced herself as Ramona. I was about to tell her it wasn't going to work out, when it occurred to me: Why not? Anything they could do would be an improvement. I could keep Pincer away as well as Burt could. I could take her to lunch somewhere. We could wait at the hospital. This was still an opportunity not to be missed.

As I led the crew into the house, they quieted, perhaps as if in shock. I realized I was somewhat accustomed to the place. The women began to whisper among themselves. I said, "Look, I know it's really bad. Today just do what you can. Thank you. I—my family really appreciates this," I said.

"We need to charge a different rate," Ramona said.

"Of course. I understand." I told her they needed to clear out completely by two-thirty. I wasn't sure how much longer I could keep Pincer away.

Before I left I poured some bleach on the crushed vial of polio vaccine, gathering it up in a towel and into the trash. Then I returned to the van, stuffing the bundled Scintillator under the driver's seat. Burt's hairpiece was sitting on the passenger seat looking wretched. It was as if Burt had melted and this was all that was left. On the floor sat the box of donuts, still pink and emanating cheer. I was very hungry and ferreted out a cinnamon donut, wolfing it down and casting crumbs all over. Then I remembered I'd purchased the donuts in order to share them with the cleaning crew, so I ran the box to the house. The women were already spreading out through the rooms, calling to each other in exasperated and horrified tones, even squealing and laughing. I set down the box in the doorway and left.

Burt's van drove like a city bus but felt solid enough. The shocks were tight, and every bump in the road came as a jolt. The steering column was tight too and let out a high-pitched whine when I turned corners. But it was probably in better shape than the old step van Sherman had bought for his grinding-and-honing venture.

Before entering the hospital I hid Burt's hairpiece under the seat as well. I didn't think Pincer would enjoy seeing it, and I also felt protective of Burt and didn't want it to become a conversation piece.

I prefer not to go into every detail of the next few hours. Suffice it to say, Pincer insisted on watching the operation in which they cauterized his bleed and suctioned his abdomen. She further insisted on offering her opinions. The surgeons showed her the professional courtesy she believed she deserved. I imagined she stopped just short of grabbing the instruments and attempting the surgery herself. All this I learned later from one of the attending nurses. But until then, I waited in the emergency room. Every twenty minutes or so, some human catastrophe presented itself. Almost worse than glimpsing the injured and ill was observing the families of those people waiting for further word. Meanwhile, using my phone, I tracked down a Lampey in San Francisco who was an attorney, and called, leaving a message that didn't sound too alarming but that conveyed the matter at hand. I could find no Lampeys in Montreal. Punctuating my search were several messages from my sister, Margaret, as well as from Doris Roofla Reshnappet, my grandfather's wife, referring to what she called the latest crisis in Arlo's home care. I'd have to call her back soon. For a second I thought of calling Sherman, as if forgetting that we were separated and that he hated me.

Finally, at close to noon, after I'd asked about Burt about ten times, a curly-haired young man in a white coat came out to speak with me.

"What relationship is Mr. Lampey to you?" he asked.

"He's my grandmother's accountant," I said. "And a friend too."

"Dr. Pincer is your grandmother?"

I nodded.

"Do you know anything about his family?"

"He has a daughter in Montreal, and a brother in San Francisco."

"Would you have contact information for them?"

"I think I've found his brother and I've left a message."

"Mr. Lampey has some serious medical issues. Do you think he'd mind me discussing this with you?"

"I don't think he'd mind. He's pretty open."

The young doctor said, "All right. Mr. Lampey has a perforated ulcer of his duodenum. It appears to have been seeping for some time, there was a lot of blood in his GI tract. He required a transfusion of three units and was in shock on admittance. He's now had laparoscopic surgery, where we applied an omental patch and performed a thorough abdominal lavage. This was a sizable perforation. We have him on broad-spectrum antibiotics for peritonitis, and we'll assume for now this is a sequela of *H. pylori*, so we've cultured for that and will be treating that as well. His stats are improving, but he'll be in the ICU under observation for at least a few days."

"Is he going to be okay?"

"Yes, the prognosis is good, the bleeding has stopped. But if he'd gotten here any later, different story."

"Should I see him?"

"Not now. He's resting. You can check back anytime, and of course, please do keep trying to reach his family."

"Of course," I said. "So, where's my grandmother?"

"Dr. Pincer is roaming the ward. I wonder—no disrespect intended, of course—if you'd have some way of coaxing her out of there? It would be helpful."

"You could tell her I'm here and that I'd like to take her to lunch," I said.

"I will do that," he said.

3

I was happy to leave the hospital, despite feeling that Burt was exerting an unexpected pull on me. I had been in the man's presence for less than twenty-four hours, yet it felt like we'd been through something together. Pincer walked surprisingly fast through the lobby, reaching up in time to catch her pin, which had come unclasped, no doubt due to the aggressive vibrations of her gait. "Take me home," she said. "I need to get out of these clothes."

"Sure. But you're hungry, and I was thinking we could have lunch," I said.

"Where?"

As we stepped out of the air-conditioned building, I felt the heat of the sun, and in the bright light noticed some fine beads of sweat on Pincer's brow.

"I was thinking we could go to Scandia's," I said, aware of the place it held in her heart.

"That's a fine-quality restaurant," she said, brightening considerably.

"That buffet is amazing," I lied.

"It's called a *smorgasbord*," she corrected me. "High-quality food."

"My treat," I said, playing my final card.

"Well, you're a good girl!"

With relief, I opened the passenger door to help Pincer into the van and was soon driving through town toward our destination. Sunlight flashed brightly off every car and shop window, while heat poured from under the dashboard of the van and my skin began to itch. I wondered if there had been fleas on Burt's couch. We still had over an hour to kill before the cleaning crew would leave, so I didn't want to rush things. I understood that Pincer's only regret about the sudden invitation was not having hidden a container in her purse where she could deposit surplus food.

"What are you doing?" she asked, as I circled the parking lot a third time.

"Just looking for a good spot."

"There's a good spot. Park there."

"I don't think it's wide enough," I said, taking every opportunity to stall.

"There's one in the shade." She pointed. "Hurry up. I'm hungry!"

I took it. Then I came around and helped Pincer out. As she slid from the seat, I assessed her shoes and stockings and marveled that she could extract such a presentable outfit from the squalor of her house. The only jarring element was her pin—I'd seen it before and wondered why she'd wear such a thing. Mounted on a gold hexagon, this pin featured the figure of a sprinting roadrunner in profile—

knobby backward knees, hideous feet with two toes in front and two in back, long jutting tail, fierce beak, and bloodshot eye. The eye was especially evil-looking because it had been set with a tiny red ruby. The rest of the little jewels followed the bird's back.

"Do you think highly of roadrunners?" I asked.

"I suppose I do," she said. "They're quick on their feet."

"Is that all?"

"I think that's enough. They're cuckoos, if that matters to you."

"They're cuckoos? I didn't know that."

"Solitary, introverted birds," Pincer said.

"Do you remind yourself of a roadrunner?" I blurted out.

"No, I don't remind myself of a roadrunner," she said, though I don't think she gave it any thought because she was already laser-focused on the buffet.

The restaurant was long and narrow, crowded with avid lunch guests. The clatter of silverware against plates struck me as unusually loud, and as we were taken to a table by our server it seemed to crescendo to a violent din, like the sound of locusts decimating a garden patch. I asked for iced tea, while Pincer went straight to the spread, and I waited a moment before joining her, steeling myself against the noise and intensity of the room. The walls were decorated with poster-sized photographs of the Swedish countryside— fields of yellow-tasseled corn, narrow lanes through gentle forests, plain red buildings atop rolling farmland. These images were to fill you with inchoate longing for a life that would never be yours except when you ate there. I surrendered and joined Pincer at the long, ladened table. She was piling her plate with gravlax, herring, cheese slices, potato salad, pickled vegetables, meatballs, and rye bread, among other things. "The Scandinavian diet is among the world's healthiest," she proclaimed. "The Scandinavian countries are virtually free of allergies. As you know, I'm half Swedish on my mother's side. And you're part Norwegian through your father. They are hardy folks and you should be proud."

Who cared? Her ideas on genetics irritated me. I took a few pieces of dark pumpernickel and some kind of soft cheese and ham and a bit of green salad. The last time we came to Scandia's I'd allowed Pincer to goad me into stuffing myself and regretted it. After we took our seats, Pincer told me she wanted to eat fast because she didn't like leaving her house unattended.

"But I thought you said you were planning to be out all day with Burt."

"There's been some funny business lately. Not sure what's gone on, but it looks like somebody's been stealing from me."

"Oh. What's missing?"

"You name it. My silver trays, my wedding gifts. Gone. All my beautiful silk kimonos from Japan, gone. My full set of Staffordshire English country china is missing. These crooks are ruthless!"

"But isn't your china packed in barrels in the garage?"

"I don't know why you think you know where everything is."

"I thought you mentioned that's where it is."

"Well, that may be, but it doesn't explain the missing trays or kimonos."

"No, it doesn't." I wondered when was the last time Pincer even saw these trays and kimonos. "Well, do you want to call the police?"

"I just may do that. I just may. It's very frightening."

I'd discovered how good it felt to hold my water glass to my wasp sting. To change the subject, I asked how long she'd known Burt.

"A while now. You know, he's been trying to get me in bed since the day we met."

"Are you serious?" I found this hard to believe, but humoring her was my specialty. "What stopped you?"

"He's a good-looking man. But if I were to get involved, I could do a lot better than Burt."

"He looked okay to me," I remarked, feeling I should defend Burt.

"Besides, somebody's been stealing from me, and for all I know, it's him."

"Well, right now he's barely alive at the hospital, so I don't think he'll steal anything today."

At that moment I became acutely aware of my grandmother's appearance, as if seeing her for the first time. It's true I was fatigued, but there was clearly something fiendish about her. Her hands gripped her utensils like claws, and she was shoveling food into the tight orifice on her face like a caterpillar chomping and devouring everything in its path in order to double itself. I continued to stare, transfixed, and began to wonder if someday I too would gobble food before a grandchild and fill him or her with horror. Furthermore, she was staring back, as if defying me to understand that she could eat as much as she wanted, including me if she had to, including the world. I realized I resented my grandmother for a number of reasons, not the least of which was that she'd never offered me a shred of comfort or sympathy when my parents disappeared. Her own daughter disappeared, and she'd glossed right over it! She had even made a horrible remark about how perhaps they'd planned the whole thing, a remark so cruel it had been hard to forget.

After consuming everything on her plate, Pincer zeroed in on the dessert table and helped herself to a number of almond, ginger, and chocolate cookies that, once back in her seat, she wrapped in napkins and stuffed into the various crannies of her pocketbook. She then pronounced herself ready to get home and remove the uncomfortable garments corseting her body. I made a half-hearted attempt to flag our waitperson before Pincer pushed the table aside and rammed her way over to the cash register, demanding the check. For a second I had hopes she'd forget my offer and pay it, but she returned to the table and dropped it in front of me. I rummaged incompetently through my bag, partly to stall and partly because my hand was throbbing and I was feeling stressed. I'd had too much iced tea and was shaking. My back ached from sleeping on the hard couch, and I continued to itch all over. Now I had to entertain thoughts of her reaction when she entered her cleaned house. I suddenly felt like I couldn't stand another second of her.

We took our leave of Scandia's. I checked my phone to see if Burt's brother Dale Lampey had called—nothing yet. Then I helped Pincer into the van and came around to take the seat behind the wheel. The moment I sat down, however, Pincer said, "What in the hell is that doing here?" She was pointing at the floor under my seat, though I couldn't see at what.

"What is it?"

"What's my old nightie doing here?"

I kicked it back under.

"I'd know it anywhere. I've had it for years. Give me that ball of cloth under your seat."

"It couldn't possibly be yours," I said, cursing myself for having chosen such a poor hiding spot for the Scintillator, and cursing Pincer for her obnoxiousness.

"Any idea how I feel about people who don't listen to me?" she snarled.

"I don't care how you feel about them," I replied.

All at once, everything about the day shifted in my thinking; I decided at that moment that I wanted to return to Pincer's before the crew left in order to let all hell break loose. A showdown was in order. There was no use pretending things were all right anymore. I wanted Pincer to have to face the facts, I wanted her to understand the mess she was in, I wanted her to rage because I wanted to rage at her in return. I tore out of the parking lot, pushing the van to go as fast as it could. I would show her!

"What's gotten into you?" Pincer asked. She was trying to secure the roadrunner pin to her blouse. But her fingers were knobby and clumsy, and the pin kept falling into her lap. We crossed the freeway and sped past the horses, the golf course, the lake. When I nearly missed a stop sign near her house and had to suddenly apply the brakes, the bundle ejected itself from under the seat.

"There it is," she said. "I knew it. Hand me that nightie now!"

"I'm driving," I said, kicking it under again.

"Pull over. This proves it, the man's perverted."

"You think he runs around in your nightgown?"

"Don't be naïve, there are many depraved uses for a woman's nightie!"

We were almost there. "Calm down," I said. "It's a rag."

"A rag it is not. Stop right now or I'll scream!"

I ignored her, but was wrong to think I could. The sting of the wasp could not compare to that of Pincer's roadrunner pin being driven into my thigh.

"Oh my god! You stabbed me!" I wailed.

I looked over at the woman in the seat beside me, brandishing the open brooch as if it were a tiny rapier, her face disfigured with rage. Searing pain radiated from the entry point in my flesh. I couldn't believe it. I pressed on the gas for the final stretch of road, made the turn for her house, and shot through the gate.

Three police cars were parked at the top of the driveway. One officer stood before the peeling garage door on his phone. Another was in conversation with Ramona, who had her arms around one of the other women from her crew.

Rolling down the window, Pincer shouted: "I am the owner of this house. Will somebody tell me what's going on?"

4

Letting myself out of the van, wondering which hurt more, the sting on my hand or the puncture in my leg, I could only imagine that a neighbor had called the police on Ramona and her crew, mistaking them for burglars. Or maybe Ramona herself had called the police, finding criminal negligence in Pincer's living conditions. A number of things occurred then in short order, and I will do my best to relay them—all I can say is that when more than one person speaks at once, my mind goes nearly blank.

Wherein:
   a redheaded detective named Ron Storke asks me for my identification,

Ramona comforts a crying member of her crew,

Pincer converses with an officer,

a city car appears, bringing three people who step out holding cameras and officious-looking metal suitcases,

Pincer pretends she's entertaining gentleman callers and says: "My goodness, the whole town's here. I have some whiskey inside, let's loosen up a little, shall we?,"

Pincer and I are taken around the house to the old pass-through shed, which my grandfather used to load up with wood, as it opens next to the fireplace on the inside,

we peer into the woodshed,

we see a human skeleton in various pieces in the woodshed, including a skull,

Pincer observes by way of the narrow pelvis and hand size that it was clearly a man,

various authorities are arriving and looking around the house,

Pincer feels the need to mention several men who were once obsessed with her,

the police want to question her further, and after hearing about the state of the house from talking to the cleaning crew, a mental health authority is assigned to evaluate her,

it is decided Pincer will be taken for a mental health evaluation,

the people with the cameras and metal suitcases turn out to be coroners,

photographs are taken of the woodshed from all angles,

detectives are gathering samples of dirt and other debris from the floor of the woodshed,

the skeleton pieces are placed on a gurney,

EMTs arrive for the second time that day,

this man named Ron Storke is asking me to explain my grandmother's situation, and we step inside,

Pincer is to be taken away in the ambulance and there's nothing
I can do about it,

her shouts reach us all the way in the house.

Rats could decompose in many different ways, it
seemed. Rats could mummify into hard furry nuggets. They could
rot away completely, leaving only a skeleton. Strangely enough, a
rat could completely dissolve on the inside, leaving behind a fully
intact rat-shaped balloon of leathery, translucent skin. All this I
learned by viewing the extensive collection of samples the cleaning
crew had gathered on a sheet on the living room floor.

Detective Storke was a man of about forty-five, with long, red,
spidery eyebrows that danced over the rim of his glasses when he
spoke. His nose was long and pointy, and beneath that nose was a
rust-colored mustache that looked strangely impenetrable. His lips
were chapped and puckered. His chin was small and crisscrossed by
red capillaries that had burst near the surface, and despite his slender frame he had several double chins bristling with ocher stubble.
He wore black slacks held up by a black leather belt that had turned
gray from numerous jabs around the belt holes, and a short-sleeve
blue shirt with a pocket on the breast, which held several pens that
looked chewed-on. The arms that protruded from the shirt were
bony and freckled, covered with billowing clouds of reddish body
hair, into which a steel-banded watch had dug a trench.

His voice sounded like a recorded message: "Mrs. Williams placed a call with emergency services at twelve-oh-seven p.m. stating that she was working for a customer and that human remains had been found at the job site. Two of our officers were dispatched. Arriving on the scene, they were told that due to an infestation of rodents, Mrs. Williams had ordered a search for the manner in which the rodents were gaining entry. One of her employees traced the perimeter of the house, examining the eaves, vents, windows, and screens before discovering a weathered door on a small shed attached to the residence with significant cracks and gaps in it. Believing she'd found the source of the infestation, she wrestled with the rusted latch and opened the old door, discovering the remains and prompting Mrs. Williams to call 911."

"That's a good summary," I said, feeling he needed a boost for some reason. There was something forlorn about the man, as if he'd never been loved.

He said, "I assume it's adequate. There's more. Follow me, please," and with that, he led me out of the living room, past the dining room and kitchen, to the wing of the house where Pincer's medical office was located. He went straight for the table Burt had been stretched out on that morning, and I noticed a damp cloth and Pincer's latex gloves at the head of it. He said, "What can you tell me about this room and what your grandmother does in it?"

I stumbled for a moment, since I wasn't entirely sure what she did in it. I said, "My grandmother still has her medical license, but I don't think she sees patients anymore."

Storke flipped briskly through his notebook. "We also have a report that an ambulance came to this address this morning and took away a fifty-seven-year-old man who we've identified as a Mr. Burt Lampey. Would you know anything about that?"

I nodded, hoping to put him quickly at ease. "Yes, I do." I proceeded to explain as much as I could, even about the Scintillator, about the plan to clean up, about Burt's condition, about how my grandmother had examined him and called the ambulance. "It's not like she was experimenting on him," I felt compelled to mention.

The detective looked at me anxiously. "Would you have any reason to believe she experiments on people?"

"No, of course not," I said, thinking perhaps humor was inappropriate at this moment. But my object had been to forge a connection with him, so I continued, "I thought maybe that's what you were imagining went on in here, like in a horror movie or something. *The Island of Dr. Moreau*. Have you read that?"

"I have not."

"It's not like *Dr. Moreau* here, is what I'm trying to say. The thought has crossed my mind once or twice in a nightmarish kind of way, but that's just me! It's about a doctor who does experiments on animals and humans and creates these monster-like hybrids. It's a great story. But not happening here!" I said, feeling like I'd only disturbed him further. I must have winced a little then from the pain in my leg, because he asked me if I was all right. I decided not to mention she'd stabbed me.

Storke then took some notes before leafing again through his notebook. "Let's move on. I also understand that a woman matching your description was seen hiding outside this house, in the shrubbery in fact, shortly before the ambulance came for Mr. Lampey. What can you tell me about that?"

"Right!" I said. "That was me. I should have mentioned it before."

"Why are you laughing?" he asked, staring at me from beneath his spidery brows.

"Sorry." I pulled myself together and assumed a serious expression, recognizing that connection with him would be difficult. For some reason, I don't know why, I said then, "Have you ever been in this house before?"

Storke said, "I have never been to this house. Why would I have been to this house?"

"I was just wondering," I said, noticing the note of doubt and accusation I'd dropped into my voice.

"I'm afraid I don't understand what you're getting at," he said. "Has this house been the subject of previous investigations?"

"Not that I know of," I said, leaving it at that. Then I added, "She's been living here alone for over twenty years," as if that explained everything.

I think the stress of the situation was making me say strange things. Maybe it was a syndrome, maybe he'd seen this kind of behavior before and understood. He got my grandfather's name out of me and asked a few questions about him. He then gave me his card and said he would keep me informed and that I was free to go. Free to go where? All I could think to do was drive back to Burt's office, where my things were.

5

Strangely, the thought of being able to return to Burt's office now struck me as a luxury, and when I was finally able to leave Pincer's, I drove back and entered the building and climbed the stairs and with the key on his key chain opened and closed Burt's office door behind me, collapsing on the orange burlap couch with indescribable relief. For the longest time on that couch I did nothing, as if my body were reconstituting itself from the cellular level up. Was it possible Pincer could have gone years without looking in the woodshed, was it possible she had nothing to do with it? Could the man have been an ill-fated hobo looking for a place to sleep, a sleep from which he never awoke? At one point I began to weep and convulse, overwhelmed, wishing I could talk to my mother about what was going on. Yet I knew exactly what she would tell me to do at this moment—sterilize my wounds! I ripped off my pants to look at my thigh.

The puncture had bled some, but not much. The entry point

was red, and the surrounding area, a circle about the size of a half-dollar, was raised and inflamed. I wondered if Burt had any alcohol in his office. I threw open his desk drawers, surprised to find, in the bottom drawer, a large assortment of prescription bottles filled with pills. Looking more closely, I could see that Burt had amassed many months, possibly years, of prescriptions for well-known antidepressants and anti-anxiety medications, leaving them untouched. Interesting. I opened the closet, where I discovered a vacuum cleaner, which I pulled out, as well as a bottle of spray cleaner and a roll of paper towels. Then I searched the cabinets on his shelves. Eureka! Burt had a liquor stash—bottles of vodka, gin, and bourbon. I poured vodka on a paper towel and dabbed my thigh and hand. I'd go out later and purchase some form of ointment for pain relief.

For now, I decided on a more old-fashioned approach. I poured a shot of bourbon into a glass and swilled it. The analgesic effect was near-instant.

It was time to remove Burt's toupee from my bag. Stuffing it under the seat of his van hadn't been the best idea, as it was now not only full of fibers and debris but somewhat sticky. I shook it out and placed it on his desk pad, with the edges tucked under so that it didn't look carelessly plunked. Then I opened the window and stood with my back to it to survey the cluttered room. A refreshing breeze blew in and I could hear the gentle rustling of tall palms along the avenue. Without Burt sleeping behind the desk, I could tolerate staying there, but if I were to stay, I might as well freshen the place up. I stationed my phone in a prominent place attached to the charger, so that I might hear any calls coming in, and then set to work. First I threw on some shorts. Next, I grabbed the laundry basket full of beer bottles and topped it with the stack of pizza boxes and carried it all down to the recycling bin I'd seen in the parking lot. Once back in the office I put Burt's personal effects, like his toiletries and clothing, into several bags and set them by the door. I wiped down the dusty windows and shelves. Then I plugged in the vacuum and ran it over the carpet in every direction. I was in no hurry; in fact, I wanted to keep cleaning for as long as I could, as it felt both productive and numbing. I threw my attention next at the couch, spending a very long time examining its rough fibers, trying to discern the possible presence of fleas or lice or bedbugs or whatever else had made me itch so much. To my relief I found no vermin, only a number of hardened crumbs, which I promptly vacuumed. I then crawled around on my hands and knees methodically parting the tufts of the carpet, seeking anything the vacuum had missed, especially mites or other miniature irritants. Maybe I did this for a few minutes or maybe I did this for an hour, I'd rather not disclose, as it reveals a somewhat obsessive side of my personality that I'm not proud of. It was during this activity that I received my first communication from the outside world.

"Hello?"

"This is Dale Lampey," said the voice. "What's going on with Burt?"

"I'm so glad you called," I said, and I told him the whole story, including my conversation with the doctor. "He said Burt would be in the hospital awhile but he's out of danger."

Dale Lampey said, "My god. What an ordeal for you. I'm very appreciative you were able to help him out. I'm not sure if he mentioned, but we haven't been in touch for some time."

This was a discordant note. I struggled to be concise in my confusion. "But—he said you're so close you share a wig!"

Dale Lampey let out a taut sigh. "He has a screw loose," he finally said.

"You don't share the wig?"

"For god's sake, who would share a wig? I'm not even bald. I mean, I'm losing a little hair, but I'm not ashamed of it. I would never wear a hairpiece."

"He made it sound like he mailed it to you every month." As eccentric as that seemed, I'd thought it was very touching, two brothers sharing a wig.

"I'm sorry you got caught up in this. He hasn't been right in the head for many years, and nobody's been able to help him. So this isn't easy to talk about."

"What about his daughter?" I said.

"Burt doesn't have a daughter!"

"Maybe I misunderstood," I backtracked, in case Dale was insane. "He's been really devoted to my grandmother, so to me he's a great guy."

"That's how it goes," Dale said. "Anyway. I'm planning to be in Santa Barbara tomorrow. Maybe we could conclude this conversation when I'm there."

"Sure. I'm actually staying in his office right now. I mean, he invited me, though I didn't realize it was an office when he invited me, but anyway, that's where I am. I can get out of here if you want to stay here."

"I do not want to stay in Burt's office."

"So you don't mind if I stay here a little longer."

"If Burt invited you, it's no business of mine."

"True," I said.

"Anyway, thank you for getting in touch."

"You're welcome."

It was now six p.m. I wasn't happy with what he'd said about

Burt and refused for the moment to accommodate any of it. Instead, I called the hospital to check on Burt. I was put through to the nurses' station in the ICU and told that Mr. Lampey was in stable condition and resting peacefully. This was a relief, and I said I would call back in the morning, but made sure they had my number if anything changed and also provided them with Dale Lampey's number.

I then called the psychiatric wing where Pincer had been taken and was told that Dr. Louise Pincer was in good condition but very angry and did not understand why she was there.

I thought about calling my sister, but the time difference made it difficult and I knew she was busy with her children and very active life.

It occurred to me then what a relief it was to have Pincer out of her house, locked up somewhere. For the first time in a while I could take some comfort in knowing someone was feeding her and watching over her and that she was not frolicking with rats. I was afraid to admit how easy it was to imagine her locking up a man in a woodshed.

To distract myself from that horrible thought, that our family's private madwoman may now have done harm outside our circle, I noted I had yet to inspect the sleeping bag I'd used the night before, the final frontier in my quest for a better night ahead. I pulled it out from behind the couch and unzipped it so that the interior was fully visible, and was shocked to see that it was filled top to bottom with large clumps of reddish fur, likely from a dog.

Now I cried. Though the day had been full of many unpleasant events, this was the one that did me in. Why had Burt given me a sleeping bag full of fur? What was I doing here?

. . .

At last, evening fell. The building quieted. Outside the window, I could see lights twinkling on the mountains.

Without undue emotion, I began to gather the fur from the sleeping bag. I soon had a large thatch of it in hand. Strangely, the fur no longer repulsed me, but rather began to suggest the dimensions and life force of the animal to whom it had once belonged. And it suggested further heartbreak in Burt's life; perhaps his beloved dog had been taken by his ex-wife in the divorce, or, worse, had died right when he needed it most. Without realizing it, I had been squeezing the fur ball so much that it had stopped shedding and taken on a solid form. The fur fibers had become felted. I realized I could stretch and mold it, and I began to work the wad into the shape of a Labrador retriever. First the body took form, then the legs descended from it, then I coaxed out the neck, head, and snout, and finally I twirled out the tail. I couldn't believe it! It even stood up on its own. I thought it was probably the most artistic thing I'd ever made.

This moment was interrupted by the ring of my phone. I could see that it was my grandfather's wife, Doris Roofla Reshnappet, calling.

"Hello, Doris," I said.

"Penny, we've got a big problem here, and you hold the purse strings, so you'd better listen up. Your grandfather and I had an agreement before we married. Call it a prenup, if you must. There was a big age difference and as you know my first husband was an invalid and I made it clear I was done with that. Arlo promised me that when he got too old to be of use, to put him on the ice floe and say goodbye. And I'm telling you, it's time."

I couldn't believe it. She couldn't really mean this, could she? "I'll be there tomorrow," I answered. "We can talk then. Okay?"

"My schedule is very busy tomorrow. What time exactly?"

"What time are you free?"

"I'm never free. But if you get here by eight-thirty in the morning we can try to come to an agreement before I have to go out."

"All right," I said. "How's my grandfather?"

"He's perfectly oblivious, as usual! He thinks everything's just wonderful. I'm getting very tired of reminding him that it's not."

"All right, Doris," I said. "See you in the morning."

She hung up.

Well. That was something to look forward to.

I thought regretfully of all the cookies at Scandia's I'd failed to stuff in my bag and gave Pincer a few points for her foresight. I'd have given anything for them now.

The night was warm. I didn't feel like driving the van because it had stiff brakes and my right leg was sore. There were places within walking distance all over, so I set out down State Street, brooding over my tasks for the following day.

It would have been wonderful to love, even just to like, the person Arlo married after his divorce from Pincer. Doris and Arlo had met on the tennis courts at the city college. Twenty-five years his junior, she was a striking woman, tall, shapely, with platinum hair and high cheekbones, a successful real estate agent who owned investment properties all over town. She sang soprano in her church choir and painted bold nudes on huge canvases in an adult education class. She spoke loudly and sprinkled her conversation with foreign terms she'd learned in a phrase book. She wore expensive, outlandish clothing, overdressing for most occasions. She regularly visited a tanning salon. Her good-mood conversation consisted of making jokes about how rough menopause was treating her, then clearing her throat and saying "excuse the expression" and emitting a strange chortle that started deep in her chest. At first she found Arlo witty and debonair, and appreciated his lifetime free pass for himself and his spouse on United Airlines.

Now Arlo was ninety-three. He had been fully independent until his recent fall, driving his year-old, optimistically purchased Honda station wagon, continuing to travel by air where United would take him. But now with a few broken toes he was moving slowly and using a cane. Doris called me one day and said that taking care of Arlo was not in her plans. My sister and I would have to find a caregiver, at least until he got better. Because Margaret lived in Australia, Arlo appointed me his trustee and explained his finances to me. Though he had some savings and a good pension, he wouldn't have enough to pay for a caregiver for long.

We decided he'd take out a loan against his house, so I took care of that. Once the reverse mortgage came through, I deposited the money in a trust account, and through word of mouth we found a kind woman named Nancy who'd come in every day and help Arlo do whatever he needed to do, including taking him to physical therapy and so on. But after about three weeks, Nancy called me one evening. "I am very sorry, Penny, but I'm afraid I can't stay on taking care of your grandfather. He is a very sweet man, but his wife is not a good person. I can't take it anymore."

After Nancy, I found Larry, a middle-aged man who came with excellent references. However, maybe because he was a man, Doris was wary of him from day one, claiming to have a hunch that Larry was some kind of degenerate, for no reason that I could tell. Arlo liked Larry, but after Doris cornered him one day and accused him of peeping at her in the bathroom, he resigned. Then came, by way of Doris's church, a con artist named Olga who tried to convince Arlo to sign over the deed to his car. Most recently I'd found a well-recommended caretaker named Lola, but last week, Arlo called and said, "I think Lola and Doris are trying to kill me."

"Oh my god, why?"

"I'll ask Lola for lunch, but she'll never bring it. So I'll go to the kitchen to make it myself, then Doris will come in and tell me I've already had it! Does she think I've lost my marbles? I know when I've eaten lunch or not!"

So I called the agency and discontinued Lola, received a bunch of angry calls from Doris, and now here I was.

I could understand why my grandfather had fallen in love with Pincer years ago in Texas. They were young and naïve. But why in the world did he ever go for Doris Roofla? To survive this imprudent marriage, Arlo had always kept an active social life outside the house.

The fog was coming in, as it did sometimes on hot days. I'd passed a few restaurants, including the one I'd eaten at with Burt, but didn't feel like sitting in a room full of people talking and laughing and enjoying themselves. My leg was throbbing and so was my hand. I wasn't that hungry after all, and I had already started circling back to Burt's office when I came upon the gas station with the mini-mart Burt had stopped at the night before. Though my first impulse was to rush past, it occurred to me to go in and thank the manager, if he was there, for going out on a limb to warn me that Burt had a problem. So into the mini-mart I went. This time a woman was at the cash register, ringing up a customer's six-pack of beer and bag of chips. She had straight dark hair pulled back in front with a pink barrette and wore a lumpy black sweatshirt under a company-brand apron.

The store had a small pharmacy section, where I picked up some painkilling antibacterial ointment. Then I saw Frosted Flakes and grabbed a box, and went to the refrigerated case and grabbed a pint of whole milk. I placed the stuff by the register.

"That's it?" she asked.

"That's it." Then I said, "Would you happen to know the man who was working here last night?"

"I know him. What about him?"

"I guess he's not here tonight?"

"Not here."

"Okay, well, I just wanted to tell him something."

"He's married and he's my husband."

"Oh. That's fine," I said quickly.

"I know it's fine."

"I mean, if you're telling me he's married because you think I'm into him, then nothing could be further from the truth," I said, realizing that sounded a little severe. "I just wanted to thank him for trying to help me and my friend."

At that point her expression changed completely, to genuine concern. "Are you with the guy who shat his guts out?"

"Yes! Yes! I mean, I'm not 'with' him, we're just friends. Anyway, please tell your husband I appreciate it."

"The guy okay?"

"He's in the hospital," I said. "He had to have surgery. And a transfusion! It was pretty bad."

"Take a free soda," she said, nodding at the machine.

"Oh, no, thanks, that's okay."

"Take one!" she said forcefully.

"Sure, okay, I will," I said, filling up a small cup with ice and root beer.

"Have a nice evening," she said.

"Sure. You too," I said.

The root beer tasted especially good. I would never have thought of having it myself. It was uncanny how a stranger might know what you needed better than you did yourself. I drank the whole thing immediately. By the time I was back in Burt's office, I wasn't hungry for the Frosted Flakes. I took off my pants and applied a large squeeze of the ointment to the welt on my leg, and without further ado, got into the bag and fell asleep, as if it were the most comfortable bed I'd ever had the fortune to find myself in.

6

I woke early and washed up in the restroom down the hall. I couldn't pretend to be shocked by what I saw in the mirror—it was me, after all, but somehow not me at all, or any me I'd ever known. It wasn't to do with my messy hair or puffy eyes, but rather with a sudden resistance to the passage of time and the disappearance of people I'd thought of as completing me. I felt flat, almost two-dimensional, a cardboard figure ready to blow over at the slightest touch. Maybe only now was it hitting me how alone I was. But I didn't need to punish myself with existential thoughts at that moment, as I had things to do and appointments to keep. So I turned to the matter at hand—that of washing Burt's hairpiece so I could return it to him in the hospital fresh. I'd found some baby shampoo in his office.

The sink looked clean but I wiped it out anyway, filling it with cold water and shampoo. Then I placed the hairpiece in the water and began to swirl it around, where it billowed like a big brown sea anemone. It was satisfying to see the water turn gray, indicating the necessity of the task. As I continued agitating it in the soapy water, I recalled a batch of images posted recently by my high school friend Claire, of bathing her baby in a sink. Well, that was the difference between Claire and me, I thought. She was in her own home washing an adorable infant, and I was in an office building washing a wig.

I was rinsing it when the door of the bathroom swung open and a sticklike woman in a crisp beige suit charged in. Washing things in the sinks of shared office restrooms was probably frowned upon and I wished I'd taken care of this earlier.

"Morning," I said, shielding the basin.

"Good morning," she replied curtly.

As soon as she went into one of the stalls behind me, I extracted the hairpiece from the rinse water, allowing it to drip over the drain for a moment. I startled moments later when I noticed her head pressed up against the door of the stall, a naked eyeball peering through the crack.

I moved stiffly but swiftly back to Burt's office with the dripping wig, wrapping it in one of Burt's T-shirts in the bag by the door to take with me. I'd go straight to the hospital after seeing my grandfather and Doris. My leg had not gotten better during the night, despite the fact that I'd slept. But I needed to ignore my aches and pains and proceed. I couldn't be late for my meeting with Doris, and before my meeting with Doris I needed some good coffee.

Soon I was holding a delicious coffee and driving Burt's van down Las Positas Road, winding along the arroyo before coming to the beach, where I'd turn to go up the hill to Arlo's. It was a neighborhood of notable botanical specimens, with bright magenta and orange bougainvillea pouring over fences and walls, with amazing mounds of yucca and agave and other Mediterranean and desert plants growing here and there in lush profusion. At last I reached his driveway and turned in, finishing my coffee to the bottom of the cup.

Doris answered in white high-heeled shoes and a pale pink dress decorated at the seams with white lace. Her blond hair gleamed like porcelain and her makeup was heavy, especially around her eyes.

"Well," she said, in her throaty voice. "Time to take care of business. Come in. I didn't make you anything because I didn't know what you wanted. Where's Sherman?"

"Sherman and I are separated," I told her, as I followed her to the sunroom. We sat on some wicker chairs near the window, surrounded by a glut of orchids in ceramic pots.

"It's about time," she said, without missing a beat. "It wasn't hard to see that you weren't, shall we say, simpatico."

"Probably so," I said neutrally. I tried to remain calm, but the word *simpatico* filled me with silent rage. I made a mental note to spend some time analyzing why.

"The business at hand is this," Doris said. "It's time to move Arlo to a facility."

I fixed my gaze on the wall behind her, covered floor-to-ceiling with her hideous nudes. The reason they were hideous was because they did not appear to have been conceived by someone who found the human form beautiful. Rather the opposite, with porcine trunks and lots of jarring genital detail. "I know this must be very hard, having all these people in the house," I managed to say.

"You bet it is," Doris said.

"But, you know, I don't think he'll need help much longer. And he doesn't want to go to a facility. He's always said he wants to stay home, that's always been his wish."

Doris said, "Maybe he doesn't get to decide at this point. Let's face it, he's only going to get worse. And he poisons these helpers against me and they treat me like dirt. In my own home! I'm through. You better find him a facility or I'm going to have the next person who steps through that door arrested."

There was no point in engaging with this heartless being. "Right. I'll see what we can do."

"He knows you're coming," she said. "You'd better break the news. I have a half dozen appointments today, so I'm going to bid you adieu."

With that, Doris gathered her purse and the little rolling suitcase that she took everywhere. I always wondered what was in it. After storming up and down the hall a few times rattling her keys, she let herself out the back door. I watched from a window as she deposited herself in her black Lexus and tore off.

Right away I heard Arlo's voice, calling from his office.

"Penny? Penny, is that you?"

"It's me!" I called out, rushing to his room, where he was at his desk. There he was, with his large handsome head and his bright mischievous eyes. I gave him a hug and kiss.

"Penny-girl, you wouldn't believe what's been going on around this place." He asked if Doris had left yet, and I said she had. He said, "I want to thank you for helping me with this mess. I know dealing with Doris isn't easy."

"No big deal," I said. "I'm glad you told me about Lola."

"Good riddance," he said. "She was the worst. What's with these people?"

"Larry wasn't bad, was he?"

"No, Larry wasn't bad. Who was that other one?"

"You mean Olga?"

"Correct. She was a real doozy."

"We'll figure something out," I said gently.

"Be sure Doris is in on it. She'll blow a gasket if she doesn't get a say."

"I know," I said.

We talked. I told him about putting my meager belongings into a tiny storage unit before moving into the weekly-rate motel back in Santa Cruz. He was sorry things hadn't worked out with Sherman, but politely didn't ask why. Then he mentioned that Margaret had been calling from Australia to check in, asking about me and saying I never returned her calls and that she was worried. I'd been busy, I told him. I said I'd call her soon. We talked about her twins, their busy schedules, that Margaret's husband, Wilhelmus, a professional soccer player, had recently scored two goals in an important match and that another team was trying to buy him but he wanted to stay in Brisbane. That would be best for Margaret, I said.

I'd noticed that talking about Margaret's life in Australia always seemed to make him sad, as it obviously reminded him of his daughter's disappearance. To this day, he was still corresponding with several people who had offered to continue the search on a volunteer basis. He'd get letters from these people reporting the coordinates of the areas they'd combed and then he'd mark them on a detailed geological map of northern Queensland. To be honest, I dreaded the idea that one day Arlo would tell me he'd received news about my parents from one of these contacts. Strange as it may sound, I preferred to imagine they had slipped unharmed into another dimension.

Finally, I told him about everything that had happened over at Pincer's house, knowing he remained interested in the welfare of his former wife. Though surprised she'd stabbed me with a pin, he didn't seem especially surprised that a body had been found on the premises. He said, "You know she buried all of my clothes and tools in the orchard before I had a chance to move out." I told him that the police had wanted his name and might come talk to him.

"At least I know it's not me," he said. "But I'm probably not the only person she's wanted to do away with. No man is safe around that woman."

My grandfather didn't like to dwell on unpleasant topics. He'd long been a 3D slide enthusiast, and asked if I'd get out his special projector and his index. One of his file cabinets was neatly organized, containing numbered boxes of his many slides, and he'd created an index covering the topics of each box. He asked me to find Box 326. Then he took it from me and began to examine the contents, holding slides up to the light from the window.

"Penny-girl, get out the screen, it's back in the corner," he asked.

I pulled out the stand-up screen and assembled it, placing it in front of his closet. Then I found the Hush Puppies box that contained all the 3D glasses. As a kid I'd always loved it when he brought out this box of glasses for his slideshows. I picked out one of my favorite pairs with red frames. Arlo took a big pair with black frames.

"Here, put in this one," he said, handing me a slide.

I flipped the toggle on the back of the projector and it roared to life. Then I placed the slide into the tray and pushed it in. The double image popped into focus as soon as I put on the glasses. Before us was a cockpit.

Arlo stood, walking slowly toward the screen.

"It's just like being there," he said, almost ecstatically. "This is my DC-8. A beauty."

"The left side was yours?" I asked about the twin seats.

"Correct. First officer on the right. Do you remember why the pilot's on the left?"

"Because," I said, "when there were propellers instead of jets, the plane torqued to the left because of the clockwise propeller. So it was easier to make left turns on the runway and the pilot could see."

"Correct!"

I moved into the illusion at his side. The cockpit glowed before us. I asked about this knob and switch and lever and gauge. He identified the altimeter and the mach meter and a rain disperser and a horizon indicator and an artificial horizon indicator and a course deviation indicator, reaching out as if to touch each one. He partook of that dimension for a long time before taking off his glasses and returning to his chair.

Later, after I'd made the tuna fish sandwiches with pickles he'd asked for, and we'd eaten them, the words were sticking in my throat, but I finally said, "I guess it's pretty hard on Doris, having these helpers in the house."

"What happened now?" he groaned.

"I guess it makes her unhappy," I said simply.

"She wants me out of here?" my grandfather asked.

I said, "I'm sure she doesn't. But remember how we talked about checking out the Palms? It's supposed to be really nice. I could take you over there. Remember, your friend Harold from the garden club is there."

Arlo said, "All right. Take me over there. Let's go. Right now."

"Right now?"

"Right now."

In the early afternoon, we set out for the Palms in his Honda. As we pulled out of the garage, Arlo spotted Burt's van. "What's that rattletrap doing here?"

"I'm borrowing it from Burt, the one I told you is in the hospital, Pincer's accountant."

"What kind of an accountant could he be?"

I explained that he'd recently gotten divorced, and Arlo nodded with the wisdom of the fleeced.

The Palms wasn't far. It sat on some beautiful grounds near the hills and looked like it could just as easily pass as a resort. Arlo was taken on a tour, while I went over the contract in the business office. Though I'd never wanted it to come to this, I'd contacted the Palms a few months before to prepare for this possibility, so there was already an approved application on file. When I joined my grandfather a little later in the dining room, he was standing with his cane saying witty things to the woman who'd been showing him around. It turned out his physician was affiliated with the place and would see him there. And in the dining room, Arlo saw several of his friends from the men's garden club, including Harold. A furnished room had just become available, overlooking a bunch of bird-of-paradise and a grassy area shaded by feathery jacaranda trees. Arlo said, "I'll take it."

"You'll take it?"

"I'll take it right now."

"You'll take it right now?"

"What do you think? Do you think it's a good idea?"

"If you like it, then it's a good idea."

There was a birthday party at the Palms that afternoon and Arlo was persuaded to stay for it. I conferred with the intake woman and it was decided I'd go back to his house and gather his things.

Back at the house, I was relieved to see that Doris was still out. So I was able to move about freely, finding Arlo's suitcases in order to start filling them up.

The stark truth was that I was now the agent of my grandfather's removal from his beloved house. After I went through his drawers and packed his clothes, I started to gather other things he might need or want. His shoes, his toiletries, his typewriter, books, especially *Diary of a Sea Captain's Wife*, his favorite. Office supplies. What of his slides? I couldn't trust Doris with his precious slides, after what she'd done with the rest of his stuff—several times she'd taken bags of his things to the Goodwill. I realized I'd have to collect just about everything, and started filling the Honda with his camera equipment, including the projector and the screen. What about his flying trophies and plaques? What if Doris threw those away? I started taking those off the wall, placing them into a box. I wondered if I should take some of Arlo's financial records, but that file cabinet was locked. Then I realized he needed bedding and linens, so I took what was on the bed in his office, then looked through the linen closet for some towels. I found an extra comforter there and a bath mat and took those as well. Then I drove back to the Palms and started unloading, using a cart they had near the door. I heaped it up and rolled it to Arlo's new room and made his bed first. I had just finished with that when the door opened and Arlo came in, accompanied by his new friend.

"Look at this, Arlo! Look at what your granddaughter has done, she's getting the room ready for you. Very nice!"

I was placing his clothes in the chest of drawers. Arlo said, "What did Doris say?"

I told him Doris wasn't home, so she didn't know yet.

"Well, she won't have to worry about hooligans around the house anymore," he said. "I'm pretty bushed, Penny-girl. I overindulged at the party. I think I better turn in."

"Of course," I said, as he sat on his new bed.

He said, "I hope Doris won't come down and read me the riot act."

"I hope not too."

"This place is pretty posh. Can we afford it?"

"Yes, we can. Don't worry about anything."

"Drive careful, Penny-girl. I sure appreciate everything. Will you let Doris know?"

"I will."

"Will you come back tomorrow?"

"Of course! I'll see you tomorrow." I gave him a kiss and said goodbye.

Out in the parking lot I noticed that my breath had grown shallow, the way it would when I had to do things I didn't like, when I wouldn't even notice until I felt dizzy. Then I detected a slight film of sweat on my forehead, and an uncomfortable dryness in my throat, and realized I could only see a few feet ahead of me. My neck was hot and so was my leg. I couldn't believe what I'd just done. I was a traitor! I should have removed Doris from the house, not Arlo! Would he like the Palms, or was he just being a good sport? What would my mother say, would she think I'd done the right thing?

It was only four in the afternoon. First I had to return Arlo's car and retrieve the van. Then I'd go see Burt at the hospital and give him his hair—I wondered if his brother had shown up yet. Then I'd go by the wing where Pincer was and check in on her. I should have asked my grandfather if I could borrow his car awhile, as it was a lot more fun to maneuver than the van. I opened the sunroof and turned up the radio and savored the new-car smell. It was poignant to see Arlo's driving gloves sitting in the niche in the dashboard.

When my sister and I were young, Arlo would take us up into the Santa Ynez in his jeep, off the road. One day we discovered the ruins of a house that must have burned down long before. The old foundations rose from the chaparral next to hardened puddles of melted glass. It was as if we were the first ever to come upon the place. Glass melted at about fourteen hundred to sixteen hundred degrees, Arlo told us. How did a fire get hotter than fire? we wanted to know. He often took us fishing at Lake Cachuma, a reservoir now blighted by drought. He taught us how to use the lathe and chisels in the shop in the garage. We made some small wooden vases out of lemon wood. Out in the back he taught us how to mix cement and make molds in sand, and we made stepping-stones with shells in them.

Such was the nostalgia I was indulging in when I arrived at my grandfather's and slipped his car back into the garage. The black Lexus had yet to return. Because my grandfather was no longer inside, because he'd never again be inside, because none of his favorite belongings were inside, the house filled me with dread, as if I were in the presence of a ghoul, a facsimile gutted of its heart with blank, soulless eyes. I wrote a note on a scrap of paper announcing that Arlo was now at the Palms and that there would never be another helper in the house again and fed it under the back door. Then I took the driver's seat in Burt's van and set off down the hill.

7

I'd only managed to travel a few hundred yards from Arlo's house when my phone began to buzz, and at a glance I caught sight of the Australian country code. My sister, Margaret, was calling. To be clear, she'd already left messages over the past few days at least ten times. I felt I had no choice but to answer.

But it wasn't Margaret. A woman with a voice I didn't recognize asked if she'd reached Penny Rush.

"*Is everything okay?*" I screamed out.

I almost drove off the road. When strangers called from Australia I was triggered to imagine the worst.

"I'm glad you asked." She introduced herself as Viola Mitchell, property manager.

"What is this regarding?" I demanded, grinding my teeth.

"A very common problem. Have you ever met a man who may

have seemed charming, but who eventually revealed something about himself that frightened you?"

"Why do you ask?"

"That's why I'm calling. It happens that your sister, Margaret Janssen, was not comfortable with Patrick Sullivan."

"Who is Patrick Sullivan?"

"A man of my profession with no scruples," she said. "I'm giving you a ring to introduce myself and find out your thoughts on the property on Banks Street. Your sister indicates she has been unable to reach you for some time."

Now I understood. By then I had parked the van in the lot by the beach and was considering hurling my phone into the ocean. "I'm not sure why Margaret has brought you, or Patrick Sullivan, in," I said. "We haven't reached any decisions about the house."

"Yes, she mentioned that you have an aversion to making decisions about the house. But I can only tell you that when you leave a house vacant, it will suffer from deferred maintenance. Neighbors may complain to the council. There's a large leopard tree on the property dropping debris into the pool of the neighbor to the south, who could lose patience. The post box on the street was struck by a car some time ago and has further deteriorated, mildew is growing on some of the windows, geckos have likely nested in the furniture, the exterior paint is peeling all around, the wood veranda has rotted dangerously in places, and possums have made a mess of the understory. Your sister believes that it's time to either put the place up for auction or clean it out to let."

It's true that Margaret had warned me about some of these problems, but I had avoided behaving in a practical manner over any of it. I always felt it necessary to defend the possibility that our parents might any day return. I had needed to believe in it, and had recurring dreams in which I saw it happen. I wouldn't even let Margaret speak of doing anything with the house, so I could see she'd gotten desperate. She'd called in professionals to deal with me.

"I understand," I finally said. "Let me think about it."

"I'm sorry, your sister says that you always say, *Let me think about it*."

"I see. Please tell my sister I'm embroiled in a scenario involving our grandparents beyond her wildest imagination and I will definitely respond in due course when I'm free."

"She mentioned you have been embroiled in scenarios for quite some time and that your time is up."

"My sister is a very understanding person, so I believe she would never say something like that."

"I won't spend any longer arguing with you, Miss Rush. You are most likely suffering from post-traumatic stress, or at least that is what your sister believes, and I can see that there is nothing to be gained by trying to have a reasonable conversation with you. Let me assure you, however, that these problems will not go away, no matter how long you keep your head in the sand. Further, fines are accruing, and no doubt interest on those fines. It could not possibly be your parents' wishes that you and your sister end up with legal problems and the expenses those problems beget. Finally, let me say this, Miss Rush. You may well continue to hope your parents are alive, and I doubt there's a soul on earth who would be cruel enough to take that away from you. Coming to a sound decision about their property is another matter entirely."

"Strange Margaret would hire you," I said.

"Goodbye, Miss Rush," she said.

I glared at my phone for a few moments after the call ended, as if it were the phone's fault such an unpleasant person had been able to worm her way into my day. Then I pressed back into the seat and let my eyes rest on the water, blue-gray near the shore, brighter on the horizon. The waves were small, lapping gently on the sand, over mounds of seaweed and scattered outcroppings of shale. I knew this beach well. There was once so much petroleum being dredged up around here we'd get our feet black with tar from all the spills, as the oil platforms offshore pumped away. After one especially bad slick our mother signed us up to clean birds. We dipped hefty brown pelicans in tubs of soapy water, their poor beaks fastened with rubber bands, gently removing the tarry goo from their feathers. We helped with grebes, ducks, murres. You could feel their hearts racing inside their ribs. You could see them wondering if we were going to eat them. We spoke to them in quiet voices and felt intense remorse over their plight. One duck shuddered and stopped breathing in my hands.

I started up the van and continued on my way.

The hospital lobby was strangely quiet in contrast to the emergency room I'd spent hours in the day before. I was given Burt's room number and took the elevator up to his floor. Though it was only about five o'clock, dinner was being served, and there was a great deal of noise up and down the corridor, with carts and trays clattering in all directions. Notably absent was the scent of anything appetizing.

From his bed, arm attached to an IV stand, Burt was watching a baseball game. He looked happy and alert and his skin was glowing with red corpuscles. I realized now how unwell he'd looked when we met.

"Penny!" He muted the TV, stretched, and yawned. "How's it going? The doctors say I'll be all right, probably out of here in a few days!"

I was very happy to see him, despite the dissonant things his brother had told me. "That's great! How do you feel?"

I came to his bedside and he reached for my hand, grasping it fondly.

"A helluva lot better than before," he said. "A little tired, though."

"Boy, do I have a lot to tell you," I said.

"Sit down," he said, letting me go. "My brother's here, but he went out for a walk. It's been terrific seeing him. I hope you can meet him." A brown corduroy jacket was draped over the back of the chair.

I nodded. Then I removed his hairpiece from my bag, handling it with unexpected affection. "They gave it to me when you left in the ambulance."

"Oh my god! What a pain in the neck I've been. Do I need it?" He took it from me anyway. "I don't know anymore. Maybe my priorities have changed."

"I think you look fine without it," I offered.

He said, "It's interesting you say that. I've noticed that more women talk to me when I'm not wearing it, but I still can't help feeling better with hair."

"Up to you, either way is good," I said cheerfully.

He placed it on his head and situated it. "Okay, I feel better. Thank you. If anything, it keeps my head warm. Now tell me everything. All I remember is driving to your grandmother's. Nothing else!"

So I told him about how he'd passed out in her house after getting on the examination table, how she had called the ambulance and accompanied him to the hospital, and how I was pretty sure I'd achieved our goal by finding the weapon-like Scintillator. "But then something pretty weird happened," I said, leaving him no time to ask what a Scintillator was.

"Weirder than all that?" Burt said.

"Yes." I described the arrival of the cleaning crew, my attempts to stall Pincer at lunch, and our return to her house. The police . . . the woodshed . . . the skeleton.

"Holy shit!" Burt started kicking his legs, making the hospital bed rattle around. "No way. No way!"

"Yes way," I said.

"Fuck! Excuse me, Penny. What the hell? What happened? What's going on?"

So I filled him in further, about the police, about the investigation, about carbon dating and DNA testing. Burt was shaking his head.

"I don't know what to say. What's going to happen now? Where is she?"

"She's actually here in this hospital," I said. "I'm going to drop over there after I say goodbye to you."

"I can't believe it. Or maybe I *can* believe it."

"I know, I know."

"Maybe this is a good thing, right? I mean, if they don't arrest her, they're not going to let her get away with living like that anymore. It'll be in the hands of experts."

"True," I said. "I just hope she didn't kill somebody. I don't think that's too much to ask."

"Sure, but it wouldn't be your fault," Burt said.

Somehow, it felt like it would be. I tended to exaggerate my own responsibility for things.

"Penny," Burt said. "I have a little news too. Don't take it the wrong way."

I must have blanched; it could only be something horrible.

"I got a call today from my building manager. He was calling to say he had reason to believe a homeless person was camping out in my office."

I could have laughed it off, but instead a feeling of abject humiliation overtook me. I felt my face burn. "Me?"

"I guess this barracuda lady down the hall, Kerry Cochren, saw somebody doing their laundry in the restroom this morning, and then she followed the drips on the carpet to my door," he said.

Someone thought I was a homeless person. And then it hit me—I *was* a homeless person.

"Did you . . . do your laundry in the restroom?" he asked meekly.

"Just some socks." I lied because I didn't want to embarrass him by revealing how much attention I'd been paying to his hair. "Very stupid of me. It was early and I didn't think anybody would come in. Are you in trouble now?"

"I told Chad that I'd look into it but that I didn't believe any homeless person except me would be staying there. Ha! No, I didn't say that. I told him I was in the hospital, so he backed off. But anyway, we've gotta be careful. I mean, technically I'm not supposed to be staying there either."

"I'm really sorry, Burt," I said. "I won't stay there anymore. I'll leave. I also wanted to tell you I've been driving your van—is that okay?"

"That's fine, Penny. Please do. That thing's like a cockroach, it'll survive anything."

I told him I eventually wanted to borrow my grandfather's car but that the situation was touchy right now, and I gave him the quick low-down on moving Arlo to the Palms.

Burt said, "That was today?"

"Yep," I said.

"What do you do for fun?"

I laughed hard at that—a bitter, barking laugh.

Just then, a nondescript man in a gray T-shirt and black jeans walked haltingly into the room.

"Dale!" Burt said. "Penny, this is my brother. Mi hermano. Mon frère!"

"Good to meet you," the man mumbled, and shook my hand. For some reason, I felt he resembled a hedgehog.

"You too." Though I must admit I did not feel like meeting anybody at the moment.

"Dodgers are up, three–two," Burt said, unmuting the TV. The brother grunted and moved closer to the screen.

I sensed with his arrival that I should reposition myself away from his jacket, as if it were too intimate to be lounging so close to it. I moved around the bed to the other side. I said, "Burt, I won't stay, I'd better go see my grandmother, but I'm so glad you're feeling better."

"You can sleep in the Dog, you know," he said. "I've done it. There's a futon back there. Grab one of the sleeping bags from the office. Please, it's all yours."

This kind offer set me back all the further, because I knew I would consider it. Maybe even do it. "Okay, we'll see." Something occurred to me then. "Do you—did you have a dog?"

"I *do* have a dog. I gotta get him back."

"Where is he?"

"One of my clients is watching him. He's a cute little Pomeranian, name's Kweecoats."

"A Pomeranian?"

"Yes, never in a million years would've thought I'd fall in love with a squirt like this guy. But never say never."

"What's his name again?"

"Like Quick Oats, but with a French accent. *Kweecoats*. Couldn't have him staying in the office. Want to see him?" He grabbed his phone and started scrolling, then held it up so I could take a look. On the screen was the indisputable bearer of the fur in the sleeping bag, a woolly orange puffball with a little face peering out.

"I gotta get my own place, Penny. I've been dragging my feet, it's clear to me now. Dale's been giving me the third degree, and he's right. This whole thing is my fault. I should have gone to the doctor sooner. It didn't have to get this bad. When you ignore things you just make 'em worse. He's beating some sense into me. He's always been the smart one."

Dale, clearly a sullen figure, said, "That's questionable."

"Anyway, a lot to figure out," Burt said. "Let me know what's happening with Grandma, all right?"

"I will," I said. "I'll check in tomorrow."

I'd said goodbye and had taken off down the hall when I heard footsteps. I looked over my shoulder and saw Dale Lampey coming after me. He said, "I wanted to clarify a few things I said on the phone. Would you have time to talk later?"

I said, "Sure, just give me a call."

"I was planning to have dinner at a Japanese place on the Mesa tonight, Hotaru, I don't know if you have plans."

I stepped back, mildly horrified.

"Are you all right?" he asked.

"I'm fine," I said. "Sorry. I need to get my stuff—"

"You're not thinking of staying in his van, are you?"

I shrugged. "Probably not. Maybe."

"That's ridiculous," Dale said. "I am shocked that he even suggested it."

"It's okay," I said. "I understand where he's coming from."

"I really don't."

"Don't be mad at him. He knows I'm on a budget right now. That's how he meant it, that's all."

"That's no excuse. He should've offered to put you up somewhere. You probably saved his life!"

"He doesn't need to thank me." Then I said, "It's great you came to see him. He said how much it means to him."

Dale scrutinized me and said, "People know my brother for two days and he's their new best friend."

I didn't deny it. Why should I? "What's so bad about that?"

Dale said, "You have to eat, don't you?"

"I should eat," I admitted.

"So meet me at Hotaru," he said.

I agreed to meet him at Hotaru.

I returned to the hospital lobby and found out where Pincer was located. As I trudged down several corridors and took an elevator, I decided I'd return to Burt's office later in the evening rather than sooner, decreasing the chances anyone would spot and despise the homeless person in their midst. I was very mad at myself for causing Burt this kind of trouble. I also wished I hadn't agreed to meet Dale Lampey, as my leg was throbbing and I felt shabby and uncommunicative.

At the nurses' station on Pincer's ward, I introduced myself and asked about her. To my surprise, rather than telling me how difficult she'd been, the two on duty described some fascinating conversations they'd had with her about medical matters and patient care, in which she'd lauded them as women in the field. That wily old goat, I thought. She knew she was in trouble this time. By the way they spoke of her, I sensed there had been no incriminating visits from the police. I asked what would be determined during her evaluation, and was told there would be recommendations on whether or not she could handle her own affairs. She was napping now, so I asked that they tell her I'd come by. My leg ached, and I was right on the verge of asking them to look at my thigh off the record, but just as swiftly came to the conclusion that looking at a thigh off the record was simply not a thing in a real place like this, and that I held a lot of childlike delusions about how matters worked in the world.

8

Standing in the hospital parking lot, I opened the back of Burt's van to assess the feasibility of spending the night in it, and because I'm practiced at seeing the potential in situations others don't bother with, I was fairly sure I could make it work. Beneath the ironing board, tire, hose, bicycle, and suitcases, I observed the presence of a futon for the first time. It was protected by a sheet of plastic and looked surprisingly clean. If I were to move the bike, hose, tire, and ironing board, it wouldn't be so bad to sleep between some suitcases and a donkey-shaped piñata. The interior walls of the van had been lined with smooth wood panels, and yellow gingham curtains protected the back and side windows. It was not outrageous, as Dale had claimed, to imagine sleeping in this van. I would save at least a hundred dollars, probably more. If I returned to Burt's office building later when nobody was around, I could use the bathroom and wash up and get my small suitcase and the sleeping bag.

I felt reasonably sure that the parking lot there would be a safe enough place to sleep.

I decided to drive to the Mesa and take a walk before the appointed hour with Burt's brother. It wasn't far from the hospital, and I found the restaurant Hotaru without trouble. But, climbing out of the van, I was hit by a wave of fatigue. I wished Pincer hadn't stabbed my leg with her ugly roadrunner pin. I limped toward the ocean, following a path to some undeveloped parkland on the cliffs, hoping the fresh air would revive me. I wasn't alone. Joggers and dogs and walkers were demonstrating their fitness in every direction, riffling through the wild fennel that grew along the paths and across the open fields. Wandering through a stand of eucalyptus, I inhaled the medicinal aroma of bark and leaves warmed by the sun. Near the cliff was a cluster of stumps and I found a nice smooth one to sit on. A grasshopper gallantly sprang out of my way.

But as soon as I settled, I had the prickly, not-unfamiliar feeling I was being watched.

I jerked my neck, looking quickly over one shoulder, then the other, studying the shadows of the trees in the grove. It was unlikely that my biological father, Gaspard, could have found me so soon after my departure from Santa Cruz, but he had become surprisingly adept at tracking me down, suddenly jumping out from behind a bush or a parked car to scare me after I had not seen him for months. As I'd stand battling the adrenaline coursing through my body, he'd laugh in triumph before announcing he had to hit the road again, and return to his tractor-trailer, wherever it was parked. Every now and then I'd look out a window and see him slowly driving past. Or I'd come out of the grocery store and see him across the parking lot. It wasn't that easy to hide in a tractor-trailer. Nor was he hard to miss, with his long, grizzled beard.

What did he hope to gain by doing this? I had to believe it was his twisted idea of staying in touch. We'd always had trouble communicating, and maybe this was the best he could do. I was glad he had a job, and hoped he'd never lose his license. He'd struggled with undiagnosed mental health issues for years, manifesting a breezy, energetic personality that attracted wounded people like my mother, who had, as a girl, been severely oppressed by Pincer. They divorced when I was an infant, so I have no memory of living with him, but still had to visit him once a year. I was eleven when he had his manic spinout, during which he believed he'd invented a recipe that was going to make him rich and famous—Steak in a Trout™. He spent money promoting it, lots of money. During my last visit with him, I witnessed signs of the obsession, the purchasing of bulk trout and steak, preparing it for neighbors, trying to find investors. To make a long story short, he contracted, likely from the undercooked flesh of cheap steelhead purchased from a fly-by-night hatchery, a tapeworm that went to his brain. Eventually he had brain surgery. Whether it was the worm or the surgery that compounded his previous problems, no one knew, but he was unable to hold a job for a few years until he took to the wheel of a truck.

The snap of a twig made me jump, and I whirled. A large gray dog was sniffing the ground, off-leash. I scanned the cliffs in both directions, reminding myself that the sale of my Chevette had given me a temporary reprieve from the possibility of his surveillance. I stopped reacting to the crackle of every leaf and twig, every flickering shadow, and soon had ceased thinking of him entirely, which was how I liked it. In the meantime, it was difficult to gauge what would need doing for my grandmother at this point. I wondered how long I'd have to spend in Santa Barbara, and what I should aim for once I left. Why did Margaret make some functionary call me, instead of calling herself? I wondered why Dale wanted to talk to me about Burt when I was hardly an expert. Was he hoping to obliterate any favorable feelings I had for his brother? At least I was getting some things accomplished. Maybe I'd make a list so I could have the pleasure of crossing them off. I looked at my watch. Only seven. I thought ahead to what I would order at the restaurant, and wondered if I'd be able to fully enjoy it with Burt's brother across the table staring at me. Suddenly I had an idea; I'd go now, early, and order my food before he showed up. I'd eat and enjoy it in peace, then stay to talk once he arrived.

Thrilled with my innovative plan, I took quick strides on the path until I was back on the street, approaching the restaurant. Dale Lampey was standing in front of it.

"You're early," I accused.

"So are you!" he said, as if he'd had the same plan himself.

It was the kind of Japanese restaurant where the sushi masters scream, *Irrashaimase!* to greet you.

As I took a seat across from Dale, I realized I had not had a good look at him until now. I'd performed visual shorthand earlier, sizing him up as hedgehog-like, but at close range his human contours took form. It was his spiky brown hair that had aroused the initial comparison. His brown eyes had a blunt, intent quality, as if they were lenses gathering information dispassionately for a data bank.

We ordered and our beers came first. A Kirin for me, a Sapporo for Dale. We said cheers. It was noisy in there, some corporate types at the next table were celebrating some fiscal news, but a few minutes of chatting provided me with some background on these brothers. Dale was a defense attorney in San Francisco, married, he muttered. Though I had nothing against wedding rings, I liked that he didn't wear one. He was younger than Burt by fourteen years, making him forty-three. They had grown up in Fresno, where their father had been a produce broker who died in a warehouse accident when Dale was only two, Burt sixteen. Burt, a star athlete and top student, became the man of the house. He turned down scholarships in order to stay home, went to a local college, then had some kind of collapse. For a few years he barely ventured out of his room. Their mother despaired. Dale realized the pressure was on him at an early age.

He knew a little about me from Burt, namely that my grandmother had been found with a body on her property.

"Look, basically I wanted to say I was wrong to criticize Burt when we talked on the phone," Dale said. "It was more about hearing news about a family member from someone I didn't know. That's not your fault, of course."

I was touched that he'd given it any thought. "I can imagine, that makes sense," I said. "I guess I can't help wondering—you said Burt doesn't have a daughter?"

"Yes, that's one reason I wanted to talk to you. I wanted to explain what I meant by that. When Burt was in his twenties he had a relationship with a woman who already had a baby, a girl, Mindy. After they broke up, he continued to call this girl his daughter, even though his ex didn't want him visiting and discouraged the relationship. I believe he sends her cards every year on her birthday, but obviously, it's delusional for him to call her his daughter, and whenever Burt does something delusional, it's very upsetting to me."

"That's a poignant story," I said.

"I don't really understand some of his choices, but it's his life."

"I guess he got it together eventually," I ventured.

Dale shrugged. "Whatever. I'm glad you think well of him. To-night after we eat I have to go bring some money to the woman who's taking care of his dog. Is that having it together? I don't know."

"Could be interesting," I said.

"Then I'm supposed to call this other woman he's entangled with and tell her to chill out. Does that sound fun?"

"What woman?"

Dale sighed and removed a piece of scratch paper from his pocket. Squinting at it, he said, "Her name is Kerry Cochren."

"Kerry Cochren?" Wasn't that the name of the woman who'd spied on me in the bathroom and reported me as a homeless person? "That's impossible, he said he couldn't stand her and that she's a barracuda!"

"That doesn't mean anything," Dale said.

"Why doesn't it mean anything?"

He said, "You've never heard that expression? I believe that means she's a hot number."

"A hot number?" I pulled out my phone, typed in *barracuda*. I was confronted by the image of an elongated fish with a huge underbite, and flashed it at him. "That's a hot number?"

"I don't think they're known for their looks."

"What are they known for?"

"They're ferocious," Dale said. "They are vicious and quick to attack. There's probably a thrill in trying to tame one."

How would he know? This made me feel disappointed in Burt, and in Dale for suggesting it was a possibility. I briefly considered prying into his personal life and asking about his wife, but realized I had no desire to hear about a marriage that was intact.

"Okay, then. Why can't he call himself?" I asked petulantly.

"Why do you care?" Dale suddenly demanded.

I felt hot and irritable and strangely unrestrained. "Why do you care that I care, not that I'm saying I care!"

"What is it that draws women to him? I have witnessed it again and again. I honestly don't understand. I mean, on an animal level, it's one thing, maybe he's irresistible. But as a functional adult, I'm sorry, no."

I was about to deny being one of those women, until I remembered that I'd imagined, for a fleeting moment, making out with him the night we met. I truly wondered why. Obviously I was awakening to the mere potential for making out with someone, someday, Burt serving as a stand-in. He wasn't my type at all, if there was such a thing. But anyway, why should Dale begrudge Burt some attention?

"Burt seems like a nice guy, that's all," I finally said. "And like I told you, he's been really helpful to my grandmother."

"I hope that's the case," Dale said. "He says he's taking his medications, but it's hard to know whether or not he's doing reliable work. I've had to bail him out a few times. Accounting malpractice suits. Messy."

This was unsettling.

"Not the best advertisement for his services, I realize. I try to stay out of it, but I don't often meet any of his clients, so here we are."

I thought of all the unused medications in the drawer in Burt's office—I should ask Burt about it directly, rather than tattling.

I had vegetable tempura and something called yam maki, like a sushi roll with fried sweet potato in it. Dale had pork tonkatsu with rice and cabbage. A few globs of wasabi went straight to my head. He told me he was reading an interesting collection of essays by Richard Rorty, and I mentioned the last thing I'd read, a novel by Murakami. We both ate rapidly and intensely, as if getting it over with as fast as possible, and in no time we were done. Dale signaled for the check, and a sudden, generalized dread of being left behind led me to blurt out, "Where is Burt's dog? Could I go too?"

"Sure, if you want to."

"I mean, if we'll get to see the dog," I said quickly, not wanting him to think I was clinging to him.

"I imagine we can see the dog," he said.

"I don't have to go, I just thought it would be nice to see a dog," I said.

"That's fine."

Perhaps simply to provoke him gratuitously, I said, "Are you looking forward to seeing his dog?"

Dale looked at me. "I feel angry about seeing his dog, if you really want to know."

"But it's not the dog's fault."

"No, it's not."

"Then why are you angry about it?"

"Isn't it obvious? Because I have found myself in the position of having to clean up after Burt more than once. He's like a child."

"Maybe that's the best he can do," I said, reflecting on an attitude I'd tried to develop toward my own relatives.

"Guilty as charged. I'm full of compassion for my clients, short of it with my own brother."

Such a quick confession could hardly be sincere.

He insisted on paying and I let him, since he had a job and I did not. I followed him out of the restaurant to a bright red sports car parked across the street. It looked fast and fun. The air was balmy, yet goose bumps rose on my arms. "Dale," I said. "I have to sort out the van and get it ready for tonight. You go ahead."

"I thought you wanted to see the dog."

"I do, but I'm tired. It's been a long day."

"Where are you going to park?"

"I thought I'd park at Burt's office building."

"It's quiet?"

"It's fine."

"All right." He took a couple of silver-wrapped mint patties from his pocket and gave me one. "If that's your wish. Look, would you do me a favor?"

"What is it?"

"I'm not going to question your choice to stay in my brother's van. But wouldn't you like to take a shower? I'm not saying you need one, by the way, but you do have cobwebs in your hair."

"I do?" I tried to look at my reflection in the car window. "Where?"

"On top and in the back."

"Why didn't you tell me?"

"I didn't really notice before. Sorry."

I felt the back of my head, coming away with clumps of the mysterious substance in my fingers. "Oh my god!" It wouldn't shake off, so I had to wipe it on my pants.

"I'll give you the key to my room, you can drive over there now while I'm dealing with the dog."

I opened my mouth, but nothing came out. In my head was a chaotic din. This only happened when I was anxious and afraid, but what was there to be afraid of now? I employed one of my tricks for emergencies, fixing my eyes just over Dale's bristly head.

"I will be okay, Dale, thank you very much, it was nice to meet you, it was good you came to visit Burt, thank you for dinner," I said in the practiced drone that enabled me to move through social interactions when I was at risk of seizing up.

"All right, Penny," he said. "Good night."

9

Should I have gone with Dale to see Burt's dog? Once I took my seat behind the wheel of the van, I felt restless and annoyed by my habit of closing down. I realized I'd been enjoying Dale's company, and in the state I was in could develop a crush on him. But he was married, so having a crush on him would be futile and detrimental to my brittle psyche, and therefore, I should try to avoid him as much as possible.

I found myself heading off in the opposite direction of Burt's office, as if unwilling to face my decision to spend the night in the Dog of the North, or at least to postpone it. I ended up at West Beach near the pier and found a parking spot. The wide stretch of sand was lit up by streetlamps and the ambient glow from the restaurant windows on the wharf, and the froth on the surf glowed blue. Cars all around were filled with people, either by themselves staring soulfully at the vastness of the ocean, or in groups, smoking joints and listening to tunes.

Though I'd have preferred to have company, there was no question that I felt comfortable being alone at that moment and was glad to see there were other people in nearby cars who felt the same. I thought about all the times I'd sat at the edges of groups in conversation, listening, enjoying myself, but surely considered the person with the least to contribute, the way the least interesting creature in an aquarium is generally agreed to be the slug over in the corner. Overall, it seemed like I had to work extra hard just to make any kind of relationship work. And in that sense, I had a lot to offer.

It was in college that my limitations, of which I was already mostly aware, became fully clear. I sensed professors didn't like me. They thought I was uninterested, furtive, contemptuous. But I wasn't at all. I was just possessed by some kind of anxiety that prevented me from revealing the chemistry I really felt toward them. Occasionally, I'd write a paper that would pique the interest of one of these professors, and they'd ask me to come to their office, but I was terrified of having a tortured conversation, so I'd never show up.

Except once. I'd taken a beginning creative nonfiction class co-taught by two grad students, Gina and Patrick. One day they asked me to stay behind to discuss the latest assignment, which had been to describe an incident in our childhoods that had made a lasting mark. My piece, more or less, relayed the following:

I was eleven years old, visiting my biological father, Gaspard, in San Diego, when I found a small fish struggling on the beach during a run. I was running because Gaspard had yelled and attempted to slap me but I'd bolted from his house and ended up down by the shore, and it was only because I was doubled over, catching my breath, that I noticed it.

"I'd better get you back in the water," I said, surprising myself with the sound of my voice, for I had not spoken out loud for almost a week.

"Please do," said the fish, surprising me more.

"Did you just say something?"

"Look, I'm not even supposed to be here. It's all been a terrible mistake."

"Why?" I asked, crouching on the wet sand. "Aren't you a grunion?"

"I'm a false grunion. It's all a big mistake."

"I know what that's like," I said.

"I'm not even female. Get me out of here! Maybe this is an opportunity in disguise."

Not willing to part with such a find so quickly, I rushed to one of the trash cans that had been placed every hundred feet or so along Mission Beach. There I found a discarded Kentucky Fried Chicken bucket, ran back to the water, and filled it. Then I dropped in the little fish.

The false grunion seemed stunned for a moment, but quickly a shock of life ran through its body and it began to swim in circles, leaping out of the water a few times.

Then it stilled and poked its mouth up my way.

"Thanks, this helps a lot," it said.

"Glad I could help," I said, feeling good about myself for the first time in weeks.

"The thing is, I can't stay in here very long. Would you consider returning me to deeper waters?"

Surely it could not have been my own idea to do what I did next—a psychologist would later tell me I invented my conversation with the fish as a way of dissociating from the peril I had placed myself in. At the base of the nearest lifeguard station sat a stack of inner tubes, some chained together, others thrown over the top of the pile. I grabbed one. Then, without further ado, still carrying the false grunion in the bucket, I stepped into the center of the tube and shuffled into the water. The sea was mild and low, small waves rumbling up to my knees. As the tube rose, I grasped the rubber under my arms, walked on, lost touch with the bottom, kicked off, and bounced over a few of the larger breakers. Once we were past the surf, the round mouth of the fish appeared again.

"Allow me to introduce myself. I am of the species *Colpichthys regis*, of the genus *Colpichthys*, of the tribe Atherinopsini, of the family Atherinopsidae, of the order Atheriniformes, of the class Actinopterygii, of the phylum Chordata, of the kingdom Animalia, of course. I'm a New World silverside, and for some horrible reason my nickname is False Grunion. What brings you here?"

It was certainly worth asking. I was now clinging to an inner tube several hundred feet from shore.

"I ran away," I finally said. "My father is mad because I don't call him Dad, and all he cares about is Steak in a Trout."

"Hmm. Well, you probably don't need me to tell you that you're now drifting south on the California current and farther by the minute from terra firma, where I believe you feel more comfortable."

"I'm scared of the ocean," I managed to say. I'd never been happier to have someone to talk to.

"Then you've come to the wrong place," said the false grunion. "I take it you'd like to go back?"

"Yes," I said. "My swimming isn't the best."

"I'm sure you have other good qualities," he said. "You see, I'm afraid I haven't many friends here to call together to give you a push. The regular grunions look right past me. I'm a bit lost myself, to tell you the truth."

"Oh, really?" I said, happy to have something else to think about. "Where are you from?"

"Long story," said the false grunion. "It's funny that two lost souls should find each other, don't you think?"

His little mouth, opening and closing in the bucket, and his fierce little eyes made him seem strong. But he was only a tiny fish.

Over the long afternoon, the inner tube drifted south, the current pushing me at around six knots an hour. Nobody suspected I'd taken to the water. When I didn't show up for dinner, Gaspard was furious. He'd made his usual rounds that afternoon, to the Marine Corps base to sell life insurance, to the used car lot, to the vacuum shop. He'd returned to his little house in the late afternoon with fifteen new insurance contracts and $225 in hard-won cash.

By nightfall, according to later testimony, he began to feel some concern. He expected to see me shuffling up to the house any moment, hungry and sniveling. He made a reconnaissance of the neighborhood and then the beach; the strand was lit by bonfires in pits from the cliffs of La Jolla to the breakwater south. He roamed pit to pit, scanning the faces in the firelight, asking if anybody'd seen a skinny kid with short brown hair and no brains.

Meanwhile, I had spent the day drifting in the inner tube, roasting under the sun, distracted from despair by conversation with the false grunion. I could no longer see land. My throat was parched, my lips dry, my eyes burned.

"I'm not sure this was a good idea," I said to my friend, who I had released but who was sticking with me.

"It doesn't appear to be," he said. "But you will do fine once this is over. You saved my life. I will always be grateful. And I will stay with you as long as I can."

"Thank you."

To keep up my spirits, he told me tales of the sea, great adventures had by his forebears. Battles with deepwater behemoths. Tidal panics. Times of famine and times of feasts. Tragedy striking when they least expected it, joy coming in on a fair morning swell. Stories handed down for generations of shipwrecks and other nautical catastrophes. He told me I would not be one of them.

"It will soon be time for me to part and direct some help your way," he told me. "We're nearing my home waters. Just don't do anything foolish. Don't try to swim. Just rest here and wait, will you promise?"

"I promise," I said.

It happened that evening that a fishing crew heard rumor of a massive school of sardines offshore and set out in pursuit. Where this rumor originated nobody ever knew, as there were no sardines to be found. But during the search, the light of the moon gathered around a dark spot in the water, something that looked like a tire at first, until a strobe from the crew detected the presence of a child.

It took a while before I was able to tell them my name. My lips were blistered, my eyes purple, my skin fiery and bubbled. I shivered like a beached fish. They wrapped me in rags covered with machine oil and called in the Coast Guard to meet us.

The episode had been overlaid with what I'd been told later, muddled by delirium, booted around by the passage of time. I'd manufactured a cartoon version of the experience, and why not? The real and the story became, in a way, the same.

Gina said she liked the piece, but that it was obviously fictionalized and that this was a nonfiction workshop. Patrick countered that I'd employed the metaphor of being lost at sea to convey my alienation from my father. I replied that I had truly been lost at sea. Gina noted that grunions, false or otherwise, don't talk. I agreed, but argued that the false grunion represented some part of my psyche that helped me get through the experience. Patrick said maybe I could rewrite it making it more clear that the false grunion was a coping mechanism. Gina changed her tune and said maybe it was fine the way it was. They wanted me to read it at our next class, which happened to be the last one of the quarter. I didn't come.

Having had my fill of introspection by the ocean, I drove back to State Street and pulled into the parking lot, looking for the best place to burrow in. Back by the dumpster stood a huge ficus tree with a thick corrugated trunk and many overhanging branches. I imagined that the spaces beneath it were prized on hot days. With only a few other cars in the lot, I had my pick, and nosed the van into the corner spot under the tree where it was dark and sheltered from the streetlights on the avenue. I hoisted the bike and hose from the back, finding room for them across the front seats. Then I crawled into the back and began to make my billet. I pushed the suitcases, boxes, and tire to the wall, put the ironing board on top, created a taco-shaped bed with the futon, and tested it. Perfectly comfortable. Satisfied that the arrangements were adequate, I locked the van and returned inside the building.

Fluorescent overnight lights cast a strange unreality to the lobby. The building was quiet, and the artificial light on the garden under the stairs made it all the more unearthly, like a tableau in a museum of lost civilizations. I climbed the stairs, passing the office door of Kerry Cochren as I continued down the hall. According to her sign, she was a suicide prevention coordinator. *Just the person for the job*, I thought. I let myself into Burt's office.

It took only a minute to roll up the sleeping bag, grab the pillow and my bag. Then I went out to the restroom down the hall to brush my teeth, wash my face, and brush my hair, removing any webs that were stuck to me. I found it embarrassing that Dale had intuited my need for a shower, and even more awkward that he'd offered me the one in his hotel room. It seemed intimate. I doubted his wife would enjoy hearing that a woman was showering in his room.

I returned to Burt's office and gave it one last look. How strange that I was now nostalgic for my nights on the couch! The good old days. The little dog I'd fashioned with fur was sitting on Burt's desk and I hoped it would cheer him up when he returned. Taking my gear, including the bag containing the Frosted Flakes I'd purchased the night before, I closed the door behind me.

Outside, there was a bright, nearly full moon. I entered the van from the front, throwing my stuff in the back and then climbing over the bicycle, which was a bad idea. I banged my sore leg on it, collapsing into the futon taco in a spasm of pain. Once it passed I laid out the sleeping bag, moved things around a little more, and settled in. The taco shape was not as comfortable as I'd expected, and I began to feel claustrophobic almost at once. I started elbowing it away, thrashing like an animal in a trap. I've always found it strange how quickly a person can lose control, how thin the veneer of civilized behavior really is. One side gave way more easily, discharging some crackling sounds, whereby I realized I was about to destroy Burt's piñata. I got up on my knees and peeled back the futon, moving the rainbow-papered thing out of the way.

Trying to settle down in the dark, I checked my phone and discovered I had a new message from Doris. I listened, holding the phone away from my ear because her voice was so shrill. She was saying that items had been removed from the house and that it was insulting that Arlo had moved without telling her and that she was going to raise hell with the people at the Palms for pressuring him to make such a major decision so swiftly. She asked that I call her immediately.

What a hypocrite!

The beer I'd had with Dale had suppressed my aches and pains, but now they were upon me again, the headache especially. I groped in my bag for my water bottle and took a few ibuprofen. Then I reached into the bag from the mini-mart for the Frosted Flakes. My hand came in contact with something it didn't immediately recognize—it was the small carton of milk for the flakes, now swollen up like a puffer fish because I'd failed to refrigerate it. I placed it near the rear door to throw out in the morning. Then I tore open the box of Frosted Flakes and began to munch them. The munching was so loud I wondered if it could be heard outside. I hoped nobody would peer in at me—once, when I was visiting Gaspard, he'd had me sleeping outside in a tent, and during the night a goblin-like head appeared in the tent window, face pressing against the mesh, prompting me to scream as if my life depended on it. I think I'd been a jumpy sort of person ever since.

The buzzing of my phone was almost welcome compared to thinking about that. It was Doris calling again, and sheer loneliness led me to answer.

She launched right in. "Penny, I've called the Palms and given them a piece of my mind. I wasn't able to speak to Arlo. These people would not put me through to my own husband. This is most likely against the law. I'm also concerned that you apparently removed things from the house without my permission. I believe this is against the law as well. I have a good mind to call the police after the way I've been treated today."

"Doris," I said quietly. "You wanted Arlo in a facility, you told me that this morning."

"I know what I said to you this morning. Don't try to pull that. I'm talking about common courtesy. You are not the wife. I am the wife!"

"Of course you're the wife. You can visit Arlo tomorrow. He'll be happy to see you."

"I cannot visit Arlo tomorrow. I have back-to-back appointments. Nothing about this was done with my schedule in mind. And another thing. I received a call tonight at the house from Mr. Gaspard Rush, asking for Arlo. I told him Arlo wasn't home and then he said he was looking for you. I said you were in town and he thanked me."

I broke out in a cold sweat. Why would he call Arlo? "Did you tell him anything else?"

"That you ransacked my house and took my husband? No, I didn't mention it."

"Doris, I think you'll be happy when you see the place. Arlo likes it. He just wanted to get it over with quickly. He talked about you every step of the way. I'll make sure you get to talk to him tomorrow, okay?"

"That would be very civil," she said. "I'm going to say good night now. Good night!"

"Okay. Good night, Doris."

Once again I was alone in the dark, realizing how stupid it was for me to have answered her call. Why did Gaspard call there? Why did I need to know this, especially now? At least he'd be looking for the Chevette. The only thing protecting me was the Dog of the North.

The next few hours, I must admit, were difficult. I was lonely and distressed, marooned. If I were to call somebody, my voice could carry and attract the attention of someone prowling around, and I preferred to keep my presence there to myself.

Alternately, the big tree under which I'd parked turned out to be a haven for creatures that flourished under the cover of night. Over the next hour or so I heard the flapping of great wings, the bowing and shuddering of branches, the sharpening of claws, and the grooming of beaks. And here and there the glottal acrobatics of mastication. Could it be a handsome family of owls? Gentle hoots seemed to answer yes. Parliament was in session. At one point, a large clod dropped on the roof of the van. If anything, the quotidian sounds of their nocturnal habits distracted me from my own problems, and I had the comforting thought as I drifted off to sleep that a benevolent force was watching over me.

In the morning I woke with a start. I was having an unsettling dream in which I was being warned by a docent at a museum about an extinct but murderous species of bird known as the "Terrifying Pea-Hen." The docent played me a rare recording of a Pea-Hen pecking something to death, and that's when I woke, though the terrible pecking sound carried on. Somebody was knocking on the van! Joyful it was not a Terrifying Pea-Hen but afraid I was about to be called out for trespassing, I peered hesitantly through the tangle of bicycle and hose to the front window.

Dale Lampey stood there, drenched in sunlight. His close-cropped hair glistened.

"Just a minute!" I said, greatly relieved, yet afraid of how flattered I was he'd come to see me. I looked at my phone. Eight o'clock.

I took a quick look at myself in the selfie setting, choosing to smooth down the tangle around my head. Then I crawled toward the rear doors and opened them.

Dale appeared at the rear of the van, holding the end of a leash. On the other end was Burt's furry auburn-colored dog.

"How come you have him?" I asked right away.

"Long story," Dale said. "Let's just say that he was not in a suitable situation."

"What happened?"

He picked up the small dog and showed me the place on its back that had been shaved to the skin and bore a patchwork of rough black stitches, just out of mouth's reach so it didn't have to wear a cone. "This woman had two unfriendly Dobermans. She hadn't even noticed he'd been bitten. I spent most of the night at the twenty-four-hour veterinary clinic out in Goleta while they took care of him. No way can he be left there! Plus he has some kind of infection of his anal glands, if you really want to know. I'm supposed to stick ointment in those for a week."

"Poor Kweecoats!" I said, looking at the hapless dog, who was glancing around frantically and pushing to get out of Dale's arms. Then I looked at Dale. "Poor you! I had to do that once when I was house-sitting. To a dog, of course. It wasn't as bad as it sounds."

"Great, I look forward to it." He placed Kweecoats on the ground and brushed several clumps of fur off his corduroy jacket. "Look, I'm on my way to the airport. I'm going to take him home with me and bring him back whenever Burt gets it together. Anyway, you said you wanted to see the dog."

"Thank you," I said. "He's really cute."

"My room is paid for until noon, you know." He dug into his pocket and pulled out a card key. "It's the Seaside, room four hundred twelve. Go ahead. I hung out the DO NOT DISTURB sign and tried not to leave the place a mess. Come here, boy," he said, looking under the van.

This time, I knew I couldn't refuse.

"Kweecoats!" Dale said then. "Drop it!"

I looked down. Kweecoats was crouching beneath the drive shaft, chewing on something.

"What is that?" I asked.

Dale pulled him into the sunlight. The dog's jaw was firmly clamped around, no mistaking it, a mammalian leg—rough and bloody on one end, a small paw on the other.

Dale attempted to grab hold of it. "Drop it, Coats!"

"Coats" had no intention of dropping this befurred trophy measuring about six inches. I guessed it had once been an essential segment of a rabbit, and I looked up into the tree, remembering the hungry sounds I'd been privy to in the night. It was at that moment that I noticed another shredded chunk of flesh on the roof of the van. Meanwhile, Dale knelt on the leash to free his hands, placing them around Kweecoats's muzzle, whereupon he attempted to pry open the dog's jaws. An extended skirmish ensued. Kweecoats growled. After considerable wresting, Kweecoats's teeth parted and the leg fell to the ground. Dale swiftly scooped it up.

"My god," he said simply, hurling the leg into the nearby bin, where it landed with a clatter.

I pointed to the roof of the van. "I know it's a lot to ask, but could you put that in the garbage too?"

Dale looked and grimaced. "I wonder if you could drive away and let it fall off."

"What if it flies onto somebody's windshield and they scream and crash?" I argued in the slightly irrational way I might approach this had we been a couple, and instantly regretted it.

To my surprise, he was kind enough to reach for what appeared to be a gored rib cage and heave it into the bin.

"My day is made," he said.

I remembered the thud I'd heard on the roof during the night and despaired. A rabbit who was the star of his own narrative had been torn limb from limb while I'd been focusing on the theme of the birds.

"Thank you. There's a restroom in the building on the second floor," I said. "I'll watch him if you want to wash your hands."

"Funny how we both spend a lot of time telling each other to wash up," Dale said, taking off at a quick pace.

I knelt by Burt's dog, who had been through a lot of trauma lately and appeared to be trembling. I spoke to him in the reassuring tones I had come to believe that dogs liked. I told him he was a beauty, while he sniffed my arm. He had soulful brown eyes, a small black nose, and a bountiful ruff of a slightly blonder shade than the rest of his coat. "Who did those Dobermans think they were?" I said in my talking-to-dogs voice. "Who did they think they were?" Gazing at him up close, I was able to read the tag nestled in his fur and was surprised to see the name QUIXOTE engraved on it. Did Burt pronounce Quixote *Kweecoats*? Presently I looked up and saw Dale advancing rapidly across the lot.

"I'd better get going," he said.

"His name is Quixote!"

"I noticed that," Dale said. "We'll have to get to the bottom of this."

I handed him the leash. "I hope Burt keeps getting better."

"That's two of us," Dale said, and he turned and walked over to his rented red sports car. There was a pet carrier in the backseat, and he loaded Kweecoats in. As he started the car, he turned and waved.

I waved back.

Before moving the bike and other things out of the front into the rear, I took careful hold of the bloated milk carton and chucked it into the dumpster, wherein it exploded like a stink bomb. Peering over the side, I observed a spray of curds in a halo around the ruptured vessel. What a relief that it hadn't erupted in the van during the night! That I had avoided being covered with sour curds surely counted as the day's first success.

I then drove to Dale's hotel near the wharf. It was a nice establishment, and I walked through the lobby to the elevator hoping no one would notice me, or the person I had become. On the fourth floor I let myself into Dale's room and gasped—it had a view of the harbor and the bathroom was huge and, as far as bathrooms go, beautiful. I went straight in and ripped off my clothes. I had no desire to see myself naked in the mirror, though it had been so long since I'd been unclothed before somebody new I couldn't help wondering if I was reasonably up to snuff. Though I was only in my mid-thirties, I had come to feel old. After a quick once-over, I was most surprised by how red my leg looked, with tentacles of inflammation radiating out from the original stab wound, one going up my thigh, a few more running down my leg to my knee. Hot water would soothe and summon white blood cells to the site. I'd keep an eye on it. I reached for the strange fixture in the shower that was too modern for its own good. It's my opinion that water taps should not be intelligence tests. Water spurted from the lower tap while I attempted to adjust the temperature. Finally I detected a secondary ring behind the handle that had to be turned by way of a minimal nub to direct the water to the showerhead, but it was so stiff and hard to grasp I could hardly manage it. I pulled and ripped off several of my already short, ragged fingernails, but at last I triumphed over the pretentious fixture and the shower surged to life, and once I stepped in, it felt so good I forgave it. I washed and rinsed my hair twice. Later I used one of the fluffy white polar-bear-sized towels the hotel supplied. Then I put on some fresh clothes from my bag, and with my hair combed out and my skin shining, I considered myself ready for the day. But it was only ten o'clock. How could I resist staying for a short while to enjoy the view and relax?

It was strange to think that only a week ago I'd started my day at the run-down Westward Ho! Motel in Santa Cruz, completely out of money, about to give up the keys to my Chevette to a man named Delbert Winkle, who would tell me a long story during the transaction about having beaten up a kid who was torturing a cat and subsequently spending the last six months in jail. I imagined I too would beat up a kid torturing a cat and sympathized. It was the same day that I'd later taken a long walk down West Cliff Drive, gazing at the waves crashing on the soft sandstone cliffs, admiring surfers in their slick wetsuits, spotting a backstroking otter in the kelp, enjoying the briny sea air, on the walk that showcased so many iconic things about the town, the town I'd been living in on and off since college, where I'd met Sherman, where we'd rented rooms and apartments and had fun for a while, the last place I'd ever seen my parents, and so on, only to receive on that walk the two phone calls, one from Doris and one from Burt, that brought me to Santa Barbara only days ago, even though it felt as if I'd been here forever.

All I wanted to do now was climb into the other side of the bed that Dale hadn't slept in and feel the cool, clean sheets. I noticed some tufts of the telltale fur of Kweecoats at the end of the bed, the very same type of tufts that had upset me when I found them in the sleeping bag, but which now seemed like a fond reminder of a plucky creature with a mind of his own. I made myself a cup of coffee with the capsules and machine in the room. I scanned the harbor and the ocean. The sun was brilliant and the water roiled. I felt a moment of hope and tried to hold on to it. This proved a struggle, however, because, for one thing, I didn't like the idea that hope came to me from something as frivolous as a nice hotel room, and for another, I quickly recognized that my presence in this room was countenanced on the fact that Burt's brother Dale had, upon sizing me up, determined that I desperately needed help. And that I was so pathetic that this, the tail end of a one-night hotel reservation, was the only way I could get it. I felt the fledgling heartbeat of the need to convince him, now that I'd framed the matter this way, that I was not as pathetic as I seemed, that I'd made choices and had priorities. I was choosing my current situation, I would tell him. I preferred to be thrifty and could delay gratification when need be. I was excellent at delaying gratification, in fact, and this was a useful attribute, one in my arsenal I had long depended on. I had no doubt that I could achieve a conventional lifestyle once I set my mind to it. Besides, a conventional lifestyle could hold just as many, if not more, horrors as the one I now possessed.

I dozed off on the bed and slept until housekeeping banged on the door.

10

It was hard to close the door to such a luxurious room behind me. Trudging down the hallway, full of the sound of vacuum cleaners and blocked by hospitality carts, I had only a fuzzy sense of the day ahead, but perhaps that was best. I would check in with Pincer. I would see Burt. I would visit Arlo. And I would try to find out what was going on with the investigation of the skeleton by contacting Storke. Finally, I would probably find myself haunted by the looming threat of an encounter with Gaspard, which added a certain extra something. But I had a slight spring in my step following my shower and change of clothes, and thought it best if I used it on the hardest tasks first.

It was thus that, after returning to Burt's van, throwing in my bag and climbing into the now-familiar driver's seat, I phoned Detective Storke at the number on his card.

After reintroducing myself, I said, "Just wanted to see if you had any news."

"News? Let me pull up the file," he said, and I waited a moment, watching a family across the parking lot grow testy as they struggled to stuff and rig their fancy SUV with their bicycles and surfboards and expensive luggage. A metaphor for this affluent era if ever there was one! "All right," he said then. "Here's what we have from forensics. This was a male, age range of fifty-five to sixty-five, height around five-foot-six, medium build. Estimated time since death twenty years. Does anybody come to mind that might fit that description?"

"No, not really." I had limited knowledge of my grandmother's life after the divorce from Arlo.

"Bones were dry," he went on. "Little to no mummified tissue. Some boring insect activity. No detectable signs of trauma on the skeleton. We're waiting on DNA analysis and matching capabilities from some of our missing persons data banks. A chemical analysis is also coming."

It was harder to tell that Storke needed love when I wasn't looking at him, yet I still detected a woebegone hitch in his voice.

"The most surprising finding is that the body was unclothed, though it had been placed on a wool blanket, which had mostly disintegrated."

"The body was naked."

"Yes. The remains of a naked corpse were found in your grandmother's shed. I hope you're mentally prepared for wherever this takes us."

"I'll do my best."

"All right. In the meantime, I've interviewed her former husband, Arlo Reshnappet, and I'm planning to speak to her accountant this afternoon if he's fit enough. I'm not forming a picture of a woman with a very happy life, if you want to know the truth."

I wondered about his definition of a happy life, but refrained from asking.

"I've just received the evaluation from the hospital," he went on. "They believe she may be suffering from a mild form of dementia caused by small strokes. They plan to release her today and recommend she have daily attention in her home if she is to remain there and will assign someone from Adult Protective Services to make sure it happens. They said she masks her frailties well and is obviously a smart woman accustomed to getting her way. All this is to say, I'm afraid, that she might well be able to stand trial if it comes to that."

"Oh!" was all I could say. "And how would it come to that?"

"I'm just pointing out that when a decomposed body is found on a person's property, that person's age and health considerations will not preempt an investigation and its consequences."

"Of course, no, it shouldn't."

"Another thing," Storke said. "You asked if I'd been at the house before. I checked the records for any history there, and sure enough, we've had officers called out to that house many times. What do you know about that?"

"I know nothing. My grandmother reinvented herself after she and my grandfather divorced, and stopped speaking to us."

"I see. Well, over the years she's reported an assortment of trespassers, Peeping Toms, and would-be intruders, though no suspects were ever apprehended."

I said, "I wonder if she'd have been calling all the time if she'd knowingly hidden a body where law enforcement might easily look."

"Fair point. Though this can be the behavior of someone with consciousness of guilt."

A discerning sound was warranted, so I produced it.

"And another thing. When I tried to contact Arlo Reshnappet I reached his wife, Doris Roofla Reshnappet, who made a number of claims about your handling of her husband's affairs. I told her I wasn't calling about that, and was finally able to extract his whereabouts from her, so I paid him a visit this morning at the Palms. He said if his former wife were capable of killing somebody, he likely wouldn't be alive."

I said, "I hope that testimony will be useful."

Storke said, "Yes, I hope so too. When there's a felon in the family, it's never a happy time."

It could not be easy to be a man with spidery red eyebrows and many rust-colored double chins. Though I found myself judging Storke's social skills, I knew he was, as they say, only doing his job. Besides, my mother would have said that Pincer was an emotional felon at the least.

"Thank you for taking my call. Will it be all right to take my grandmother back to the house today?"

"We are finished with the interior, but the area around the wood-shed is still off-limits."

"No problem," I said. "Thank you for everything you do. For the years it's taken to accumulate this expertise. For your attention to detail. For showing up, day after day."

After a long pause he said, "I'll take that as I hope you meant it."

I turned the key in the ignition and departed the parking lot of the Seaside Hotel like an eel slinking out of the reeds. I drove Burt's van to Pincer's so as to look the place over before bringing her home and also called the psych ward and found out she'd be ready to go by three. Mostly I had to figure out how to provide her with the help she needed without having to provide myself. I didn't think I could take having to stay with her, even for a night. One time, a few years ago, Sherman and I had come to visit. The house wasn't as bad then, not nearly. She told us to take a stroll while she prepared dinner. When we returned, we discovered she had been dicing raw chicken on my laptop as if it were a cutting board. She feigned confusion, but seriously, some part of me thought she'd done it on purpose! Another time I came down alone, but woke in the middle of the night because she was in my room with a flashlight, looking through my suitcase. At the moment I felt myself on the verge of panicking, thinking about grappling with her later in the day. Without Burt's help, I honestly wasn't sure I could take it.

Pincer's gate, I was surprised to see, had been carelessly left open by whoever had been there last. I stopped to collect the mail from the box and then drove up the driveway, parking by the garage. The chorus of insects and birds rang out from the untended foliage on the property with all its bowers and thickets. Thanks to the efforts of the cleaning crew, I counted twenty-two large black garbage bags full and bulging in a cluster under the electric lantern that hung by the garage door. I walked down the brick path and let myself in. I'd been too preoccupied with the police presence the last time I'd been here to register all the progress that had been made. The house smelled a lot better and I was very glad the crew had been able to accomplish so much before making their unfortunate discovery. I went straight to the kitchen and was thrilled to see that all the jars on the counter that had been filled with mystery substances were now washed out and neatly lined up at one end of it. The floor had been mopped, the inside of the refrigerator detoxed, the stove shined.

The living room had been picked up and vacuumed, though the rat carcasses were still arranged in a museum-quality display on the sheet. I was struck then by the light in the room, which seemed brighter than ever—perhaps the windows had been washed or the curtains were more widely parted than usual. It was as if her absence had freed everything, even the light, from her shadow.

Shrubs grew up over the lower part of the great windows that looked out across the wilderness of the yard, and all at once I realized that there was a face among them staring in at me. I jumped. But it was only the girl I'd met while hiding in the front hedge, the girl with Casper the dog. Our eyes met and for a moment I had the eeriest feeling that I was seeing myself some years in the past, perhaps in the very place I'd hidden and played in this garden, doing something innocent but for which I would soon be rebuked. I smiled because I understood why she was there and I wanted her to know I didn't mind; her curiosity was fully understandable to me, and the gate had been left open, after all, and there had been so much activity at the house in the past few days. Just as I waved, she vanished.

I ran outside and called for her. I didn't know her name, but I said, "Don't worry, it's okay. You don't have to go!" I skirted the house, pausing and listening. I called out a few more times, and then heard a voice, not a girl's but that of an old woman, answering me.

"Come here," the voice croaked. It was coming from the neighbor's fence. My leg was considerably stiffer than it had been following my shower, so I moved slowly, climbing over the trunks of fallen trees and through an expanse of brambles. A lizard darted from the leaves. Small finches sat in a robust patch of matilija poppies, swaying on their leggy shoots.

Then I saw her white head peering through the chain-link fence.

"Come here," she said again. She was a frail figure all in white, holding on to the links.

I surmounted the final obstacle, a stack of wood now grown over with ivy and studded with fungus. "Hi! I'm Penny, Louise Pincer's granddaughter," I said, hoping to present a good face.

"Has she passed on?" the woman said.

"No!" I corrected her at once. "She's coming home today."

"We thought she'd passed on," the woman said again, as if disappointed.

"She's alive," I insisted.

The woman said nothing, appraising me with a steady gaze through the fence. Finally she rasped, "Let us know when she does. My son is interested in the property."

I wondered if I'd heard her correctly. I stood frozen for a moment before seizing a large, barbed pine cone from the ground with the intention of pelting her with it, but it's obviously not advisable to pelt an old woman with a large, barbed pine cone, so I restrained myself. But I was enraged and wanted her to know it. *You vulture!* I could yell. Or, *Art thou buzzard or human being?* I wasn't practiced enough at yelling at people. Frustrated at my inability to lob an insult in a timely fashion, I backed away. Retreating to the house, I experienced an unpleasantly familiar feeling of negation and exile. Pincer had complained many times about her neighbor, but I'd always assumed it was her fault.

Still, the lowest points of the day were yet to come. I needed to check the state of the bedroom to make sure it was ready for her, and was glad to see the bed had been freshly made. (I refused to look in the bedside drawer; that would have to wait.) But as I scanned the room, now much more orderly than it had been, I noticed on Pincer's desk by the window a stack of unopened letters, and it quickly became apparent that a number of them were from the IRS. Why were there so many and why had they not been opened? All at once I remembered what Dale had said to me about defending Burt against accounting malpractice suits and felt my skin prickle. I grabbed one sent certified mail, tore it open, and thereby learned that Pincer owed the United States Treasury $197,628.69.

I folded up the letter and put it in my pocket, walked to the front door, and left the place behind, reaching the Dog of the North and feeling as if my bit of the world was now too mangled to set right. What was she thinking, or not thinking? What had Burt done? Was he even a real CPA? Or was his judgment impaired because he'd been seeping blood for untold months?

11

I got out of the van and walked toward the entrance of the hospital. It was a rambling white stucco building with a red-tiled roof and what looked like a bell tower. I hadn't noticed how attractive it was on my last visit, presumably because I hadn't been in the state of mind to find anything attractive, least of all a hospital. But if that were true, it should look even worse now, leaving me to wonder if I was becoming a little more hardened and bureaucratic about the problems of others.

In short order, I'd taken the elevator, passing the paneled walls featuring the works of local artists, lots of dogs and flowers and beachscapes, and entered Burt's room. A nurse had placed a cuff around his pale upper arm while chatting it up with him and laughing. Burt, who was not wearing his hairpiece, cried, "Penny! Come sit down." Then he said, "You're the best, Judy," and she said, "Enjoy your company, Burt," and left the room.

I moved to the bedside chair. "How are you feeling?" In the after-glow of Judy's attentions, he looked almost radiant.

"Not too bad. They're still poking and prodding and testing. Now they're talking about my heart. Hope I can get out of here soon."

"I hope so too," I said.

"You hear about my dog?" he asked. "He got mauled at Evelyn's."

"Dale stopped by on his way to the airport and showed me. Your dog looks good, he's definitely going to be okay."

"I never thought Evelyn would let her dogs do something like that," he said morosely. "Dale came through. He got the job done. He's going to take care of him until I'm better."

I asked about the Quixote/Kweecoats discrepancy.

"Ah, good question. Jenny named him," he told me. "She was in a literature class in college with a know-it-all who'd done a paper about 'themes of madness and sanity in *Don Kweecoat*,' and every-body was like, *Huh?* I guess she started lecturing them on how Cer-vantes was as important as Shakespeare and that *Don Kweecoat* was the bestselling novel of all time." Burt chuckled wistfully.

I chuckled too, imagining the downfall of a know-it-all.

"She called him Kweecoat to honor that great moment, then it morphed to Coats and sometimes Coatsy. Boy, a lot of things look different from a hospital bed." He sighed. "I feel like I have some new insight on who my real friends are."

"Burt," I said gently. "I found something at my grandmother's house I don't understand. Could you look at it?"

"It's not a dead rat, is it?"

"Nope." I pulled the folded envelope from my pocket.

"Could you hand me my glasses over there?" he asked.

I gave him the envelope as well as the glasses, and as soon as he saw it was from the IRS, he said, "Jeez." He removed the letter and read, then set it down on his chest.

"Penny," he said at last. "This is very disappointing."

"Yes, it is."

"I imagine you'd like to know how this happened, seeing as I'm your grandmother's accountant."

"I am kind of curious."

"I'm telling you, Penny, she's made things very difficult. It's almost impossible to do a good job for someone if they fail to reveal all of their income."

"Where is her income coming from?" I'd been considering asking Pincer if I could borrow some money, already a stretch but now probably impossible.

"She's got some stocks and bonds salted away but my theory is that she pretends she's broke so no one can prey on her. So every year notices come in and I'll tell her to pay what's owed and, forgive me, Penny, then she blames me and says I messed up and it's all my fault and then another year goes by. I don't know what to say. This is terrible."

The man looked shattered.

"Sorry, Burt."

"You have power of attorney, don't you?"

"Supposedly, but she's never given me the document and obviously doesn't want me to use it."

"You're going to have to use it. You're going to have to take out a loan against the house or find out where her stocks and bonds are."

"I know how to do the loan-against-the-house thing. I did it for my grandfather."

"Arlo Reshnappet?" Burt said.

I nodded.

"Now, there's a grudge that never dies. Your grandmother sure hates that guy. You wouldn't believe the things I've heard."

"I'm sure they weren't very good."

"Oh man. You better believe it. Terrible things. I can't even repeat some of it."

"I really love my grandfather, so I'd rather not talk about it."

"Sure. Got it," Burt said.

"Burt," I said quietly, "when I was staying in your office I was looking for some alcohol to put on the place where my grandmother stuck me with the pin, remember?"

"I do. I've got plenty, did you find it?"

"I did eventually. But I looked in your desk first. I really wasn't meaning to pry. But I saw a bunch of prescription bottles in there, and, well, I noticed they were for antidepressants and stuff, and that they weren't ever opened. Are you supposed to be taking those?"

"Caught red-handed," Burt said. "Yeah, I'm supposed to take a whole medicine cabinet full of stuff, but it's awful, Penny, it ruins my libido."

"But when you don't take it, doesn't it interfere with your work?"

"I don't know. I need to be myself. My libido is important to me!"

I nodded.

"Don't mention this to my brother, would you?" he asked.

"All right," I said. "I won't."

"He's got a heavy case right now, he's trying to defend a woman who strangled her own baby. Can you imagine trying to defend a woman who strangled a baby?"

"No, I can't."

"He takes it really seriously. He looks at how society and the system let her down and what might lead to someone committing a crime like that. He doesn't see her as a monster. I appreciate that stance, that it takes a village to create a monster."

"I guess people can snap," I said. "Today I almost assaulted a senior citizen with a pine cone."

"Penny the assassin! Why?"

"Have you ever met my grandmother's neighbor on the south side?"

"No, but I've heard plenty about her being a freak."

"She is!" I laughed.

"So, speaking of freaks and stuff, what's happening with Grandma? Have they hauled her off in the paddy wagon yet?"

I told him what I knew from speaking to Storke. In so doing, I felt as if her current troubles might start to overwhelm me. And when Burt changed the subject right away, I wondered if he felt the same, and what, considering his own difficulties, would possibly compel him to continue to help out.

"When I get out of here, I guess I'll need the keys to the Dog. Think you can use your grandfather's car now?"

"I'll ask him," I said.

"I gotta get my own place. That woman down the hall is making trouble for me. We had a little fling and now she's gone batshit-crazy."

"Sorry, Burt." I sighed. "I'll try to get my grandfather's car today, and just let me know as soon as you're ready to check out. I'll be here."

"I'm waiting for word right now. The doctor should come by any minute."

"Should I wait, then?"

Burt reached out and took my hand. His was large and warm.

"You go ahead, I'll call when I hear something."

"Thank you. Thanks for everything."

"You're a good person, Penny. I'm glad to know you."

"I'm glad to know you too," I said.

I was very touched by what Burt had said to me, so much so that I left his room blinking my eyes. It was impossible to be mad at him. I could well imagine how impossible it would be to work with Pincer on anything. She'd brought this on herself, as with everything else, in my opinion. But I felt the burden of the tasks facing me as a result of this mess—hours trying to work it out with the IRS, the paperwork for a reverse mortgage, and, horribly, having somebody out to assess the value of her house, and how would that work because she'd obstruct it, and maybe I'd have to ask Burt if he felt like taking her away again. I couldn't unspool it all right now. I didn't feel generous, but rather angry and oppressed.

Walking out through the parking lot, the sun bright and the minerals in the asphalt shimmering with heat, I received a call from Arlo. "Penny, are you coming by or what?" he said, unusually agitated.

"I'm coming right now." It was just about one, so I had a couple of hours before I had to pick up Pincer.

"I need to talk to you about something important," he said.

"I'll be right there. Are you okay?"

"I'm fine," he said. "Get here soon."

I was a little distracted as I said goodbye, because at that moment I saw a familiar red sports car pull into the parking lot, finding a place in the shade of an oak. The next thing I knew, Dale was getting out. Now what?

"Dale!" I called.

He turned and waved. He was lifting the dog from his kennel.

I traversed the lot in the sun. "What are you doing here?"

"Did you just visit my brother?" He took off his brown corduroy jacket and threw it into the car. He wore a white cotton shirt with the sleeves rolled up, dark glasses, and a watch with a brown leather strap. A ridiculously well-put-together married man.

"I did, he seems good."

By now he'd placed Kweecoats on the pavement.

"He's not good," Dale said.

"What do you mean?"

"I was just about to board the plane when I got a call from his doctor. He said I should know that Burt's got some other issues and I might want to stay. He was going to talk to Burt as soon as he got a few more test results. So I got the car back and here we are. Did he know any of this when you saw him?"

"No. He said the doctor was coming any minute. He thinks he's about to be released. What do you think's wrong?"

"I don't know. It must be something serious requiring choices of treatments."

This was horrible, hard to take in. Kweecoats was urinating on a nearby tire. "Can I watch him for you? It's too hot for him to be in the car," I said.

He mumbled something. I think he said: "I wouldn't want to trouble you."

"It would be fun, I'd enjoy it. I'm on my way to visit my grandfather and it'll make his day. I'll be back here right after, because I have to pick up my grandmother."

Dale said, "All right. I think that makes sense. Thank you."

He hefted the crate and followed me to the van. I threw open the back doors, he shoved it in. Then I opened the crate and placed Kweecoats inside, where he circled and stomped his blanket awhile before settling.

"I hope Burt's okay."

"I do too."

"The shower was great," I mentioned, but quickly wished I hadn't. It sounded as if I were inviting him to imagine me sudsing up.

"Good to hear," he said.

"I'm really worried about Burt. I'll be back soon."

"Thank you," he said.

I drove straight to the Palms, fretting about Burt's condition and fighting off quasi-erotic thoughts about Dale, but nevertheless hoping to foster erotic thoughts about someone soon. It was surprising how quickly my world had been recast since arriving in Santa Barbara. Where the stage had once been dominated by the scowling visages of Sherman and my gloomy office mates, now the brothers Lampey had seized the starring roles.

Upon parking, I let Kweecoats bound from his kennel to the ground. It was fun to hold his leash and bring him inside, provoking a great deal of commotion from various passing residents while I signed the guest registry in the lobby.

"May I pat your pup?"

"What a little bundle of love!"

"That's not a dog, that's a fur ball. Get the vacuum cleaner!"

"Come here, baby, you're a sweetie. Yes, yes, you are."

I felt proud of his magnetic appeal, much as I used to feel validated as a girl standing beside my mother when she was at her best. Truly, I was a natural-born sidekick. After Kweecoats received his due, we navigated the halls to Arlo's room. I knocked and Arlo called out, "Come in!" He was not in bed, but standing, dressed in his brown slacks, plaid shirt, and warm cardigan, his back remarkably straight, his handsome, reassuring head looking at something freshly attached to the wall. I could see at once that it was his topographic map of Queensland, the map on which he'd been recording the information received from his contacts since my mother and Hugh disappeared.

"Who's this?" he asked, staring down by my feet.

"This is Kweecoats, dog of Burt, accountant of Pincer," I announced.

"Kweecoats?"

"Like Quick Oats pronounced with a French accent."

"Why Quick Oats?" he asked. "Why not Cream of Wheat?"

"It's a mispronunciation of Quixote," I said.

"I see," he said. "That explains everything."

Arlo said next that he'd had the best sleep of his recent life and that getting away from Doris hadn't come a minute too soon. Then he turned and placed a finger on the map, on a spot just south of Mount Isa.

"I got an email this morning from one of the trackers down under, Jocelyn Reese. She says some ground opened up recently in an area down there riddled with caves. There were some man-made items found. Nothing that belonged to your mother and Hugh, but she thought we'd want to know."

"So you think they fell into a cave?" I asked quietly. Opening up this subject made me feel queasy and infirm.

"I hope not, but I want to poke around a little before I can't travel anymore. Nobody cares about this as much as we do, and Margaret, of course. I couldn't think straight at home with Doris breathing down my neck. But listen, I fly gratis and I'll get a ticket for you. We'll visit Margaret and her family and then rent a car and see what's out there."

I sat down on the end of his bed.

"You feel up to traveling?" I said.

"I'll never be better. I have a valid passport, do you?"

"I do," I said, as I had been planning to go to Australia for some time, but kept avoiding it.

"The thing is, I want to go before Doris finds out. She'd wreck everything."

"You mean you wouldn't tell her?"

Arlo took a seat in the institutional blue wingback in the corner. "She comes by this morning and tells me she's driving to the port of Long Beach tomorrow to board a cruise to Baja. I'm the last to know! Well, I want to go on a trip too. I'll call her once we're there."

My god, it seemed Doris couldn't wait to be rid of Arlo. All the while pretending she was so busy and making a fuss about the manner of his removal! I now despised her more than ever. Kweecoats was tenderly sniffing Arlo's leg. "I hear you had a visit from Detective Storke," I said, to change the subject.

"I'm getting a reputation around this place before I'm here a day. Police detectives coming for me, Doris dressed to the nines, then funny little dogs. Sounds like Louise is in some trouble. I didn't have much to tell him, seeing as we haven't spoken to each other in twenty-five years. He asked about her character. I'm probably the last person to ask about her character. Things got ugly. I didn't want to talk about that. That's between a husband and wife."

"I agree," I said, flashing on hideous moments in my final days with Sherman.

"I'll tell you what I think of Detective Storke," Arlo said. "Lonely man."

"You thought that too?"

At that moment Kweecoats sprang into Arlo's lap. Arlo said, "I'm sorry, but I'm a cat man. What do you call this thing?"

"A Pomeranian."

He began to dig his fingers into the pelt of Kweecoats. Then he started to laugh. "Funniest-looking thing I've ever seen."

I was staring at the map of Queensland.

"So what do you say, Penny-girl?" he asked.

The southern continent filled me with unspeakable dread. I didn't know what to say. It had taken everything from me. It had even laid claim to my sister. Why should I pay it a visit? Normally I'd do anything for my grandfather.

I asked if we could talk about it later, because I had to pick up Pincer at the hospital and bring her home. He grunted, as if he understood that this could be a distressing assignment. He said, "Decide soon. And do me a favor, would you? Ask her if she remembers the Floating Gardens."

"What's that?"

"Just tell her I asked. I want to know word-for-word what she says."

Before I left, I asked if I could borrow his Honda. He said okay, but he hoped I wouldn't be needing it because we'd be leaving for Australia, and whatever the case to wait until Doris left on the cruise the next day so as to avoid riling her up. That sounded reasonable. Today I could give Burt back his keys and stay in a motel somewhere. One step at a time.

I'd wanted to have lunch with him but Arlo had already been to the dining room and back. (The diet to live to ninety-three appeared to be two pieces of bacon, half a grapefruit, and coffee for breakfast, a tuna fish sandwich on wheat for lunch, a very large martini at cocktail hour, with dinner have-what-you-will.) So I told him I'd see him later after dealing with Pincer and gave him a kiss. I was glad I'd brought Kweecoats, purveyor of joy. On our way across the parking lot, he pulled on his leash and yipped, seemingly at nothing, making me think for a moment that Gaspard might be hiding somewhere between the cars about to jump out, but thankfully, no such thing happened, the yips directed at that other dimension only dogs can discern.

12

If I can get through this afternoon, I thought, *I will get a motel room, I will make Pincer pay for it, I will watch TV, I will put an ice pack on my leg, I will sleep as long as my heart desires.*

I was sitting across from the entrance to the psychiatric ward of the hospital on a generic blue wingback chair like the one in my grandfather's room awaiting Pincer's release, next to a stack of sticky magazines that felt as if the last people to look at them had been sucking on lollipops and drooling. A doctor had already come out and outlined much of what Storke had told me that morning.

At last, the door opened and a wheelchair emerged with Pincer in it, fully dressed in the clothing she'd been wearing the day we went to lunch. The evil roadrunner pin was properly fixed to her blouse, its tiny ruby eye aglint with menace. She said, "Help me up, Penny, I need to speak to Burt right this minute."

"Burt?" I said. "Why?" I gave her my arm while the nurse moved the footrests of the wheelchair out of the way. Pincer took to her feet and charged forward.

"Why do you want to talk to Burt?" I said.

She said, "I need to make Burt an offer he can't refuse."

"You know he's still in the hospital."

"I imagine so, that's why we'll take care of it now."

"What's the offer? Maybe you'd like to go home first."

"I want to talk to Burt, that's what I want!" she said.

Was she not chastened in the least? Did she not remember what had precipitated her incarceration in the psychiatric ward? She walked briskly, as if she'd spent the last two days rejuvenating herself at a fabulous spa. I wondered what she thought was happening. Maybe she thought she had been brought in as a consultant.

We took the elevator to the ground floor.

I said, "I guess Burt's got some more problems besides his stomach. Maybe something with his heart."

Pincer said, "That's why he'll appreciate this. I'm going to offer him the back room at my place. He can do chores to earn his keep. I'll make sure he has an excellent diet and keep an eye on him. His own personal physician. He'll never get that close to a crisis again."

Despite my previous insistence that Pincer was no Dr. Moreau, I shivered to think of Burt receiving in-house care from her. Would he be interested in such an offer? For his sake, I hoped not. We left the building, skirting the outer flank of the hospital. I said, "Do you by any chance happen to remember that police are investigating a skeleton found in your woodshed?"

"What is it to them?" she said angrily.

"Don't you understand how anything works? Why is it there?"

"I know why it's there," she said. "I'm not going to keep radioactive bones in the house."

We were rapidly advancing on the main entrance. "Why are the bones radioactive?" I demanded.

"They belonged to Dr. Hiroshi Matsumoto. We worked together in Nagasaki. He was in love with me. It was before Reshnappet and I split up. I loved him too, but couldn't fully reciprocate."

"That's too bad."

"Yes, it is. It was very nice to be treated like a desirable woman after years of darning Reshnappet's socks for not even a thank-you."

"All right. But why did Dr. Matsumoto send you the bones?"

She stared at me like I was a fool. "The bones *are* Dr. Matsumoto."

"He sent you his own bones?"

"He didn't send them. He came to the house. Hiroshi had no family in Japan. He wanted to give his body to me and to science. And that's what he did."

"What do you mean?" I nearly shrieked.

Now she was hustling through the quiet lobby with keen determination. "I mean that we were both involved in the documentation of disease in those exposed to radiation from the dropping of the bomb in Nagasaki. He was fifteen years old in 1945 and lost his entire family. He knew it would catch up with him someday. He charged me with evaluating his condition upon his death and that's what I did. It was what he wanted. I've got all the papers saying so!"

We were waiting by the elevator. I felt stunned and disordered.

"He came to the house to die?"

"You could say that. You could also say he came to the house to finally live."

I cringed.

"Will you tell all that to the police? Why didn't you tell them before?"

Again she looked at me as if I were a simpleton. "It's very personal," she said. "I'm not going to blurt it out at the drop of a hat."

We emerged on Burt's floor and I quickened my pace. I led her to Burt's room, where the bed was unoccupied. Dale, however, was sitting in the chair doing something with his phone. He looked momentarily pleased to see me, but before he could say anything, Pincer said, "Where's Burt?"

I introduced them to each other.

"Where's Burt?" she said again.

"Well," Dale said, "Burt is now being prepped for heart surgery."

"Now?" I said. "Is he okay?"

Pincer threw her hard black pocketbook down on the bed. Dale offered her the chair, but she stood her ground. She said, "Tell me what you know or I'll go find the attending."

Dale glanced at me and began to explain. He said that it had been discovered by way of an angiogram that Burt had two blocked arteries around his heart. The discomfort he'd reported over the past couple days had been chalked up to the ulcer repair. Fortunately, somebody had the foresight to investigate further. Emergency surgery was required, and thus, Burt would soon be in the operating theater. Dale looked tired and disheveled. "It's considered fairly routine," he said soberly. "Burt should be in better shape once it's over."

"As long as there's no bleeding from the graft, no atrial fib, no blood clots, no adverse reaction to the anesthesia," Pincer said. She looked at her watch. "I wonder if I can get in there."

"You know what? You've been away for days. We can see Burt tomorrow after his surgery and you can confer with the doctors then, all right?"

Persuading her to do anything was generally impossible, but to my surprise, she said, "All right. Take me home. I'm dying to get out of these clothes."

"Kweecoats is fine," I told Dale. "I'll keep him this afternoon and we can talk later, okay?"

Dale nodded bleakly. "I appreciate it." Then he reached for something on Burt's bedside table. It was Burt's hairpiece inside a plastic sleeve. "He says he's not going to wear this anymore, and wants it put in with his dog until they're reunited."

I took it from him.

"Let's go, Penny!" Pincer hectored from the doorway.

"The good thing is they discovered the heart problem now," I said. "Right?"

"This is true," Dale said.

"Okay," I said. "Talk to you later."

Dale nodded again, looking past me at the ogreish figure in the corridor. For some reason I cared enough to hope he did not see anything of me reflected in her bearing.

As we emerged from the hospital, Pincer mused aloud on the chances of Burt's survival, concluding that his chances were reasonably good. "Now there's no question," she said. "There's no better place for him once he's released than with me." I couldn't help but disagree.

Then she said, "What's the matter, why are you walking like a peg leg?"

I said, "Somebody stabbed me with a pin."

"Don't swing it out like that. Bend it at the knee."

"Do you admit that you stabbed me with a pin?"

"I have more important things to think about right now, and so do you."

Having her examine my leg was the last thing I wanted, so I let it drop.

I showed her the Pomeranian when we returned to the van. She wasn't impressed because she'd met him before, Burt had brought him around many times, but she took note of the quality of his stitches and said the vet had done a fine job. For the same reason I'd dropped the subject of my leg, I avoided mentioning his anal glands. At Burt's behest, I removed his toupee from the plastic sleeve and placed it in the kennel. Kweecoats drove his snout right into the center of it, duly inhaling a straight shot of Burt's scalp. Up front, Pincer climbed into the passenger seat without assistance and told me to hurry up.

I took the road along the highway while she chattered about the state-of-the-art equipment she'd seen over the past several days, the hospital's preeminent programs, its world-class staff, and so on. I was working on my escape plan. I didn't fully grasp her explanation of the bones, and didn't want to. Further, any moment now, my new friend Burt, the nicest person I'd met in a long while, was going to be sliced into on an operating table. Only a couple of hours ago he was telling funny stories and defending his libido.

Despite Dale's complaints about Burt, I was beginning to believe that he cared about his brother a great deal.

Pressing on me was the question of whether or not I should call and tell Storke what Pincer had confessed, or simply let him know that she had something to say. As we neared her house, driving past the hedges and gates, I remembered my promise to Arlo.

"By the way," I said, "do you know anything about a place called the Floating Gardens?"

"Sure, I do," she said. "Reshnappet and I went to the Floating Gardens in Mexico on our honeymoon. We climbed Teotihuacan and then spent a week in Taxco. It's a silver mining town. I have a beautiful little pin from that trip. Why do you ask?"

"Just wondering," I said.

"Why? Did Reshnappet put you up to it?"

"Actually, he did. He wanted to know if you remembered the Floating Gardens. So I guess you do."

"What's it to him? He's got his own floozy now."

"I mean, since you're both pretty old and still alive, maybe he just couldn't help wondering if you shared any memories."

"Tell him I don't remember anything!" Pincer said.

I couldn't wait to tell Arlo she remembered it all.

We drove up the driveway and parked. I intentionally angled the Dog of the North so that when Pincer climbed out she wouldn't see all the garbage bags lined up in front of the garage. I'd have to haul them somewhere soon before she had a chance to reclaim any of their contents.

I removed Kweecoats from the kennel, putting him on his leash, while she marched up the brick path with her keys in hand to let us in. I never sought to remind her of my own keys—including one for the house in Texas—lest she suddenly find it appalling that I had them and demand them back.

Upon entering, she stood transfixed, taking in the rooms she could see at first glance. I braced myself against the shock waves that were coming. The lingering silence was terrifying. Finally, she remarked: "It's always nice to come back to a clean house."

"It is?"

"I always clean extensively before I go away," she said.

"You do, do you?"

"I'm not afraid of hard work."

I saw the whole thing, her brain trying to make sense of it, fabricating a reasonable answer. I was spared.

The dog and I followed her to her room, where she rummaged in her desk drawer, finding another wad of keys and taking them to a large old ornate trunk in the corner. It had wood slats and a domed top and because it was locked I'd never known what it contained. I knew I was supposed to be keeping my eyes open for the power-of-attorney document so I could start working on the IRS problem, but didn't feel like it at all. In fact, at that moment I couldn't care less. After trying several keys, she found one that fit, wiggled the trunk out a few inches, opened the heavy lid, and rested it against the wall. My eyes must have widened; it was like beholding a pirate's bounty.

A stack of richly colored silk kimonos sat on top.

"I thought you said your kimonos were stolen," I said.

"Those were other kimonos," she contended. She removed them, while Kweecoats sat beside me. Soon other items came to light. A black-lacquered box that she opened to reveal a string of pearls. "Hiroshi brought me many gifts," she said. Next she produced some indigo-colored garments made of cotton, less formal than the kimonos. There were short little pants she called mompei and waist-length jackets. There were casual yukatas. A short blue robe with a heron on it that she referred to as a happi coat. A few metal tubes that she said contained hand-painted scrolls. Then she lofted a curved steel sword in a golden sheath. "Hiroshi's family were samurai," she said. "Nobility. This was his grandfather's."

More items came to light, untouched by rodents, perfectly preserved. A flat box holding woodblock prints—chrysanthemums, bamboo groves, waterfalls, ancient trees. A ceramic tea set, a lacquered tray. An old RCA Victor LP of *Madame Butterfly*. At last, a stack of letters and a folder of papers. From the folder she removed some photos and showed me one of herself in a kimono standing on a bridge beside a Japanese man who was holding her hand.

At that moment, it occurred to me how completely unwell I was feeling. It came over me abruptly. My face was flushed and my eyes felt glazed. The hoarding side of her personality was depressing the life out of me. The feeling of being suffocated by delusions. The cold indifference to the disappearance of her only child, my mother's unhappiness growing up, likely why she wanted to leave the country in the first place. Suddenly I said, with great emotion, "If you loved him so much, why did you put his body in the woodshed where it's cold and dirty? You took better care of your souvenirs!"

"Where do you think most people are buried? In the cold dirty ground. If you're accusing me of heartlessness, you don't know a thing. I don't have to explain anything to you."

"You'll have to explain to somebody."

"What do you think I'm doing? I'm preparing for the interrogation. I know what's coming. As you know, my brother was the assistant attorney general of Texas. I know a great deal about the law. If you want to be useful, get me some groceries. Make sure you get bananas. I eat at least two a day. Skim milk. Some chicken breasts, celery, carrots, rice. I have things to do. Take that pedigreed half-pint with you!"

"Um, okay," I said, shivering. I watched her a moment, going through her folder of papers, her mementos spread around her in a tight box of sunlight coming through the window. I had a strong memory of times when, furious with Sherman, I'd waited until he'd turned away from me and then given him the finger, putting every shred of my energy behind the gesture, baring my teeth, shaking the pitiful digit at him with rage. I always felt ashamed too, despite it being a secret between me and the universe.

I drove about a mile and then pulled over, breathing hard. I stopped by a low white fence, over which I could see two chestnut-colored horses grazing in a paddock, their coats gleaming in the sunlight, their flesh rippling with vitality. Then I imagined them as skeletons with Pincer pulling off the meat, and let out a cry of horror. I had to call Storke. The sooner this was dealt with, the better.

He answered, and in short order I'd told him everything she'd said. I could tell he was taking notes, and that he seemed slightly overwhelmed, if not stumped. "I'll need her to tell me this and more," he said, once I'd finished. "You say she has some kind of documentation?"

"She says she does."

"I don't know what to make of it. I have to look at some statutes. I imagine she must have signed the death certificate herself. That should be on record if this is true."

"If it's true, is there a crime?"

"I really can't tell you that right now. I appreciate the promptness of your call."

Was I hoping she'd be arrested and taken away?

"You're welcome," I said.

My eyes felt as if they were floating in warm soup. I drove from there to Burt's office building parking lot because I had decided to take a nap. I was lucky to find my spot under the ficus tree where it was shady; it was likely no animal carcasses would fall upon the van at this time of day. Of course, I had to unload the bicycle and hose and jam them up front, which seemed a lot more arduous than it had the night before. As I was doing this, I happened to glance over at the office building and discovered I was being watched from an upper-story window. It was a sticklike woman in an ill-fitting business suit. I recognized her! It was the barracuda, also known as Kerry Cochren. The malevolent, twisted face glowering down at me seemed spurred on by my proximity to Burt's van. Well, let her stare and brood, I thought. I hoped nobody considering suicide was depending on her while she was wasting her time on this.

I left the windows open a few inches and climbed in back, let Kweecoats out of his kennel, and took great pleasure in watching him settle beside me. I thought how inconvenient it would be to get sick right now, threw down two ibuprofen, and collapsed. I had the sense I was forgetting something important, but was too weary to care. The temperature in the van was just fine. A person can get used to almost anything. The relief I felt at being able to stretch out in a relatively quiet place was enormous. I prayed for Burt's well-being, and hoped Dale would call soon with good news.

I slept. I slept a long time. By the time I stirred, it was dark and I was disoriented and damp with sweat. It took me a minute to remember what was going on. I'd been dreaming about the radioactive pigs running wild around Fukushima, thousands of them, which I'd read about recently. In the dream they were able to run right through walls and I was hopelessly in charge of stopping them.

There was a strange smell in the van, like paint fumes. I sat up and opened one of the back windows. Kweecoats was perched near my head, panting. I grabbed my phone. It was nine p.m. Many calls had come in during my time-out. There were two from Storke, several from Arlo, several from Pincer, and one from Dale. Who to call first? I didn't have to decide, because a call came in at that very moment from Dale.

"He's all right," he said.

"It's over?"

"It's over. He's in recovery. They say everything went well and his vital signs are excellent."

Tears sprang to my eyes. "I'm so glad!"

"Me too," said Dale. "Very glad. So, where are you?"

"I'm over in Burt's parking lot. Should I meet you to give you Kweecoats?"

"Yes. I was thinking of picking up a few tacos, can I get any for you?"

Maybe I should eat something. "Okay. That would be nice. Thanks."

"Meat? Vegetarian?"

"Anything is fine."

"All right. I'm staying at the Seaside again. Meet you in the parking lot in about half an hour."

"Great," I said, appreciating his abilities.

Next I called Storke.

"I've been trying to get hold of you," he said. "I spent several hours with your grandmother and heard quite a story. She produced a number of documents to support it, which I now have with me. She herself signed the death certificate and I've been able to determine she did file it properly. I'm going to have to consult with some experts on postmortem law. It's not clear to me there's a crime here, which may come as a relief."

Did it? "I still don't understand," I said. "Was there—did she—perform an autopsy?" I couldn't believe what I was saying.

"According to the death certificate, an autopsy was performed. Cause of death was multiple organ failure due to carcinomatosis, attributed to radiation exposure in 1945 and thereafter."

For a moment I couldn't speak.

Finally, I said, "You're okay with that?"

"No, I'm not. I was told growing up that Truman had no choice and it was the only way to stop the war, but I've changed my mind and now feel it was the greatest mistake ever perpetrated on humankind."

"Yes, exactly, but I mean, isn't there something wrong with doing an autopsy on someone you know, someone you love?"

Storke judiciously cleared his throat. "Look, it's not for everyone. It could be . . . a doctor thing we don't understand. I can't say I've heard of it before."

"Me either."

"Well. It's not for me to decide how palatable someone's actions are if there are no laws broken, so I'll leave the fine points to others."

"Understood," I said.

"You were expected to return with some groceries," he added.

"That's right. I totally forgot!"

"Well, you don't have to worry about it now," he said. "I did my good deed for the week and picked up a few things for her."

She was a mastermind!

"That's beyond the call of duty," I said. "Thank you so much."

"I'll be in touch," he said.

Last but not least, I listened to the messages from Arlo. In each, he asked if I'd decided about Australia. He said he'd been inquiring into seat availability on upcoming flights. He said there was no time like the present. He said he'd even called Margaret, who was ready to receive us anytime. The pressure was on. I couldn't sort that out now. I'd call him later. Same with Pincer. Her messages were rambling. In one she was complaining about the boneless, skinless chicken breasts she'd received from Storke, who clearly didn't know that the nutrients were in the bones.

I had to get going to eat my tacos with Dale. Kweecoats needed his dinner too. I started unloading the bicycle and hose from the front to stow them in back but immediately noticed a change in the appearance of the exterior of the van. It had been painted with graffiti during my nap. I stepped back and realized that the words WHORE COW had been applied in big black letters to the side.

What kind of insult was that? Was this the work of Kerry Cochren? If so, she was even worse at insults than I was. I pitied her! Still, it did not feel good to drive through town thus marked.

13

I made it to the Seaside Hotel without incident. Those I passed along the way were apparently untroubled by the presence of a whore cow.

Dale was standing by the red sports car in the parking lot, holding a six-pack of beer and a paper bag that looked deliciously greasy. I could see him assessing the graffiti on the van as I pulled up.

"Is this the work of the barracuda?" he deduced, once I joined him.

"How can you tell?"

"I spoke to her. She's full of bile and thinks you're to blame."

I contributed further supporting evidence, having seen the spiteful figure in the building window. Dale set down the greasy sack and retrieved an item from a bag in the trunk of the car, a black Sharpie.

"I don't think we can remove it easily. Let's change a letter or two so it says something else."

This made sense. We studied the words, and after conferring over several possibilities, including WHOLE COW and WHORL COW, we arrived at CHORE COW, drawn to its utilitarian sound. In short order he transformed WHORE to CHORE, sweeping over the W many times with the pen, matching the style of the rest of the scrawl.

"I do apologize," Dale said.

"For what?"

"For my brother's foolhardy ways."

"Getting involved with a disturbed individual could happen to anyone."

"Why does it always seem to happen to Burt?"

"Anyway, it's his van, and he's been very nice to let me use it," I said.

He capped the pen and stood back to examine his work. "I'm glad he's been good to you. I thought maybe we could eat on the beach," he said, and I agreed.

We crossed the road. The Pomeranian followed on his leash, attempting great sniffs through his tiny snout. Companionable groups were scattered like patches of seaweed and driftwood across the sand. The air was balmy, the surf low and steady. We sat midway to water's edge. Dale tore the bag in half lengthwise so that it became our tabletop, and before us sat a pile of tacos wrapped in foil and a sack of tortilla chips. He offered me a Dos Equis and I took it, reducing it by half in a few quick gulps.

Kweecoats rolled in the sand, which I suddenly noticed had many lumps in it, like a cat box that had not been cleaned out in days. I wondered what we were sitting on and drew in my legs. "Do you think it's okay for him to get dirty sand in his stitches?"

"They itch, don't they? Come here, boy. Come here." The dog came and sat in Dale's lap, and he leaned over to examine the status of the wounds.

"Stitches intact," he announced. "Anal glands I'll check later."

This made me laugh, as if anal glands were a private joke between us.

I was surprised that Dale seemed to enjoy my company, if I dared presume as much. I'd been surprised that Burt did too. I wondered what their mother had been like, and if any reasonable interaction with a woman spawned excessive gratitude.

There was a lot to unpack. We went over the events of the day, mostly to do with Burt and how close he'd come to having a coronary occlusion.

"I should tell you something interesting he said, right before he was taken into surgery," Dale added.

"What?"

"He said, 'If anything goes wrong, give Penny the Dog of the North. And everything in it, it's all hers.'"

"Really?"

"It's more of a curse than a gift, but I suppose it's the thought that counts."

"That's incredibly touching. But what about the girl he calls his daughter?"

"She doesn't care about him, she doesn't want anything to do with him," Dale said. "Maybe he's finally realized that. Anyway, I'm not sure why he thinks you'd want it, but I know he's sentimentally attached to that van, so it *is* a genuine token of his esteem."

"I can't believe it, really." This news affected me more than Dale perhaps understood. It was the first time I'd ever known of somebody leaving something to me. Pincer had bragged of the scholarship she was setting up for women at the University of Texas with whatever remained of her estate. Arlo had apologized to me once for having been drained by Doris of his.

"You'll be happy to know he stressed *and everything in it*."

"I am happy. I've always wanted an ironing board and a good hose."

"All yours."

"Well, no, because Burt's fine. So there's no reason to even talk about this," I said hastily, hating the topic of people's deaths.

"Indeed."

By now I'd finished the first bottle, drilling it down into the sand. Dale offered me another. It was a safe bet he'd had a harder day than I had. Waiting hours in the hospital through his brother's surgery could not have been fun.

I turned to my tacos. One was chicken and the other was beans and cheese, and they looked good. Yet I did not want to devour them in front of Dale, nor did I want them to go cold. I wished I could send him away on an errand. Somehow my bad leg felt formless, like it had disintegrated into the sand. Though I hated to volunteer information without absolute certainty it was of interest to the other person, I went ahead and mentioned that my grandmother didn't appear to have murdered anyone, and relayed the strange tale she'd told me of her relationship with Dr. Hiroshi Matsumoto that had led to the discovery of his bones. I realized I was plugging Dale into the role Sherman once occupied when things were better between us, confidant, and, recognizing that he was receiving my daily briefing without any context or familiarity with the contours of my life, I started to laugh, the kind of laughter that can be triggered by the mordant and brutal.

Yet he received the briefing without complaint. All through the story, he was kicking his feet, scattering the irregular sandy lumps of unknown origin, saying, "No way. No way!"

"That's exactly what Burt says when I tell him stuff about her."

"You're saying that she gave this man an autopsy herself and filed the paperwork."

"I'm pretty sure that's what the detective said. Sometimes I mishear things."

"In her own home."

"Stop rubbing it in!"

"So here's the question. Is it a love story for the ages, or scientific fastidiousness run amok?"

"Maybe both."

"She's eccentric to the breaking point, but likely not a criminal," Dale finally deduced.

"I hope so. He's still looking into it."

"They won't pursue it," Dale said. "She's eighty-five? I think they have better things to do."

"Shouldn't every crime be investigated, no matter the age of the defendant?"

"Of course. I'm just saying, practically speaking, this isn't going to be a high priority in a busy district attorney's office."

"Because it's unlikely she'll strike again?"

"Right. Unless there are a bunch of men planning to donate their bodies to her. Can you find out?"

I was in the mood to laugh, obviously, but abruptly curtailed my mirth when a horrible thought crossed my mind.

"She wants Burt to live with her," I said. "That's why we came by the room in the hospital."

Dale started choking on his taco.

"Are you okay?"

"I don't think it's a good idea," Dale said, coughing something up.

"It's not," I said. "Tell him it's not, and I will too."

"I'm sorry, I don't know her at all, but I wouldn't want to find out one day that she'd dissected Burt."

"I understand, it's settled, he can't accept the offer, we'll have to make sure."

Dale uncapped another beer, gazing at the dark horizon as if contemplating the mortality of all beings, but particularly his brother's. We ate for a while in silence.

"I was going to say something candid about Burt, but realized it wouldn't sound right," Dale finally said, crumpling the foil of a finished taco.

"What?"

"I was going to say he easily attaches himself to people, but in your case, I think he made a good choice."

"Ha!" I said.

I had a trait that worked against me, which was that if I ever received a compliment, a loud roar, like a great fire crackling on a ridge, would fill my ears and the compliment would thus be vaporized. If that failed, the compliment would receive the treatment once witnessed by my mother of a cane toad. Shortly after they moved to Australia she saw a neighbor savagely beating the ground with a broom—a poisonous cane toad had met its match. Such beatings, she surmised, were to be common household tasks in her new life in Queensland. Compliments, and sometimes just plain good news, were the cane toads of my consciousness, dealt with likewise.

The roar of the compliment vaporizing/thrashing process had muddled my thoughts, but into the awkward pause I pushed forth. I asked if he'd ever spent time in Santa Cruz, what neighborhood he lived in in San Francisco, and so forth. He had a good friend who was a public defender in Santa Cruz and liked to come down on weekends for the beaches. Also went to concerts at the Kuumbwa Jazz Center and had a few favorite restaurants, including Tacos Moreno, which was a favorite of mine too. In the city he lived on Sacramento Street near Laurel Village. I wondered why he never said "we" to indicate that he did these things with his wife, and suspected him of either trying to disarm me or of having a very uncompanionable marriage.

I came from a lineage of marital failures.

Arlo and Pincer divorced with tremendous rancor.

My mother and Gaspard divorced within a year, just after I was born. My mother always said she knew the marriage was a mistake within weeks.

It was a generational certainty, then, that I would divorce Sherman. Almost preordained. A pattern that could not be broken. I should have known. I had sensed it coming but had resisted as long as I could.

"Thanks for meeting me again," Dale said, breaking into my thoughts. "It's helped a lot."

"Sure," I said. "Me too."

"Are you feeling okay? You look a little flushed."

I did not feel okay. But I hated getting sick, and with nowhere to go, now wasn't the time.

"Nothing, really. Just a little dizzy."

"I'm not sure how much longer I'll stay here," he said. "I might need to leave tomorrow after making sure Burt's all right."

"I understand. You have a life to get back to."

"I guess you could say that. Are you missing anything in Santa Cruz right now?"

A profound question on many levels. But I answered, "No. I quit my job right before coming down."

"What were you doing?"

Perhaps due to the second beer, I failed to censor the cynicism of my next remark. "Oh, general surgery. Teaching in a medical school."

"My god. That's impressive."

"Ha ha. Only kidding." The joke was not funny. "That's my sister. I was working in a dental office. As the receptionist."

"Oh. Okay." I could see him working to steer around my abject declaration of inferiority with as much finesse as he could muster. "How long were you there?"

"Over three years." I felt ashamed all around, of both my extended tenure and abrupt departure.

"Oh. Was it one of those dental offices where it's like a big happy family and you put up seasonal decorations and everybody loves each other?"

"No," I said.

"Then are you interested in teeth?"

"No, teeth aren't very interesting, to me, anyway."

"That must have made it easier to leave," he said.

"I'd been looking forward to it for a while," I said, realizing I was free now and should be enjoying myself.

"Jobs are hard to find in Santa Cruz," he added.

"That's true. Initially I felt lucky."

Dale seemed to be growing fonder of his brother's dog, and was now squeezing him like a muff. "What are you going to do now?"

"I've been in kind of a weird limbo for a while, I guess since my parents disappeared. It's been hard to make plans or move on."

"Tough situation," Dale said.

"My grandfather wants me to go to Australia with him and try one more time to find out what happened."

"Good for him. You should do it."

"I guess I'm afraid to find out what happened."

"It must be terrible not knowing."

"Maybe it's better than knowing," I said.

He said he could understand that.

The great dark ocean surged at our feet. Kweecoats widened his nostrils to parse its brackish, tangy scents. The rhythmic sound of waves pounding and pushing the sand, over and over, was putting me in a mood that was far, far too relaxed, so relaxed that I might do something I would regret, and I suddenly felt I had to get out of there. Was this how it started with Sherman and Bebe Sinatra? A few beers and tacos at the beach?

"Dale, I think I should go, but thank you for the tacos and beer, it was fun," I said, standing.

"Oh!" he said. He stood too, dusting himself off. "Is that it?"

"Yeah, I think I'm kind of done in," I said.

"Same here, I'm pretty fried myself. But I guess I'll stay a little longer."

"Okay, good night, then!"

"Good night!"

Back at the van, I yanked out the dog crate and dropped it on the hood of the sports car. Looking inside, I could see that Burt's hairpiece had been fully integrated into the circular nest Kweecoats had fashioned with his blanket. Although it was heartwarming that the dog had taken comfort in it, it also looked like Burt was being composted, and it gave me a chill.

I tore out of there, to the extent that the Dog was able to tear. I'd come very close to crawling over to Dale and kissing him, my attraction to him exponentially enhanced by the beer and the beach. It would have been a terrible mistake.

Ten minutes later I was in the parking lot of the Palms, and eleven minutes later I was climbing through a mound of bird-of-paradise outside Arlo's windows.

The curtains were drawn but the windows were open, and I whispered to him through the screen.

"Penny?" he immediately replied. "Where are you?"

"I'm outside your window."

"Just a minute," Arlo said.

I could hear him groping around in the dark. His bedside light came on. Then the sound of him shuffling toward me. The curtains flew back, light bathed my face.

"I want to go to Australia," I said.

"Thatta girl," he said. "Let's go tomorrow."

"The sooner, the better," I said.

"This place is full of nice people, but I can't wait to get out of here. We'll depart from LAX. The flights leave in the evening. We can take a shuttle from here around noon. Where are you staying?"

"In that van."

"Ugh! Sleep in here. I have my own bathroom."

Arlo yanked out the screen without waiting for a response. I threw myself onto the sill and hoisted myself over, landing facedown on the carpet like a failed projectile.

Arlo said, "I don't know if I can sleep. This is pretty exciting stuff." He moved to his closet and began to rummage.

"I hope it's okay with you, but I think I'm going to sleep right now," I said, looking around for something to make a bed with. I pulled some of the linens I'd brought from his closet and threw the seat cushion of the institutional wingback down for my pillow. It smelled like the marshaled flatulence of many anonymous butts. Even at a fancy place like this! I pushed it away and made a pillow with my sweater instead, and fell asleep wondering why I was still hurting so much.

Part 2

14

The long cold metal tube in which I sat, in the second-to-last row in a universally despised middle seat, aroused memories of trips I'd taken to the southern hemisphere in the past. In those days the captain would wake us when the plane crossed the international date line, and upon landing in Sydney, we'd be sprayed with some kind of insecticide.

Back then, the reasons to leave the country had been adding up. Some years before, my mother had been very unhappy about the things Pincer had falsely accused Arlo of in the divorce, and she and her mother had not spoken since. Meanwhile, her hopes for a more stable relationship with Arlo had been dashed when he married Doris Roofla. And though it had been a slam-dunk case to revoke Gaspard's visiting rights with me following my mishap at sea, Gaspard continued to challenge the case and send her vicious letters. Finally, since she and Hugh had felt that America was going down the tubes for some time, Hugh set out to find a new job on the southern frontier. In 1996, when he obtained a Fulbright and a year-long appointment, off we went.

I was in ninth grade, Margaret in seventh. We spent a year in Canberra and went to school. Hugh made contacts in the library world and two years after our return he was awarded a full-time position in Brisbane. They would leave the United States for good. Before long they would become dual citizens. They would alienate what relatives they still had in the States, who would ask, *What's wrong, isn't America good enough for you?*

I remained in Los Angeles to finish high school, staying with my friend Claire and her family, but Margaret went with our parents. And she too never came back.

In those days, I'd visit as often as they'd buy me a ticket. And they'd come visit from time to time too. Eventually, after Sherman and I married, they'd bring us both. As soon as we'd arrive, he'd want to take off exploring, but I wanted to hang out with my family. I was surprised that he didn't understand that. On both sides, resentments built.

I'd returned to Queensland only once since the disappearance—shortly after it happened. Margaret and Wilhelmus had infant twins then (our parents had planned to be back for the birth), and I stayed almost two months, in a fugue state of which I have almost no memory, adding to their burdens rather than helping them, I'm sure.

Now Arlo was up in first class, as befits a retired pilot with full seniority on an international flight. I was in the seat already described, between a woman with a baby and another young woman with loud, leaking earbuds, as befits someone who has purchased a ticket last-minute at the airport.

We'd spent the morning making sure we had all of Arlo's prescriptions and deciding what he needed to pack. For the great-grandchildren, Margaret's boys, he asked me to go shopping for some swag. So I went out to do this with the idea of ending up in the parking lot of Burt's building, where I would leave the van.

I also provided Arlo with the latest installment in Pincer's melo-drama, to which he said, "Boy oh boy. I was a sucker. I wouldn't blink an eye when she'd take off for Japan for weeks at a time."

"Who knows if it's even true?" I said. "I think she makes up stuff all the time."

He agreed. He also said he'd call Margaret to confirm our plans.

By the time I reached the lot, I'd rounded up some Santa Barbara T-shirts and an assortment of stickers and two soft stuffed sea ot-ters. Then I phoned Burt. The call went to voice mail; this wasn't surprising, as it had been less than twenty-four hours since he'd had surgery. I said I'd call again and I hoped he'd be feeling better soon and that I had to leave for Australia to settle some things there, but that I'd see him as soon as I got back. I told him where the van was parked, and where I was about to hide the key, on the top of the right front tire. (I looked up to see if the barracuda was watching from her post—thankfully, she was not. I hoped she would not fur-ther attack the blameless Dog.)

At last, wholly unplanned, just before ending the call, I said: "Take care, Burt. Lots of love!" And then felt exposed, a feeling I couldn't stand.

I walked it off returning to the Palms. What made me think Burt wanted my love? It was clear something about the past few days had taken a toll. Much as I'd looked forward to the train trip the day I came down to Santa Barbara, I now looked forward to the enforced immobility on our flight and the chance to shut down.

I was within sight of the Palms when Dale phoned. He was at the hospital and had seen that I'd tried to reach Burt.

"How is he?"

"Sleepy but recovering."

"I'm so glad. I left him a message about going to Australia tonight with my grandfather, so he'll know I won't be around when he gets out."

"Smart decision," Dale said. "You'll get to see your sister and spend time with your grandfather even if nothing conclusive turns up about your parents. Burt will be staying here at least three or four days, if not longer. I'll go home today and come back when he's discharged."

"The Chore Cow's back at the office building," I added.

"My worries are over. Have a good trip. I know the purpose is sobering."

I thanked him and said goodbye, slightly disappointed by the flatness of the exchange, yet still trying to gauge the degree of warmth present in it. On a scale of 10, I'd rate it about 5.5.

Finally, I made the call I looked forward to least. Pincer answered immediately.

"I got a lot to deal with right now, Penny. Are you coming over soon?"

"No," I said. "I'm going to Australia today."

"Today? Why?"

"I need to deal with some stuff over there and help Margaret." I didn't mention Arlo, it wasn't worth it.

"This is very inconvenient. I was hoping you'd help me prepare the back bedroom for Burt, but like usual, I'll just have to take care of it myself."

I didn't feel like arguing about Burt, but said, "Don't count on that. He probably has other plans."

"I know he doesn't have other plans."

"Have you heard anything from Detective Storke?"

"Yes, I have. Somebody stole my Scintillator."

Indeed someone did. It was still under the front seat of Burt's van. "Why would they, and what is it anyway?"

"It's a highly sensitive instrument designed to detect radioactivity, and was of utmost importance to me in my research."

"Do you ever point it at people like it's a gun?"

"Penny, when you're a woman living alone you need to be quick on your feet. I'm not afraid to use any resource at my disposal. In the meantime, I've been in touch with my attorney this morning. I have nothing to worry about there. What I need to do now is make arrangements for Hiroshi's interment and demand they return his remains rather than locking them up in some old evidence room."

"Well, good luck with that." I didn't bring up her massive tax problem, as I'd have to deal with it when I returned. She ought to be able to survive the next few weeks. "By the way, my leg is killing me where you stabbed me."

She said, "I don't know what you're talking about. If your leg is killing you, do something about it."

"Thanks," I said.

Later that day, the joy Arlo experienced arriving at LAX was almost contagious. It had been his base for almost twenty years after previous posts in Denver and Chicago when my mother was a girl. He'd flown the maximum number of years a pilot could fly in a career in commercial aviation, and, having been the face of United for years on billboards and magazine advertisements, he was greeted with all due respect from the ticket counter forward. As we waited in the lounge for the flight, crew members came by to say hello. As we came closer to boarding time, the captain presented himself and told Arlo he'd invite him into the cockpit during the flight. When first class was called, Arlo and I said goodbye to each other for the next fifteen hours. He said, "Know anything about shrimp cocktail and warm nuts?"

"Never heard of it," I said, as he disappeared through the gate.

Eventually the last rows were invited to board. The woman in the aisle seat with the baby had short blond hair and wore a blue sweatshirt, stretched out of shape and over-laundered. I pictured the baby pulling and hanging on it, curving her spinal column, grabbing her breasts, and trying to suck the life out of her. Perhaps my views on motherhood were overly apprehensive.

Before long we exchanged pleasantries. Her name was Jean. She was an American returning to Geelong, near Melbourne, after visiting her parents in Tallahassee. She'd married an Australian and was happy in Victoria. She played the oboe in the Geelong Symphony Orchestra and was an active member of Democrats Abroad, and would be working hard on voter registration for the presidential election the following year, torn between Bernie and Hillary. I told her my sister had also married an Australian and was happy in Brisbane.

"How old is your baby?" I was making mental comparisons to the pictures Claire had been sending but that I usually ignored.

"Six months. He's done well on the flights so far, but I'm prepared to drug him, don't worry. I know how people feel when they see us coming down the aisle."

"I don't mind at all. What's his name?"

"Sherman," she said.

The noise I produced would be hard to describe. Something between a gasp and a warble. "Sherman?"

"I know, it's not a popular name these days. It comes from *shearman*, such as the man who cuts the wool, and my husband's family has a station out near Broken Hill."

"Forgive me. My ex-husband's name is Sherman," I said. "I didn't mean to react in any way that could be construed as negative."

"Oh no!" She laughed and covered his ears. "Don't hold it against him!"

I realized I was looking at the infant with an antipathy that I needed to make every effort to disguise. I did not feel the world needed another Sherman, but there was nothing I could do to stop them from proliferating. Here before me was the prototype, the nascent version that prefigured a future, full-on Sherman who would have the capacity to ridicule anyone who believed in anything, whose cynicism would know no bounds, who thought life was misery and one ought to get used to it, who thought all endeavors ended in sorrow and disappointment, who stepped on any bud of possibility that dared form in his path.

Not long into the flight I began to shiver with alarming intensity. I released the paper-thin blanket from its plastic and wrapped it around myself, but it provided little warmth. I felt miserable; following the watery distraction of the drink and meal carts I tried to sleep; I took more painkillers. Wretched hours passed in the cold roaring tube. I twisted and turned, trying to find a comfortable position within the space allotted me. Perhaps I still looked normal enough, for at some point during the long hours of darkness, as we followed the night across the Pacific, Jean asked if I'd hold Sherman while she went to the bathroom.

Sherman was now awake, staring at me with his beady little eyes.

What would he become, what would any baby become? I wondered if an intervention at this stage could change everything. As I sat there holding him, wondering what that intervention could be, he began to whimper, perhaps suspecting me of plotting against him. "Dear little Sherman," I said, bouncing him a little. "Your mother will be right back. Don't worry." Sherman's lower lip trembled. "She'll be back, dear little Sherman." Was I saying it with enough warmth and conviction? The last time I'd held any babies was when I visited Margaret after our parents disappeared. The babies were her twins Boaz and Bram. I remembered telling them that their mother would be right back, then wondering if my own mother would be right back, and starting to weep. This caused one to weep, which caused the other to wail, and that's how Margaret found us, where-upon she decided I was a very poor babysitter. "Sherman, it's a rough world out there," I murmured. "And you have a chance to resist its grinding toll. You don't have to become what the world wants you to become." Sherman closed his eyes, as if he could bear the situation he found himself in no longer. Shermans tended to feel that way around me.

"Are you all right?" The woman with the earbuds by the window asked then.

I turned to look at her. It was the first time she'd spoken the whole flight.

"I'm merely suppressing some unpleasant memories," I replied.

"No, I mean, I happened to see your leg a moment ago and it looks seriously inflamed."

I brought Sherman to my shoulder and peered over his heavily padded backside, lifting my leg. Between the top of my sock and the hem of my pants I could see an expanse of mottled, purplish skin, which probably warranted attention.

"I had a puncture wound earlier this week, and I think maybe it's gotten infected," I said.

"I'm in med school at UCLA," she said. "I think it's quite advanced, actually. You could be on the verge of sepsis. You really need to start taking some antibiotics immediately."

"You mean before we get there?"

"Do you know what sepsis is?"

"I've heard of it."

"It's when a small infection triggers a whole-body response, and it can lead to organ failure and, frankly, death. How are you feeling right now?"

"Not that good," I admitted. "I'm kind of queasy and I ache all over."

"May I take your temperature?" she asked, pulling a digital model from her bag, and I said sure. She held it near my forehead and it beeped moments later. "A-hundred-and-two-point-six. I think this is serious enough to find out if anybody on board is carrying antibiotics. What was the puncture from? Is your tetanus shot up to date?"

I wasn't sure about the tetanus shot, but admitted that the puncture was from a piece of my grandmother's jewelry. I didn't mention that she'd stabbed me intentionally. Then, sensing it might be pertinent, I added: "It's possible that rats might have been crawling around on it." Saying this was very unpleasant, but I liked her very much because instead of shrinking from me, she nodded and took the information in stride. I also appreciated that she didn't ask why I'd let it advance this far, because I wouldn't have known how to answer.

After a short session on her tablet, she pronounced that I may have contracted and incubated any number of bacterial infections, possibly leptospirosis, but that tetanus or hantavirus or the plague itself could not be ruled out. No matter what it was, the potential for sepsis had to be dealt with at once. Without hesitating, she pressed the call button on her seat.

Shortly a flight attendant answered the call, and the medical student, whose name was Fernanda, articulated her concerns. Before I knew it, the classic announcement rang out through the cabin—was there a doctor on board?

I wondered if Arlo had heard this or if he was too intoxicated on shrimp cocktails and warm nuts to notice. But it was so much better this way than me hearing a call for a doctor and worrying it was for him.

There were eight doctors on board! All of them piled to the back of the plane as if eager to get a piece of the action. By now Jean had returned and taken possession of Sherman, staying in the aisle to clear the way. I was helped to my feet and asked to remove my pants in the bathroom so they could assess my condition, and one by one, as I stood in my underwear in the frigid, urine-suffused compartment, its floor sticky, its bin overflowing with used tissues, they opened the flimsy bathroom door, introduced themselves, asked questions, and viewed my naked leg. Some of them touched it. One said he was an ophthalmologist but was hoping he could be helpful anyway. It was a startling shock when a gray-haired man peered in and introduced himself as a recently retired pediatrician by the name of Fountain-Goose.

"Dr. Fountain-Goose?" I exclaimed.

The man standing in the bathroom doorway was my childhood physician, older now, but unmistakable, especially with that name. "You were my doctor when I was growing up. I'm Penny Rush. Do you remember me?"

It did not take him long to say, "Penny Rush. Yes. If I'm not mistaken, I saw a lot of you."

"This is amazing," I said. "Why are you going to Australia?"

"My wife and I are enjoying our retirement and Australia's been on our list," he said. "Now, what's going on with your leg?"

I'd had mixed feelings about Dr. Fountain-Goose when he'd seen me as a child and adolescent. While he was certainly competent and kept Margaret and me in reasonable health, he'd seemed lacking in other ways that I'd never quite put my finger on. In those days, he'd served, at my mother's behest, as a counselor for my emotional problems.

"That's a terrible story," he said, once I'd elaborated on the source of my wound. "Wasn't your grandmother a physician of some kind?"

I nodded, leaving it at that.

Now, more than twenty years later, after examining me in the back of an airplane, he told me he'd confer with his ad hoc colleagues, and soon I was sitting in a jump seat in the galley with a blanket around me, shivering intensely. To my surprise, I heard them tossing around the possibility that the plane should make an emergency stop in New Caledonia, which we were soon to fly over, but it was felt I could survive the three remaining hours to Sydney because my heart rate wasn't elevated, nor was my blood pressure too high or low. (It was strange to hear people discussing my odds.) There was no way of knowing which pathogens were raging through my system until I could have blood samples taken to a lab, but in the meantime, the team of physicians produced the means to begin my treatment. I was given an injection of corticosteroids in my leg and a massive dose of antibiotics with as much water as I could glug down.

The highlight of the journey was when I looked down the aisle and saw my ninety-three-year-old grandfather making his way to the back of the plane to see me. One of the flight attendants who knew I was his granddaughter had told him about my condition.

"You're moving to first class," he said upon reaching me.

"I am?"

"I hear you need to stretch out that leg. I'm tired of the place anyway. It's like a coffin, nothing like first class used to be. There's nobody to talk to! I can't stand it."

And so I was led up to first class, where I climbed into Arlo's "coffin" and slept the rest of the flight. Arlo spent those hours chatting with Jean and Fernanda and even playing with little Sherman, having nothing to hold against him.

15

Sydney was immigration, customs, and a terminal change. It took all my stamina to make it through, helping Arlo along as well. Next came the short flight north to Brisbane. Arlo, who had been invited for a full hour into the cockpit of the 747 during the long night, was in the highest of spirits, peering down at farms and forests and river deltas from his window seat, while I sat beside him, recalling uncomfortable conversations long ago with Dr. Fountain-Goose, evaluating the status of my sepsis, and wondering if I had any number of rodent-borne diseases. The infection itself appeared to be responding rapidly to the antibiotics, as the color of my skin was changing. No longer a deep plum, it was now the hue of a slightly unripe strawberry. My fever was down as well. I'd been given instructions by Fountain-Goose on behalf of the entire medical team aboard the flight to get to a hospital or doctor as soon as possible to obtain an official diagnosis, continue the treatment, and monitor my vital signs. Nevertheless, my instinct was to hide my condition from my sister. I said to Arlo, "Don't tell Margaret about the medical intervention on the flight, okay?"

"Why not?"

"I don't want her to think something's wrong with me."

"If you say so."

Obviously I looked forward to seeing my sister and her family. But I was deriving much-needed feelings of purpose by keeping my thoughts focused on the trip to Mount Isa and whatever awaited us there. I imagined we'd stay a few days with Margaret, during which time we'd secure a vehicle and equip ourselves. Over the past twenty-four hours I'd read up on road travel in the far reaches of Queensland and it sounded as if we'd be wise to rent a satellite phone. Cell phones simply wouldn't cut it. And we'd need food and bedding, in case we had a breakdown in the far-flung quadrants Arlo wanted to focus on.

I was also preoccupied with what I'd left behind in Santa Barbara. Removing myself from the place geographically was not enough to put my new concerns out of mind. I wondered what Pincer would do next. I wanted daily updates on Burt's condition. I calculated the time difference and realized Dale and Kweecoats would be, by now, back in San Francisco. I felt jealous knowing Dale's wife would be fondling Kweecoats and cultivating his affection. I wondered what Storke had to say. I even wondered how Doris was faring on her Baja cruise, and what she'd do once she learned where Arlo had gone.

Margaret was visible as soon as we emerged into the waiting area, standing up front to claim us. My sister—the newer, improved expression of our mutual genes, shapely, statuesque. She had always been the articulate and commanding one, serious and disciplined about her interests, and I'd always been in awe of her, knowing she was an example to us all. As I limped toward her, I couldn't help but note that she looked stronger and better than ever.

We hugged. By way of clasping her elbows, which were uniquely knobby, I knew it was really her. It seemed I'd mostly dropped the habit of fearing my family members were imposters. That began when I was young and I'd return home from visiting Gaspard, and had actually been something I'd tried talking to Dr. Fountain-Goose about. (He'd posited the obvious: that I was afraid of losing my family when sent away.) But this was the real Margaret, in a nice sleeveless rayon dress that suited the Brisbane winter weather perfectly. Overwhelmed in my bundle of clothing from the flight, I felt grossly in need of a shower. Margaret, who was clearly not an imposter because, as Fountain-Goose had trained me to understand, why would anybody go to all that trouble, had us wait in front with our luggage while she fetched her car, a new Honda Odyssey minivan that soon pulled up gleaming and brilliant in the sunshine, unrusted, unattacked by spray paint, smelling inside of its supple leather seats, its one-upmanship of the Dog of the North not lost on me, and shortly we were on our way, Arlo up front, me in back.

"Your sister has a problem," Arlo said, first thing out of his mouth.

"Guess who was on the flight, Dr. Fountain-Goose!" I interrupted.

"What kind of problem?" responded Margaret, with an edge.

"Nothing!" I spoke up. "I just need to get some antibiotics."

"I can get those for you," she said. "What for?"

"Just a little infection."

"Was it really Dr. Fountain-Goose, or just someone who looked like him?" she asked, proving she had not forgotten another of my childhood idiosyncrasies, of mistaking strangers for people I knew.

"What kind of name is Fountain-Goose anyway?" Arlo wanted to know.

I said, "Of course it was him." I mentioned that he was vacationing with his wife and would be coming through Brisbane later in the week and might even give us a call.

Margaret said, "It's a busy week here. Tomorrow I have the day off and we need to go to Banks Street."

This was our parents' house. I knew this was coming and could do nothing about it at this point but say, "Great, let's do it." Then I added, "You don't sound excited about seeing Dr. Fountain-Goose."

"It was probably a different name once," Arlo continued to muse. "Fountain-*Geüsze* or something like that."

"Is there something to be excited about?" Margaret said. "If you want to get together with Dr. Fountain-Goose when I hardly ever see you, be my guest!"

Her response puzzled me. Was she really that eager to spend time together? All at once we disappeared into a tunnel, a bypass under the city that had been completed since my last visit; no longer would we take the quaint meandering road from the airport down the Brisbane River as the city came into view. Every time I visited, Brisbane had leapfrogged further over its past. My experience in this new tunnel was most notable for how queasy I began to feel as we rushed past its walls. Mercifully, when we emerged into daylight again, we were nearly there.

I saw it as we rounded the final corner. Their rambling old Queenslander, overlooking a nature strip on a hill just to the west of the city center. It had a wide veranda and filigreed latticework on the eaves and rose from a steamy tangle of fan palms, cycads, staghorn ferns, grevillea, and other fertile foliage decking it on all sides. The frangipani trees in front were still winter-bare, their blunt naked limbs providing not a hint of the sweet-smelling flowers and glossy leaves that would burst forth from them anytime now. It was beautiful, it was lived-in and festooned with toys, it represented a domestic ideal that I both longed for and derided, and just as Margaret said with utmost cheer, "We're here!" I began to vomit profusely, as if my innards were shouting, *We're here too.*

"Holy smokes, take cover," I heard Arlo say.

"Penny! Oh my god!" Margaret parked and rushed around to open the sliding door, reaching for my hand to guide me out onto the sidewalk, where I continued to retch into the plants. She knelt beside me, offering some tissues from her purse.

"Sorry, Margaret. Your car. Sorry."

"Let's get inside," she said, putting her arm around me, leading me in.

It was approaching noon. Nobody was home. Wilhelmus was at practice with his team and the boys were in what Margaret called *kindy.* She assigned Arlo to the guest room on the ground floor, while she'd fashioned a corner for me in her office upstairs with the kind of inflatable bed blown up with a vacuum cleaner.

"But I need to clean the car," I kept saying.

"Forget that. What's going on?"

It was then that I had to confess the extent of my condition and what had occurred on the plane. As I'd suspected, she was appalled. I really didn't like arriving with a problem. I didn't want Margaret to think I was always in a bad way. She may or may not have questioned me about how this could have happened and why I hadn't paid attention to it sooner. I prefer not to remember. The upshot was that she'd take me to work with her and have me seen. I couldn't protest; it was necessary. I then took a shower that rivaled in my estimation the one I'd taken in Dale's hotel room. Margaret even had plush towels. Thinking about the desirability of my naked body was not a high priority at the moment, but I did notice that my leg looked like a sausage.

To my chagrin, Margaret had spent that time decontaminating the seats and floor of her van. Perhaps because she had two children or because she was exposed to bodily fluids on a daily basis, the job was less vile for her than it would be for others. Or maybe Margaret was just a great sport. She'd made us tuna sandwiches and a fruit salad of papaya, banana, mango, and kiwi, but I was not ready to eat. We would soon have to leave for the hospital. As she rushed about readying herself, Arlo had lunch at the kitchen table looking over *The Courier-Mail*. "Catherine may drop by," she told Arlo. "She picks up the boys every day and she's eager to see you."

Catherine was Margaret's widowed mother-in-law.

"I'll try to make myself presentable," Arlo said.

While I waited for Margaret, I read a recent article on Wilhelmus that had been framed and hung on the wall in the hallway:

RECLUSIVE HUNK TAKES ON ROLE
AS CAPTAIN OF THE ROAR

Don't expect Wilhelmus Janssen to talk about his Asian Cup winnings or his elevation to captain of the Brisbane Roar. Known to his fans as "The Reclusive Hunk," the 32-year-old Brisbane-born Socceroo is notoriously quiet, and his teammates respect him all the more for it.

"We have great understanding," says Flynn Patrick, teammate and the club's vice-captain. "Wilhelmus is a man of few words but his decisiveness and strategic brilliance provide us everything we need."

Coach Lachlan Hughes thinks Janssen is a natural for the captaincy. "He sets an example for us all, on and off the field. He's got the experience and the respect of his mates, and that's what counts."

Being known as a "hunk" doesn't come without its drawbacks. Many fans are no doubt disappointed to learn that he's happily married to Dr. Margaret Janssen of the Royal Brisbane and Women's Hospital, with twin boys at home.

The previous captain of the Roar, Angus MacMillan, upon appointment released this statement: "It's an honor to find myself captain of this storied and beloved Brisbane team. I hope to build on our team's fantastic record and spirit in the year ahead."

Janssen could not be reached for comment, but we believe he would have said the same thing.

Our parents had adored Wilhelmus, always comparing him, I'm sure, to Sherman, who did not have articles written about him, nor was he called a hunk, reclusive or otherwise. I supposed the best thing about Wilhelmus was his devotion to Margaret, and for that reason he clearly deserved our regard.

In a car so redolent of a eucalyptus-based cleanser it made our eyes sting, we drove to the hospital, where Margaret is a surgeon educator for the University of Queensland medical school. In other words, she is a person upon whom people depend. People within the organization depend on her. Patients depend on her. Their families depend on her. She had, at the right time and place, taken the necessary steps to place herself in this position. She had achieved it methodically, as if following clearly marked instructions. Emotional neediness had not waylaid her. Bouts of depression had not thwarted her. She approached everything she did logically and without undue hesitancy.

"Have you heard anything lately from Sherman?" she wanted to know.

"No."

"He moved in with that woman?"

"Yep. He'd been staying over at her Christmas tree farm for months and I didn't even know it."

"When you thought he was in Berkeley doing research?"

I nodded grimly. "I still remember the day he mentioned some lady with a tree farm who wanted her axes and saws sharpened. But things were already bad."

"Just because things were bad didn't mean he had to run off with somebody."

She urged me to file for divorce as soon as possible. I sensed no regret that Sherman would soon be amputated from our family like a gangrenous limb, but my energy level for that topic was low anyway.

"And Doris really left on a cruise the day after Arlo moved out?"

"Yes, after saying she was too busy to visit him, and also complaining that we moved him out right after telling me he had to move out."

We could only begin to imagine how angry and upset our mother would have been about this.

At the Royal Brisbane Margaret had me seen by a gruff, bearlike colleague, who drew blood and put me on a supplementary dose of antibiotics by IV and monitored me for several hours while I rested on a gurney in a corridor. At one point, groggy and disoriented, I heard some people speaking near me in hushed tones and raised my head, whereupon I was swiftly introduced to Meg, Bryan, Sarah, Colm, Rose, Abimbola, and Kelly, all in staff uniforms. They surrounded me and began asking questions from all sides.

"You haven't visited Margaret in ages, have you? She would have said!"

It's been a while.

"Penny, where do you live in the States?"

California.

"Are you here for long?"

Not sure yet.

"What do you do, Penny? Are you in the medical field as well?"

In the field—yes.

"What branch?" one asked.

Mmm, *dentistry*.

"Ah, you're a dentist," the older woman said.

"From California," another said.

"They have lovely teeth in California," another said.

I didn't correct them. I didn't want them to know Margaret had a sister who was actually like me.

The older woman said, "I hope you don't mind me asking, but I recently had a bone graft where I've had a tooth removed, and was told it would fill in, but it's very tender and I'm wondering if it's infected, would you be willing to take a look?"

I suggested it would be better if she went to her own dentist, since he or she would know her mouth better than I did.

"Yes, I would, you see, but my dentist is on holiday and I don't know if I ought to go to someone else. I don't want to trouble anyone if it's nothing, you see."

With that, she leaned over and opened her mouth wide like a hippo, giving me a full view of her oral cavity, which included the aforementioned gap. I had never seen a dental bone graft before, but the gum did look rather inflamed there. Based on my own recent experiences with deferred treatment, I found myself urging her on. "Yes, I think it's possibly infected and you should contact another dentist for an opinion as soon as possible."

"Yes, I was afraid of that, it just doesn't feel right," she said. "I worry it all day with my tongue and make it worse, most likely."

I said it had been a long day, and they all wished me well.

Shortly after, Margaret appeared, looked appalled. She whispered, "Why did you tell people you're a dentist? You gave *advice*?"

"It was a misunderstanding!" I claimed weakly.

Later, once Margaret's colleague checked me again and I had the antibiotic prescription filled by the hospital chemist, Margaret sent me home in a cab. There I was greeted by the enormous, six-foot-six-inch Wilhelmus, whose footfalls made the wood-framed house shake, and the two little boys, who gave me shy hugs and called me Aunt Penny. That touched me so much! Arlo was in a bathrobe, sipping his martini and watching the news. We were served a pot roast Margaret had thoughtfully prepared in advance, though I still hadn't found my appetite. Wilhelmus is a man of few words; he looks great in knee socks and probably knows it. I do remember Wilhelmus ordering the boys to brush their teeth, saying, "There are more organisms in your mouth than people on earth."

My scientific contribution: "No matter how small they are, I just don't see how that many could fit."

"They cannot all fit!" cried Boaz, pleased to be receiving backup.

"No, they cannot!" screamed Bram.

The role of the aunt was to aid and abet, I decided.

Before bed, Boaz and Bram introduced us to their guinea pigs and serenaded us with a duet on recorders. Next, because they were taking gymnastics, they treated Arlo and me to a spectacle of cartwheels and somersaults. Finally, to round out the evening's entertainment, we observed a choreographed sword fight, the boys' wooden weapons clacking noisily for what seemed like a very long time. I could barely keep my eyes open. I fell onto the air bed in Margaret's office at some point, happy to be under the roof of people who seemed glad to take me in.

Sleep patterns are generally disturbed for those who cross many time zones and are recently septic. Further, inflatable vinyl beds are hot and prone to deflate little by little. I found myself waking in the night, sweating, being consumed by rising folds of vulcanized rubber, churning with feelings and memories stirred by our arrival in Australia, by seeing Margaret and her things, and especially by the fluke encounter with Fountain-Goose. Despite all Margaret and I had shared growing up, I'd had a shadow life outside our family that had burdened me. Margaret knew about my yearly visits to Gaspard, but I'd kept the emotional side to myself. After all, I had everything I needed at home. Hugh loved me and considered me his daughter and the four of us were very close.

Thus my appointments to see Fountain-Goose to discuss my problems were not a topic that came up around the house. My mother scheduled them secretly, as if to spare me the embarrassment of having to admit something was amiss. I wondered now how much of that Margaret knew about. I'd never thought to ask.

The night dragged on. I contemplated the years that had passed since I'd last seen my mother and Hugh, and a familiar lump rose in my throat. My mother and I used to speak nearly every day on the phone, eager as she was to stay connected no matter the distance.

Back then it was almost as if nothing had seemed real until she'd heard about it. Was that why nothing had seemed real since?

From outside the window came the intermittent scuttling of neighborhood possums, and at dawn the cries of hundreds of birds filled the sky. In the breaking light I could see a number of pictures of my family in nice frames surrounding me on Margaret's shelves.

To distract myself from the raw feelings these photos were provoking, I searched for Pomeranians on my phone. I discovered they were originally from a part of Poland and Germany once called Pomerania, on the shores of the Baltic Sea, that they used to be full-sized, and that they had been popularized by Queen Victoria, who at one time was in possession of thirty-five of them. One site described them as having wedge-shaped heads, which I thought highly inaccurate and unflattering. While I was perusing many photos of white, tricolor, orange, and cream-colored Pomeranians, a text message came in:

> Hi Penny,
> It's come to pass. Burt has installed himself at your
> grandmother's. He went straight from the hospital.
> He's been evicted from his office on State Street,
> and I believe the notorious barracuda had something
> to do with it. Also, his van was towed and is now
> impounded somewhere. I will try to straighten things
> out this weekend. I'm sorry to bother you while
> you're dealing with other things there, but thought
> you'd probably want to know.

I was starting to resent Dale's attractive and attentive manner. I put down the phone and regrouped. A spotted gecko was eyeing me from one of the blades of the ceiling fan, but they were harmless and produced cute yips from time to time. After a moment's considera-

tion, I realized I had no choice but to call Pincer at once. The hour
was optimal there, late afternoon. When she answered, I couldn't
help but notice how cheerful she sounded.

"Hello, Penny. Have you finished up your business?" she asked.

"Are you kidding, I just got here! And I hope you remember poking me with your very ugly roadrunner pin, because my leg got infected and then became septic and they had to call for doctors on
the plane to start me on antibiotics and today I threw up in Margaret's car and had to go to the hospital!"

She paused a moment before saying, "Well, I didn't tell you to take
a trip across the world right now, that's your doing."

"Doesn't that make you feel sorry?"

"Penny, I have my accountant Burt Lampey here now, so I'm on
my toes morning, noon, and night. It's like my rotations at Harbor
Hospital all over again."

"How's he doing?"

"Very well. I've got him up and walking around and he's taking
his antiplatelets, beta-blockers, ACE inhibitors, cholesterol meds, di-
uretics, and vasodilators. He'll get the hang of it. It's a lot to keep
track of when you're still groggy from surgery. He's obedient and
grateful as a lamb."

I could see the distinctive profile of a kookaburra in the branch
of a tree near the window and hoped it would start cackling on my
behalf. I said, "You're sure it's not too *taxing* for you?"

"Work keeps you young. I'm at my best when called to duty. Your
generation doesn't understand that. It's a nice distraction from this
business with Hiroshi's remains. But I believe that's simmering down.
Detective Storke's another nice man, by the way. He's been coming
by on his rounds to check up on me."

I didn't have the heart to mention that Dale would soon be removing Burt from her clutches. For now it sounded as if she were taking Burt's care seriously, and it was great not hearing her complain about what imaginary things had been stolen or how disappointed she was by the latest purchase of chicken breasts. Who knew, maybe she and Burt were a match made in heaven. Or maybe Storke was the man for the job. Maybe she required them both. Whatever the cause for her good cheer, I was grateful for it—though in retrospect, I should have been very suspicious.

16

Before long came the bustle of the boys preparing for school, the clattering of dishes in the kitchen, footsteps up and down the stairs, shouts, grumbles, rushing water, doors creaking and slamming, and, finally, silence. I got up and dressed in my usual—jeans and T-shirt—and found Margaret on her laptop sipping a cup of tea, Arlo at the kitchen table with coffee. I greeted them with the news I'd received in Dale's text, that Burt had moved in with Pincer straight from the hospital. Arlo emitted an instinctive sound of dread, but Margaret seemed unmoved by the significance of this. I realized that she knew nothing about Burt, let alone Dale, so I foolishly grabbed my phone to show her some pictures. I'd taken one of Dale unloading the dog crate from the sports car without his knowledge. "Okay, this is Burt's brother, Dale. He's really nice."

Margaret glanced at the phone and said, "Burt's brother Dale. Okay."

Still unaware that I was exposing myself to unfavorable judgment, I scrolled for a picture of Burt, which I'd taken the night we'd had Mexican food in the restaurant. I'd gotten used to him without his hairpiece, so the sight of him wearing it made me smile.

"Here's Burt," I said. "He's a friend of Pincer's, her accountant, and he was the one trying to help me deal with her, but then he had a bunch of medical problems plus got divorced and lost his house."

Margaret took a look.

"He's funny. You'd like him," I added.

"What's with the wig?" she asked.

"Yeah, he decided not to wear it anymore and gave it to his dog. Not to wear! Just to curl up with."

"As one would. Is he still capable of helping?"

"I don't know, but he's a friend now, so I'm worried about him. Here's his dog." I held up a magnificent portrait of Kweecoats from the day I took him to the Palms, backlit by the sun.

"Cute little guy," Arlo vouched.

"Dale's keeping him until Burt's better. Their father worked in a produce warehouse and was killed by a crate of vegetables when they were kids. Isn't that horrible? And Burt had an athletic scholarship but gave it up to help take care of Dale, who's fourteen years younger." I mentioned these things as though they were features of some new cosmology I was privy to. But Margaret looked indifferent, almost repulsed.

"Is there something wrong?" I asked.

"Didn't you just meet these people a few days ago?"

I said I had, but so what?

She said, "I mean, what about the people you work with? Where are the people that matter to you? Those are the people I want to see pictures of."

What a gross miscue, how could she be so dense? "I couldn't stand the people I worked with!" (This wasn't strictly true; they were okay. Actually, they were fine.) "Anyway," I added, "I don't work there anymore."

"You left?"

"That's why I had time to go to Santa Barbara, and here."

I had a counterproductive trait when it came to Margaret. When I sensed I was annoying her, I would try to annoy her more.

"What's that?" she asked, as I placed another image before her.

"Burt's van. He loves it. He calls it the Dog of the North."

Margaret visibly recoiled, her nose wrinkling up like a small cabbage.

I added: "A woman in his building is obsessed with him and thought I was invading her turf, so she spray-painted *whore cow* onto the van when I was sleeping in it."

"You were sleeping in it?"

Arlo interrupted. "Penny, I'm making a list of everything we need for our trip, but I want to see some koala bears first with the kids."

"Penny needs to recover," Margaret said, looking at me with fatigue. "I really don't think it's a good idea to take off quite yet. It's a twenty-hour drive or more. Maybe you should fly?"

"We're driving," I said tersely. "That's the plan, period."

It was then that I retreated with my coffee to Margaret's office, where I petulantly kicked the bed, possibly hoping to pop it. I was simultaneously offended by Margaret's trivialization of Burt, Dale, and Kweecoats, and disconcerted to recognize, by way of her blunt remarks, what tenuous ties I had to them, and that once Burt's life settled down, the infrastructure of these friendships would surely crumble. The idea that we had become great friends was obviously questionable, and all-knowing Margaret had the perspective to see what I could not. Yet at the same time, I wanted to shield Burt, Dale, and Kweecoats, even the Dog of the North, from her dismissal.

The trees in the nature strip were quivering in a light breeze, their leaves shimmering like silver coins. Powerful clouds could be seen in the direction of the coast. From the tops of several lofty eucalyptus trees, the squawks of magpies and cockatoos echoed. The day was inviting me to enjoy it. Feeling oppositional, I briefly considered crawling back into bed and hiding under the covers, but knew I couldn't get away with it. Margaret would roust me in no time.

The truth was, I had regained, over the past months, some equilibrium existing outside of the scrutiny of intimate relationships. Being challenged by Margaret was hard to bear.

I looked up to see if the gecko was still perched on the blade of the fan, but it had moved on. The absence of the gecko seemed like a sign to snap out of it; my grandfather and my sister and her family were close at hand. I was more surrounded by loved ones than I had been in some time. Now was not the time to brood, especially once Margaret knocked on the door moments later and said that she didn't mean to sound unfriendly about the pictures of my friends. "Talk about them all you want," she said, adding that she really appreciated my efforts with Pincer and Arlo. I almost said, *What's so great about* your *friends?* but didn't. Margaret always came through, I had to admit. So I came back downstairs, poured some more coffee, wrote a brief reply to Dale to offer reassurance, and soon, with a map spread out on Margaret's table, Arlo and I were discussing our route to the northwest, which was of course to be the same route that my mother and Hugh had taken. I had to promise Margaret we would not get lost.

And so it was that later that morning, Margaret and I stood together as a team on the street in front of our parents' house. The time had finally come. It wasn't hard to see that the garden had greatly changed, becoming an interesting blend of the predatory and the dead—many specimens had simply given up, overtaken by more robust flora, giving the property a savage, unruly appearance.

"I stopped paying the gardener," Margaret said.

Anything that she'd stopped attending to counted as one less thing for me to feel guilty about.

"Let's go inside."

The house on Banks Street sat on a ridge, with a view from its back veranda of Mount Coot-tha. It was there that our parents regularly sat for lunch, gazing out past their leopard tree at the onslaught of wilderness just beyond the city limits. Our mother always took pleasure in how ready the natural world was to envelop them.

We had a big backlog of topics to discuss besides the house. Driving over, we covered the grotesque situation at Pincer's, Arlo's relationship with Doris and his move to the Palms, and a little more about my final days with Sherman. She brought me up-to-date on her professional life and what it was like balancing that with the needs of the boys. Her mother-in-law appeared to play a large role in keeping things sane for the family, and Margaret was very grateful to her.

Now, seeing the house, I understood why it would nag at her psyche. Margaret turned on the air-conditioning as soon as we stepped inside in order to dry up the damp smell pervading the rooms. We opened the wooden shutters all around and stood back to take it in. Based on the call I'd received from the property manager, Viola Mitchell, I'd expected much worse.

It was just as it had been five years ago. A saltshaker sat on the little table between their leather armchairs facing the television set, likely used during their last dinner there. The books they'd been reading still lay by their bedsides—a study of the artist Milton Avery by my mother's, Sir Edmund Hillary's *High Adventure* by Hugh's. A laundry hamper was half-filled with their last dirty clothes. Not everything was frozen in time—Margaret had long ago emptied the refrigerator and unplugged it, and cleared the pantry of food.

"I've come over a few times and borrowed things," Margaret said. "I didn't think you'd mind. I took the Dutch oven and that big black salad bowl."

"That's fine," I said.

"Well, what should we do?"

It was tempting to leave it as a museum, a place where we could drop by and do research on them for years to come, but I knew Margaret wouldn't go for that. "You tell me. It weighs on you the most."

Margaret said, "Remember what I've told you about the missing persons laws in Queensland?"

"Tell me again."

"The court will only issue a death certificate after someone's missing for seven years. That's two years still to wait. At that point, we can decide whether to sell the house or keep it and rent it, that's another discussion. But there's another choice, in which we file papers and 'swear death'—showing evidence to receive the certificate sooner."

"*Swear death?* That's sick! Why would we want to do that?"

"It's reasonable at this point."

"But we don't have any evidence, and besides, we don't want to believe it."

"Of course we don't want to, but do we have a choice? We've done everything reasonable that can be done." This was true. Margaret had checked in regularly with the police in the area, and in the beginning we'd hired our own investigators. "There is no reason in the world they would stage their disappearance to take on new identities—"

"That we know of," I stubbornly said.

"—and most of all, they'd never gone anywhere without telling us exactly where they would be at every moment, and obviously, Penny, how could you think they could still be alive and doing this to us?"

"Margaret, what you say makes sense, it's just that I can't help wondering if they slipped into another dimension or are being held against their will."

"Slipped into another dimension? Are you serious?"

"How do we know?"

"I can't even respond to that. Held against their will, that's even worse. Do you actually prefer thinking something like that?"

"I like to think about how they might escape and suddenly we'll get a call from someone telling us they're all right."

"I would like that too, but isn't it better to understand that they were probably outwitted by natural forces beyond their control?"

"No, that's not better at all. You mean wandering around until they perished?"

"Like Burke and Wills," Margaret said. "You're right, it's no better that way. It's no good any way at all."

We decided to be constructive and spend a few hours cleaning and sorting. Margaret put forth the idea that perhaps if we cleaned and cleared enough we could rent the house out furnished to keep it from going to rot. She thought she could possibly find someone at the hospital or in the choir she sang in who might agree to a casual arrangement.

"Do you understand why I didn't want to do this without you?" Margaret asked.

"I do. I'm sorry I didn't come sooner."

"Well, you're here now, and that means a lot."

Some rooms were simpler than others. Five-year-old creams found in bathrooms were easy to throw into a garbage bag. Margaret began to sort the clothes in the bedroom closet, but when I caught a glimpse of a few of our mother's gray hairs on the shoulder of one of her jackets, I thought I might faint. I moved to the office. Hugh had been a superb record keeper and kept very tidy file cabinets filled with tax documents and receipts and correspondence and general memorabilia. There were even a few Penny files and Margaret files, filled with our report cards, graduation programs, and other keepsakes of our childhoods. It was while prowling through the contents of these filing cabinets that I came upon a folder of old letters from Gaspard and, with a certain dread, placed them with my bag to look at later.

I found myself preoccupied with Burke and Wills as I explored the artifacts of our parents' lives, owing to Margaret's mention of them. I recalled clearly how fascinated my mother had been by their disastrous expedition, in which they set out in 1860 from Melbourne well supplied with gear and a fleet of camels to explore the interior of the continent. In the end, they stopped just short of reaching the northern coast, flummoxed by impenetrable mangroves, out of provisions, desperate to make it back to their camp at Cooper's Creek, where other members of the party waited with their store of goods. Alas, due to wet weather, failing health, and the deaths of several of the camels, they made slow progress returning, and the men at Cooper's Creek finally gave them up for lost, setting out for home. The tragic twist: Burke and Wills arrived later *the very day* the camp had been abandoned. Further mishaps to do with crossed communications and delays interfered with rescue attempts. At last, starving and sick, they remained by Cooper's Creek until they perished, nearly a year after setting out.

The year we lived in Canberra, determined to make this an educational experience for us, our mother and Hugh compiled a reading list of Australian classics. We had read, among many others, Miles Franklin's *My Brilliant Career*, *The Merry-Go-Round in the Sea* by Randolph Stow, Patrick White's *Voss* and *The Vivisector*, Nevil Shute's *A Town Like Alice*, Mary Durack's *Kings in Grass Castles*, Thomas Keneally's *The Chant of Jimmie Blacksmith*, and the wonderful *A Fortunate Life* by A. B. Facey. Needless to say, she'd been especially moved by Alan Moorehead's *Cooper's Creek*, as if to take part in a doomed expedition would have been an unparalleled opportunity.

I pulled *Cooper's Creek* off the shelf. *They gave their lives to pierce the secret of the Inland*, was the catchy copy on the cover. Ha! How many people could say their parents had done the same?

The protracted tragedy of the Burke and Wills story spoke to her in some way that seemed almost personal, some way I never quite understood. As did the fateful 1848 outback trek of naturalist Friedrich Leichhardt, fictionalized in *Voss*. From the dog-eared condition of that book, filled with pencil marks and underlinings, I was reminded of how deep this obsession had run. Yet it was impossible to imagine that she and Hugh could have planned to have a doomed expedition of their own. The thought had crossed my mind from time to time but made me feel perverse for even considering it.

Margaret received a steady stream of calls and texts while we worked. She was obviously in demand and dispatched her opinions on various matters without losing her stride. At one point, after a brief conversation, she announced that the results of my tests were in. The lab had performed a rapid test on my IgM antibodies and confirmed a diagnosis of leptospirosis.

"Leptospirosis? What is it?"

"It means you're lucky since it's been caught fairly early, and that our grandmother stabbed you with a pin that had likely been urinated or defecated on by rats."

"That's entirely possible. How lucky could I be!"

"Truly. You're negative for tetanus, plague, and hantavirus. It could have been much worse. But the sepsis part was one hundred percent your fault."

"I realize that."

"But really, it was."

"I get the idea!" I yelled.

"Don't do stuff like that!" she yelled back, but in a caring way, I could tell.

Leptospirosis. I returned to work with renewed vigor, proud that I was infected with a famous disease and still carrying on. We managed by early afternoon to make the place reasonably presentable. We laundered, vacuumed, sponged. Every item I came in contact with felt charged with meaning, so this process was more grueling than anything I'd done in a long while, and that was saying something. I teared up more than once, and borrowed one of my mother's handkerchiefs, ironed and folded in her underwear drawer, to mop my eyes. We called Arlo a few times to check in, vowing to bring back kebabs from Margaret's favorite Lebanese take-out place in Red Hill. As we prepared to leave, closing shutters, turning off lights, a thread of texts appeared on my phone.

Thank you for the reassurance. I will still go this weekend.

I finished that Rorty book I mentioned to you. Really struck by an essay written as if from the year 2096, looking back at our present time when we were evidently taken over by tyrants because the fraternity among our fellow citizens had been fractured by the cruelty of income inequality.

He says it's hard to understand how Americans of our time could have tolerated the horrific inequalities in our society, much the same way now we don't understand how slavery was tolerated. Do you follow politics? I wonder who among the current crop of candidates for next year's election is the tyrant in the making!

My god, though, Rorty wrote this in '96 and everything he says is coming true. I see crimes of desperation and hatred on the rise all over. Sorry to

go on. I'll let you know what happens this weekend.
I can't say I'm looking forward to it.

A warm glow spread through me. Sensing that something unusual was happening, perhaps that I was happy, Margaret asked
what was up.

"Oh, it's another message from Burt's brother, Dale. About an
essay he read."

"That seems to represent a significant development. Is Dale
single?"

"He's married," I said.

"Why is he writing you a long text like that?"

"I guess maybe he values our friendship more than you think."

"A married man does not write texts like that unless he's up to
something."

"He doesn't seem like the up-to-something type," I asserted.

Margaret turned off the air conditioner, shutting the place
down. "Are you sure he's married? Maybe he's in the same situation
you are."

"Maybe. He never mentioned his wife when we were together."

"I would find out what's going on with that," Margaret said. "I
mean, if you're interested in him. Are you interested? Or is it too
soon, since you're not even divorced yet?"

I did not commit to an answer.

But while Margaret phoned in our lunch order, I wrote back:

The Rorty sounds uncanny! Scary to think things
are trending that way. I hope you'll find Burt in good
shape and that you and your significant other are
doing well.

And received this reply, almost immediately:

> My SO is keeping me busy but the pleasures seem
> to outweigh any inconveniences.

I can say with certainty it had been better not knowing for sure.
The inconveniences? How droll. His unambiguous affection for his
wife made me feel more bereft than ever. Why did I listen to Margaret? But who else could I listen to?

17

The next few days were full as we prepared for the trip to Mount Isa. I worked to free myself from fruitless daydreams and my physical condition continued to improve, though my leg remained stiff and bruised. It was hard not to imagine Burt at Pincer's house and feel some concern, especially when I tried calling several times and he didn't answer. But for all I knew he was basking in Pincer's attentions, freed from the deranged lady in his office building, rejoicing in bowls of chicken soup, sleeping in a bed, not on the floor or hard couch, and best of all, knowing that his brother cared and would soon be back to see him.

Margaret made every effort to arrange her schedule so as to have the most time with us that she could. We went with Boaz and Bram to the Lone Pine Koala Sanctuary one day after school, and Arlo was able to hold one of the placid, somewhat bristly creatures for a photo. This thrilled him. One evening at dusk we sat by a place on the river to see the fruit bats, endearingly known as flying foxes, emerge from their cave, thousands of them, and light to the sky. And Arlo and Catherine Janssen saw each other several times that week. She was in her early eighties, cheerful and fit. She would appear with freshly baked lamingtons, little cakes with chocolate icing rolled in coconut, and they'd play chess.

When Margaret could spare her fancy van, Arlo and I took some jaunts around town to collect our supplies. The river twists and turns through the city in all directions and we'd cross a bridge unsure on which side we'd end up, but we didn't mind getting a bit lost. Downtown, cranes loomed beside new buildings going up all over, City Hall and Parliament House now dwarfed relics of the sandstone quarrying days. We had certain favorite arteries lined with jacaranda trees just coming into bloom; we drove around hilly neighborhoods to look at picturesque houses and subtropical gardens and to catch vistas of the cityscape and hinterlands, our windows down because the air was mild and full of fertile scents. But what Arlo prized seeing most were places he remembered from past trips, such as the bulk fruit market in Rocklea, where, he told me, my mother had taken him once to buy melons.

Eventually we put together a box of food, and from Margaret and Wilhelmus borrowed a small butane stove, sleeping bags, flashlights, none of it to be used, presumably, but to have in case of emergency. I reserved a new Toyota Land Cruiser with a roo bar and hired a satellite phone as well. It would take two days to get there if we pushed. Occupied with the logistics of the excursion, I was able to disassociate from its ultimate purpose, at least for the moment.

Nevertheless, when I retired to the wretched bed in the evening, I studied the copy of *Voss* that I'd brought over from the house. I'd venture to say that, boiled down to its essence, it's the same story as *Picnic at Hanging Rock*—Europeans falling prey to a land they don't understand. I'd also say that White is a writer who can find the disgusting in everything, and his language and syntax create primal unease. He won the Nobel Prize for it. It was a pleasure to fall into a literary novel again—I'd been unable to concentrate the past year or two when anxiety about my life had overwhelmed me.

But as absorbing as White's novel itself were the marginal comments made by my mother, revealing what she had chosen to focus on in the narrative. Penciled in throughout were notes like: *classic karst! Uplifted peneplain. Variable ferruginous zone. Bedded cherts! Calcareous shales! Mineral rich pre-Cambrian basement*. It appeared that the love story at the heart of the novel was incidental to her, the hubris and megalomania of the explorer Voss but a trifle. She'd read the novel as a geological expedition. It was so odd, yet so like her. She'd always said she didn't feel comfortable around people, though she craved their attention and approval. Every social encounter for her was fraught with peril and difficulty. In a world of rocks, she was serene.

White, as described in the introduction by Thomas Keneally, had himself been something of a misanthrope, living for many years on a farm in New South Wales with his partner as a gay man in exile. Perhaps knowing he would not have children, he hoped to "people the Australian emptiness in the only way I am able." I'll interject that this European concept of emptiness was likely not shared nor conceptualized by Aboriginal Australians. Keneally goes on to describe White as a Gnostic, with an affinity for deserts, where all is "unmade, undefined, and so untainted." How easy it was to romanticize arid lands! Of course, I resented it. In such a state my mother and Hugh had vanished.

On our fourth day in Brisbane, on the eve of our de-parture, I received the promised call from Dr. Fountain-Goose. He and his wife would be sightseeing in Queensland for the week so he thought he'd check in. I told him I'd been diagnosed with leptospirosis, but he wanted to know if the sepsis had responded to treatment, and went on to say that he'd taken a renewed interest in my "case." When I asked him what he meant, he reminded me of his diagnosis of *selective mutism* when I was ten years old, and I felt something like an electric shock go through me. In fact, I could barely speak, which was fitting, given the diagnosis he had just reminded me of.

"We don't need to talk about that," I finally said, feeling as if I'd been contacted by an assassin.

"Oh! Pardon me. I somehow imagined it would be of interest, now that it's behind you."

"I guess it feels overly familiar for you to blurt it out like that," I managed to say. "I'm telling you this as a tip, in case you run into other former patients."

"Oh! I'm terribly sorry. I was interested in your case and remembered you well. I was pleased to see you again on the plane, despite your unfortunate condition. So, you say your family's moved here?"

I explained that my mother and Hugh were "no longer with us"—without going into detail.

He was sorry to hear that too. "I remember your mother vividly. You may not be aware how often she called our office."

There seemed no end to the disturbing material this man had ready to spring on me.

"Very anxious woman, to put it mildly," he continued.

"I'm sorry, but I'm not sure what makes you think I want to hear things like that."

After a sharp intake of breath, Fountain-Goose said, "I was your doctor for many years. I believe you trusted me. You obviously did, you spoke to me about many things that were troubling you. It may surprise you to know that I cared about my patients and thought about them a great deal. I was not a machine that simply processed what I was told, then discarded it. It was the substance of my days, the work I devoted my life to!" My god. I had cut an authority figure to the quick. Had I overreacted because I myself had failed to integrate past and present? He was not a god that needed bringing down, evidently, but a waning organism in search of its own significance.

"I see what you're saying. I just wasn't prepared for that."

"We spent a lot of time on your issues."

"Yes, I know." Then I added, "But things only got worse, actually."

"I see. And I'm to blame?"

"No, no, I'm not saying that."

"On the plane you mentioned an impending divorce, is that correct?"

"Yes, but—"

"What I'm trying to tell you is that you will continue to reenact your relationship with your father with every man you meet until you recognize the pattern and put an end to it. And that includes me. I am not your father dancing naked in front of you in the shower. I hope you'll get some help before it's too late!" Then he hung up!

Shocked by this horrible exchange with Fountain-Goose, I nearly screamed and took off from the house, walking around the block twice, violently kicking pods off the sidewalk, my fists bearing down so hard in my pockets I was at risk of pulling my pants down. By the time I'd cooled off a little, I'd decided to very uncharacteristically face the accusation head-on and delve into the letters Gaspard had sent to my mother when I was a child. Just how bad had it been? As I read them, sitting on the veranda in a wicker chair, my agitation was sustained. The letters were as she had described them— rambling, nearly incoherent screeds accusing her of ruining me, of destroying his relationship with me, of creating a child who was a nervous wreck, and so on. My breath grew shallow as I worked my way through them, and such was the state I was in when my sister came home from work and I asked:

"Margaret, do I seem like someone who is forever reenacting rage towards father figures?"

"Not that I've noticed," she said. "Why?"

Somewhat relieved, I said, "When we were growing up, did it seem like something was bothering me?"

"Like what?" On the other side of the room, Boaz and Bram were feeding old produce and vegetable trimmings to their guinea pigs. The greengrocer at the shops loved Margaret and gave her big bags of the stuff for free whenever she stopped by.

"Did you ever wonder why I couldn't sleep and had nightmares all the time?"

"I just thought that was you. Why?"

"Fountain-Goose called. Did you know I used to go talk to him about my problems with Gaspard, and that I had something called 'selective mutism'?"

"No," Margaret said.

"Do you know what it is?"

"I believe it's a disorder in which a person chooses not to speak in certain situations. I think it's included in the *Diagnostic and Statistical Manual of Mental Disorders*," she added, unnecessarily.

"But I never *chose* it. It just happened."

"Is that what he diagnosed? Because he wasn't a psychiatrist, he was a pediatrician, and not a great one either. Who, incidentally, practically pulled my arm out of its socket when I broke it that time."

"But I couldn't talk when I was around Gaspard, so maybe I did have that."

Margaret said, "For a long time, I didn't even know Gaspard was your father! I thought he was some distant relative that you were chosen as the oldest to go visit. Mom always seemed upset while you were gone, and then of course I remember when we had to go pick you up at the hospital in San Diego. That was the last time you saw him, wasn't it?"

"More or less," I said.

"Whatever happened to him?"

I told her he had been hospitalized several more times and ended up working for a trucking firm, and that I'd occasionally seen him lurking around and driving by.

"Lurking? Then what happens?"

"Nothing, he just leaves."

"That's not very nice!" she surmised.

"It's always been hard for him to be nice," I said. "But it doesn't matter, because I had Hugh."

"That's what I thought. To me our family was the four of us, so it was simply out of my sphere of awareness to imagine what you were dealing with. Did it seem strange that I never cared about him or asked about him?" she asked, as the aroma of cruciferous vegetable matter reached our corner of the room.

It had seemed completely normal. The topic of Gaspard never came up in our household. Only a few times when my mother and I were alone, when she described her unbearable attraction to him that led to their brief, disastrous marriage and my birth. She had said it was a relationship built on raw lust. As a girl of ten, I'd thought of the way he often cleared his throat and spat, of his cigarettes and tattoo scar, of his shallow laugh, of his big yellow teeth with metal caps, of his beady blue eyes rimmed in pink coming at me when he was mad, and wondered if raw lust was something I too would have to experience.

Arlo had been listening. "You know what, Gaspard Rush calls me every once in a while. I think he's had a rough life. Your mother always said he never grew up, couldn't stick with anything, was always on the make for a quick buck. He still calls me Dad."

"Ew," I said, feeling pathetic by association. "What does he want when he calls?"

"It's hard to tell. I always think he's going to ask for a loan, but he hasn't tried that since he and Ardie were married."

Processing their veggies, the guinea pigs produced the sound of a teletype machine in a newsroom.

"I got into a fight with Fountain-Goose," I then told Margaret, sheepishly.

"Why, what happened?" She was aptly pouring us glasses of white wine. Arlo was already equipped with his martini.

"He started talking about my childhood problems without asking if I minded, and made a remark suggesting our mother was a

pest. I said I didn't like it and he accused me of attacking him because I have rage towards father figures, and then he hung up."

"Now we don't have to see him?"

"We're free of Fountain-Goose."

But I thought of times I'd attacked Sherman. Really let loose
with some words. Shredding the fabric of our connection one failure of sympathy at a time. Had I been drawn to Sherman as a substitute for Gaspard, in a futile attempt to right what had been wrong,
thereby poised to rage against him once that proved impossible, to
avenge the helplessness of my youth?

I didn't know. What if it was my fault things with Sherman had
ended in such ruin? I took a long drink from a cold glass.

18

And so Arlo and I set out to do what we came across the world to do, which was to travel the 1,850 kilometers to *the point of no return*. At dawn there was a groggy though cheerful parting ceremony in front, for which the entire household had been dragged from bed to hug us and wish us well. Margaret said she hoped the trip would be cathartic, which alarmed me for some reason I'd have to consider later.

That morning we crested the continental divide, winding up onto the plateau on a highway slowed by tractors hauling several trailers and the one and only incline on the route. Once atop the tableland, we headed onto the great flat beyond. We saw license plates from all the states except Tasmania on everything including vans, trailers, fire trucks, utility vehicles, double-decker sheep trucks, cattle transporters, hay wagons, fuel tankers, and long flatbeds carrying tractors and other equipment.

Strangely, as soon as we'd set out, I began to look in every car we passed and at every person near the road as if we now had the opportunity to catch a glimpse of my parents gadding about. All my impossible hopes began to well up. At Dalby we picked up some coffee and stretched our legs in a small park by a sluggish creek, and there came upon a stone memorial to a beige moth that had saved the state from ruin—*Cactoblastis cactorum*. I was certain my mother and Hugh would have stopped here. I felt sure they would have stood right where we were. This was a piece of regional history they had known about and relished relaying to others. Prickly pear cactus had been introduced to the continent in the 1800s to create natural fences, but the conditions were so ideal that the species went wild, spreading over fifty million acres. A Prickly Pear Board was appointed by the government and "Pear Plan" prepared, which included the introduction of this moth that eventually destroyed them. Biological warfare at its finest. Hugh had been amused that it was illegal to have cactuses in Queensland, having learned that if one were spotted in the wild, it had to be reported to a governmental biosecurity officer within twenty-four hours. I told Arlo we'd once visited a botanical garden where some meek little cacti were being held behind bars as if they were criminals! He said he'd heard about this in one of my mother's letters.

It was then, as we stood beside the monument, that I experienced an intense shock. As if we'd summoned them, a man and woman who looked like—exactly like—my mother and Hugh were walking down the road bordering the park. "Wait here," I said to Arlo, and dashed across the grass.

They had rounded a corner by the time I crossed the road. Rushing ahead, I spotted them ambling down the sidewalk in the sun. Their backs were so distinctive. My mother's magenta tunic, billowing! Hugh's plaid shirt and olive-green Dockers! His tennis hat, my mother's shape, her short brown hair! They turned abruptly into a shop, and when I reached the door and entered, the two simulacra turned around and were so completely and utterly not my mother and Hugh that I could only perceive them as body-snatching monsters.

The two people I had mistaken for my parents were not monsters, of course, and, having been chased by an unhinged woman into a shop only to have her cry out at the sight of them, became rather distressed themselves. The woman came forward and clasped my arm. "Are you all right, dear?" she asked. "Is it the sun's got you? Sit over here," she said, directing me to a chair.

We were inside a small and tidy thrift store. By the door stood a plastic life-sized yellow Labrador retriever, collecting loose change for Guide Dogs for the Blind by way of a slit in its head. I wondered if I should explain my overheated presence there, but thought perhaps the explanation, that from the rear they were dead ringers for persons who'd vanished, might make the kindly couple feel cursed. "I'm so sorry," I said. "I'm fine. Nothing to worry about. I recently had a septic leg. I'm taking antibiotics but they make me a little funny."

"Oh my," said the man. "Drink plenty of fluids in this climate."

"I will," I said. "Thank you."

They told me their names—Harold and Ann Farrar—and I told them mine. They were from Brisbane, visiting their daughter and son-in-law, and loved popping into this op shop to find books in good condition for their grandchildren.

"It wasn't them," I said to Arlo, when I found him on a bench in the park.

Arlo nodded and then said, "Penny, I want to talk to you about something."

"Sure, what is it?"

"When we set out on this trip, were you hoping we'd find Ardie and Hugh?"

There was no judgment in his voice; he sounded tender and concerned. This made me stop and try to put into words what I was hoping for.

"I'm not sure," I finally said. "Have you ever read a children's book called *Sylvester and the Magic Pebble*?"

"Don't think I have," Arlo said.

"Well, it's about a family of humanlike donkeys," I began.

"Humanlike donkeys? Do they have skin or fur?"

"I guess they're not really humanlike, it's just that they wear clothes." Arlo understood. "Sylvester, the donkey son, finds a magic pebble and wishes he was a rock, which he then turns into, and the parents think he's disappeared and sorrowfully search and search, and one day they go to the rock to have a sad picnic, and they wish he was there, and because they're next to the magic pebble the rock turns back into Sylvester and they all dance around for joy."

"Why did the donkey son wish he was a rock in the first place?" Arlo wanted to know.

"A lion was coming!"

"Do you think Ardie and Hugh wished they were rocks?"

Together we chuckled, wistfully or bitterly, it was hard to tell. The question felt profound.

Back in the car, Arlo mentioned the time my mother had been "lost" once before.

"Was it on a river trip?"

Arlo said, "It was. You were a baby, staying with Louise and me. I got a call from your mother's boss at Atlantic Richfield, where she was working as a paleontologist. They'd received word that a rafting expedition was presumed lost in the Grand Canyon and that one of the missing persons was my daughter.

"I was home alone with you. Louise was at the hospital. I started calling in favors with the U.S. Air Force base in Phoenix, asking them to fly over and see what they could see. Also made contact with some United buddies asking if they'd take a look flying over on their night flights, for a flicker of fire or any kind of light. Twenty-four hours go by, and we're sweating bullets and trying not to look you in the eye for fear you're now an orphan, and then the phone rings and it's your mama. 'Dad,' she says, 'did you happen to hear anything about our group?' Boy, she had no idea how much she'd scared us. She was fine, though they'd lost their supplies and capsized a few boats.

"She went on other river trips later, so I guess she wasn't too scared." This reminded me of a file I'd seen in the cabinet at their house, and I made a mental note to check it out when we returned.

"She went in for that kind of thing," Arlo said, reminding me of another episode from our time in Canberra. My mother and Hugh had befriended an ornithologist, a sturdily built woman named Jane Farquhar, who arranged to take us on an expedition into the bush to observe mallee fowl and their mounds. For some reason we went in two cars, Margaret and me with Jane, our parents in the other. The male fowl were good fathers, Jane told us, building the mounds for the eggs, tending to the temperature by adjusting the depth of the eggs on a daily basis. (I remembered asking her if *all* the males were good fathers, or if some abandoned the mound and kicked their eggs around like soccer balls. She'd replied that in the animal world, if you didn't do your job the others ostracized or put an end to you, which sounded somewhat threatening, since we didn't know her very well. Maybe she thought Margaret and I were slackers.) We set up camp in a frenzy of helpfulness, and when our parents didn't show up we worried all night. In the morning they finally appeared, happy and rested, saying they'd merely strayed a little off course.

What could it all mean, had it been my mother's destiny to be lost? What about Hugh, had it been his as well? Or was he simply a casualty of a more dominant destiny?

We drove all day, passing through Roma and Tambo and Barcaldine, over long flat stretches through pastureland and endless tilled fields yielding crops I couldn't identify. Every so often Arlo would ask me to find him a gas station, and after the brief stop he would recline his seat apologetically, as if it were impolite to nap, and nod off. In the afternoon, light played tricks on the road, and, holding the wheel of the Land Cruiser on the long straight highway with the drone of the tires below, it seemed to me time had jumped. I would feel, in a split second, as if I were suddenly in a different time and place, as if I were living in an impressionistic collage of my own life lacking temporal or spatial continuity. I wondered if this was symbolically relevant—a miniature version of the past ten years or so, a mess of jagged pieces that had never found a way to assemble into a sensible whole.

Whatever was going on, I needed painkillers and lots of iced tea to make it to Longreach, where we made our first night's stop. (Margaret had said no one in their right mind would drive that far in one day, but we'd valiantly pushed on.) Though we'd refueled and stopped a few times for breaks, my leg felt petrified, and I was aware of dragging it like a piece of luggage. Our pet-friendly motor inn was a low-rise orange brick building surrounded by a profusion of golden wattle in full bloom. Two brindled cattle dogs were tied to a picnic table in front, and around a small pool were a handful of people in shorts and singlets dangling their naked legs into the water. None of them resembled my mother or Hugh. The place had its own restaurant and we were hungry, so without hesitation we went straight there. Arlo laughed when he looked over the menu. "You've got just the right item for me," he said to our waitress. "Aged rump."

Later, back in our room with the two queen beds, I checked in with Margaret, while Arlo discovered he'd received a number of messages from Doris, who had apparently returned from her cruise. Margaret answered right away and I reassured her all was well, though I made the mistake of telling her about the look-alikes. She didn't like that kind of thing, and so asked if I'd remembered to take my antibiotics. When I was through with my call to Margaret, I could hear Doris's voice growling from Arlo's phone: *"Listen here, mister, don't act so innocent, you're as responsible for this charade as anybody, and let me tell you something else . . . "* Arlo turned to me and said, "I'm paying for my sins." And hung up.

I think we both felt a little subdued. Something about discussing our chances after the pointless excitement of seeing the imposters, Harold and Ann Farrar. Though we'd felt compelled to trace their steps, what was there to look forward to? Later, as I arranged my body under the sheet in order to find a satisfactory position, the sweet fragrance of wattle flowers drifted in through the screen along with the clicks and trills of mysterious insects. My grandfather was already asleep, breathing quietly. I wondered if anyone in the world might be thinking of me at that instant, decided probably not, and felt momentarily like a tearful child. Then I wondered what I might do to remedy the situation when I returned from this trip, how I might start over. And soon, whether through coerced optimism or exhaustion, I fell asleep.

We rose early the next morning. Arlo was able to order his classic breakfast of coffee and bacon, though he had to substitute pineapple chunks for grapefruit because it was not available, while I filled up on coffee and a surprisingly good scone, trying again to call Burt to check in with him. No answer. Had Pincer confiscated his phone? God help us all. I didn't feel like calling Pincer again, but maybe I'd have to.

Arlo said, "I'm starting to think Doris isn't right for me."

I cleared my throat, sorry this was such an understatement. But I asked, "Why do you say that?"

"My first morning at the Palms, she came to see me and said she would torture me every day until I die, and that she hopes I have cancer." Then he added, "And to top it off, she never laughs at my jokes. Catherine Janssen has laughed at more of my jokes in the last few days than Doris the whole time we've been married."

"It's important to like someone's jokes," I said, thinking it was also important not to be like Doris in any way, shape, or form.

"They weren't great jokes, but she's on my wavelength," Arlo said with feeling.

Catherine had impressed him with stories of her childhood spent on a cattle station in New South Wales. She'd grown up rough-and-ready. They'd made their own butter, slaughtered their own beef, maintained their water bores, covered great distances on horseback to mend fences, rescued cattle stranded in flash floods. "When the cattle had bloat from bad grain, she said they'd stick long pins straight into their swollen gut to release the gas," he said. "Quite a gal. Good at chess too."

If only he could have met someone like Catherine instead of Doris or Pincer!

And so on we went into ever-more-uncultivated terrain. We began to spot termite mounds in the scant brush. As we journeyed northwest, massive thunderclouds rose on the distant horizon, suggesting the possibility of storms at our destination. Road trains rose up from shimmering mirages at the vanishing point in the road, blasting the Land Cruiser with gravel when they passed.

That morning we stopped to refuel at a petrol station in a town called Winton. As I approached the store, it was no small shock to see a poster featuring pictures of my mother and Hugh.

MISSING

HAVE YOU SEEN THESE PEOPLE?

Hugh and Ardis Fielding were last seen in Mt. Isa on April 15, 2010, at the BP station on the Barkly Highway. They had been exploring and were expected the next day in Camooweal. They did not arrive and have not been seen since.

Their vehicle was a beige 2006 Holden Commodore station wagon that has also never been found. It had Queensland registration plates 224 LBD.

Hugh Fielding was 58 years old at the time of the disappearance. Ardis Fielding, a.k.a. Ardis Rush, a.k.a.

Ardis "Ardie" Reshnappet, was 50 years old. Mr. Fielding is described as 184 cm tall, of medium build, with grey hair, green eyes, and a salt and pepper beard. Mrs. Fielding is described as 180 cm tall, of medium build, with short grey hair and hazel eyes.

An extensive search of the area in radius of 400 km from Mt. Isa has failed to find any trace of the Fieldings.

Anyone with any information about this couple should contact Inspector Roger Kwabble from Mt. Isa Police. A reward of $25,000 has been offered for any information leading to the discovery of their whereabouts.

Why were my mother's maiden name and former married name on the poster like aliases, as if she were on the lam? And where did they get these grainy photos that made them look like bank robbers? Who made this poster, and why was it so fresh? Inside the store, a man in a white smock was tending the register. He had thin blond hair, under which a bright pink scalp peeked through, and he was sinewy, with hairless arms spotted with inflamed hair follicles, and he wore a large Celtic ring, the kind with a pair of hands cradling a heart. I asked if he knew anything about the origin of the poster.

"Reckon I've been hearing about those folks a few years now. There's a woman comes round every few months and puts up a new flyer. Of course, many are hoping to get the reward money. There's been heaps of dodgy claims, I hear."

"People think they've seen them?"

"Everybody loves a good mystery. And you can't just disappear off the face of the planet. Some say they planned the whole thing."

"Some say that, do they?"

"From what I know, complicating the case is the three-day period before it was noticed they were gone. They could have driven
anywhere within three days of the Isa. Then again, they may have
had car trouble. They could have stopped the wrong person for help,
been kidnapped or thrown out of the vehicle, the wagon taken to a
chop shop and rendered unrecognizable. Their fate in that instance
would be anyone's guess."

I shrugged as if to concede, but he went on:

"Have you heard about the bloke with the vat of sulfuric acid?"

I shook my head.

"North of Isa, up near the Gulf. He's being investigated. May be
responsible for some disappearances."

"What are you saying?"

"Well, think about it. Then, you know, the mining conglomer-
ates over there are always in the crosshairs of the conspiracy theo-
rists. If these folks were part of any of the environmental protests a
few years back, they may have been taken out."

"Thanks for sharing your thoughts," I said. I bought two bottles
of cold water and got out of there. Standing by the door, gazing at
the notice, Arlo was dabbing his eyes with his handkerchief. I put
my arm around him and we returned to the car. I decided I would
not mention a word about what the man in the station had said. Nobody close to my parents deserved to hear that.

Back on the road, I gave Arlo some time to recover. "So, that's
part of what your tracker does?" I finally asked.

Arlo again dabbed his eyes. "True to her word. But I sent her a
beautiful picture of Ardie and a fine one of Hugh! I don't know why
she used those dogs." He sipped some water and ate a few chips from
our supplies, crunching quietly.

"And she combs the countryside?"

"I send her five hundred a month," he said. "Don't tell Doris."

I took a deep breath and pressed on. I imagined this was money Arlo felt compelled to spend, whether it was useless or not. I wondered if the tracker Jocelyn Reese had shared with him any of the things I'd just heard in the station.

By noon we'd seen a pair of gangly emus sprinting through the Mitchell grass, and cattle at a distance, baking under the sun. The soil reddened under spinifex growing in green and golden clumps. A few rocky outcroppings began to appear—I tried to see the landscape as my mother would have, as telling a story of metamorphosis, molten rock, and the sediments of ancient seas. But the only thing it told me was that they'd worked hard to get as far from humanity as possible.

Not infrequently did raptors and corvids rise from the bitumen ahead of us, where they had been feeding on the carcasses of poor mowed-down kangaroos, wombats, and wallabies. The sun in the west scorched our eyes, and potato chip crumbs on the seat dug into my legs because I was wearing shorts. We were just under two hours out of Mount Isa when my bad leg began to cramp, and I entertained wrathful thoughts about Pincer. I had to stop and get out and pace up and down for a while before it settled down. Applying pressure to the pedal seemed to set it off, and about twenty minutes later it happened again. I pulled over onto the gravelly shoulder and told Arlo I needed a minute to rest. To which Arlo said, "Let me drive. My license is good. I'd love to try out this machine."

"You're okay with the right-hand drive?"

"Sure I am."

I thought, if we die in a wreck because Arlo had the chance to take a spin on the open road, so be it!

And so we switched places. The air was warm, with a slight

breeze coming over the dry grass and rocky ground. Flies buzzed our heads as we rounded the hot body of the Land Cruiser. The light was so bright it felt like it could peel back your skin. Arlo took the driver's seat and began to familiarize himself with the dashboard. Back straight, he tested every knob and switch before starting the engine, hands at ten and two.

"Ready?" he said.

"Let's go."

"Nice pick-up," he said, getting us back on the road.

Arlo's wiry arms had grasped a thousand wheels. He drove commendably, even taking care to move to the far left when a road train went by spraying rocks and sand. It was thus that I relaxed completely, dozing off until I felt the car slowing on an unsealed surface.

I sprang up. "You okay?"

He said, "Penny, I'm seeing camels."

"Where?"

"Back there. I'd better turn the wheel over to you."

"Sure, of course. But there are camels around here, you weren't seeing things."

"Are you sure?"

"I'm sure. There's supposed to be a bunch of feral camels all over."

"You're trying to make me feel better."

"No, I'm not! But let me drive, I feel better now."

It seemed the missing persons poster was everywhere in Mount Isa. As we cruised into town, we spotted one immediately on a telephone pole, and Arlo asked me to pull over so we could take it down.

"Really? Are you sure?"

"I'm sure," Arlo said.

I stopped, jumped out, and ripped it from the pole. Arlo had his arm out the window, waiting for me to place it in his hand.

We drove a few hundred feet and saw another taped to a streetlight. Again I stopped and removed it, handing it over to Arlo.

So it went the rest of the way to our motel. They were fixed to streetlights, telephone poles, benches, the sides of buildings. In short order, Arlo had a pile of them on his lap. On one, someone had drawn a mustache and bushy eyebrows on my mother, fangs and devil horns on Hugh.

We had cell service as we entered town, and my phone began to hum. Over the course of the past few hours it appeared several calls had come in from Dale.

"That's strange," I said.

"What's strange?"

"The brother of Pincer's accountant's been calling, I wonder why."

"Let's get to our room first," Arlo said. "I need to use the facilities."

We located and checked into our lodging, an economy place with bulky AC units mounted in the windows, red plastic geraniums in a pot by the door, and an old yellowed linoleum kitchenette that smelled like natural gas. Only blocks away loomed two towering smokestacks spewing plumes of sulfur dioxide from the smelters. I stood in the parking lot to listen to Dale's messages. In both, he asked me to call when I had a chance.

I was just about to do so when the phone lit up in my hands. Dale!

"Hello, Penny!" he said. "Where are you?"

"I'm in Mount Isa in northern Queensland. Where are you?"

"In Santa Barbara. Have you heard anything from your grand-mother or Burt?"

"No," I said. "Why, what's wrong?"

"They're not here," Dale said. "I'm at your grandmother's right now but I'm getting ready to leave. There's nobody here. I also went to where the van was towed and they told me the owner came with a locksmith two days ago. I've been calling him all day and he doesn't answer."

"Well, maybe they went out for a drive and they're having dinner out somewhere. Do you think we should be worried?"

"I told him earlier in the week I was coming on Saturday. I made a list of apartments for us to go look at together. His name's been torn off the door of his office. I don't know what else to do. I didn't realize he was in good enough shape to be out all day."

I thought I heard a yip in the background. "Did you bring Kweecoats?"

"I did," Dale said. "I thought maybe Burt would want him back."

"Sorry this is happening," I said, tamping down some instanta-neous dread. I didn't like the sound of this but didn't want Dale to worry. "I guess it means he's feeling better, which is good news."

"I suppose so," Dale said.

"How long are you staying?"

"I've got a room at the Seaside, flying back late tomorrow. Hope-fully they'll be here when I come back in the morning. How are things going over there?"

I briefly told him about our stay in Brisbane and our two days of driving.

"I'll send you a text as soon as I hear anything," Dale said. "Sorry to worry you."

"I'm not worried," I said. "I'm just sorry you're having to wait around."

"And you're not even here to join me for dinner," Dale said.

I ignored this peculiar remark. "Well, better go," I said. "Give Kweecoats a pat for me."

"All right," said Dale.

I'm not sure I'd ever stared as intently at the ground in a parking lot as I did at that one, a warm but furtive feeling rising in my chest. It was a rough, gray surface, full of cracks, in and out of which poured steady streams of ants. Focusing further, I saw an ant carrying the corpse of another ant back into one of the cracks, and shuddered at the implications. But Dale's voice had activated a bittersweet ache within me, despite all the reasons it should not. I must have stood there long enough to invite a reconnaissance and felt a few ants crawling up my legs. After a flurry of shaking and flicking them off, I returned to the room.

"What's happening?" said Arlo, when I came back inside. He was sitting on an ugly blue chair in the corner, ripping up the posters one by one and dropping the shreds into a wastebasket.

And so I told him. That Pincer and Burt weren't home hardly struck him as a crisis.

"Any chance we could eat in the room tonight?" he asked. "I'm bushed."

I agreed. "Let's stay in and watch TV."

"How about some cheese sandwiches?"

"Great idea. Is it because of the terrible pictures you're doing that?"

"No, Penny," Arlo said. "It's because it's time to call it quits." He picked up another and tore it in half.

"You mean you don't want to look around?"

"I want to look around. But I'm not going to be looking around the same way."

What had changed? Perhaps the posters looked pitiful to him. Perhaps they reeked of futility. Perhaps seeing an unflattering photo of his beloved daughter plastered all over the place seemed disrespectful to her memory. Perhaps the posters made him feel foolish.

If Arlo was ready to move on, I thought I had better catch up. I knelt beside him and took one of the remaining posters from the pile and joined in with him by ripping it in half, then in half again, then in half again. I then ripped the shreds into smaller and smaller pieces, until I was producing bits the size of snowflakes that floated down into the can.

Eventually I brought our supplies in from the car and made the sandwiches on paper plates in the kitchenette. The bread hadn't gone stale, nor had the sharp cheddar grown mold, so in that way we were in luck. We'd even brought some gin and vermouth for Arlo's martinis, and I chilled a beer in the mini-fridge. I took my antibiotics with dinner, left a message for Margaret to assure her we were alive, and then Arlo and I watched a couple of episodes of an old detective show called *Blue Heelers* from a box set of DVDs in the room. It was a show I fondly recalled watching with my parents years back when visiting them, usually accompanied by Hugh's specialty, a bowl of vanilla ice cream covered with passion fruit pulp. When it came time to turn out the lights, Arlo said, "Tomorrow's another day. I want to go back to Margaret's and spend time with living people. I'll have plenty of time for ghosts later on."

19

Wind had kicked up sand during the night, and by morning the air was thick with orange grit. It was a primordial grit, a grit of ancient rocks and seabeds, old bones and extinctions, a particulate history cast as a scrim. Arlo and I woke early, had coffee and toast in the room, took our respective pills, grabbed our dark glasses and hats. The Land Cruiser, once white and gleaming, was now barely recognizable. As I studied the silt on the hood, I noticed a number of nicks and dimples that had not been there when we picked up the car in Brisbane. Then I noticed three small pits in the lower reaches of the windshield from which several cracks were creeping through the glass. I hoped Arlo would not be presented with a huge bill for damages.

Just as we were climbing in, my phone began to buzz. Dale!

"Are they back?" I asked, gulping my words.

"No," he said. "It's afternoon, I'm still waiting around. I'm not too happy about it. I'd like to look inside the house, if you don't mind."

"Of course, go ahead!"

"I've been casing it already. If you were going to break in, how would you do it?"

It was strange they weren't back, and I started to worry now too. I told Dale he could go ahead and break a windowpane. He said he'd prefer not to. I suggested then he try the woodshed—perhaps he could bust in through the little doorway by the fireplace.

"All right, I'm over there right now," he said. "It's still taped off like a crime scene."

"This is important. Go ahead and see if there's a way to get through."

I could hear him opening the shed door. "Dark in here," he said. "I need to use my phone as a flashlight. Hold on."

I heard some shuffling sounds. A moment later he said, "I see the little door. It's got a hinge on it with a padlock but the wood's all rotten. Hold on a second, I'll see if it gives way."

"Sure," I said, and then I heard a scream.

"*Fuck!*"

"What's happening?"

More screaming, further groans and gasps, Dale wheezing, running somewhere in pain.

"Dale!"

"I'm being attacked by wasps. Oh man. Oh man!"

"Oh no!"

"They're all over me!"

"Now what?" Arlo asked.

At that point his phone must have hit the ground. I could hear him yelling and slapping and struggling at a distance, and there was nothing I could do about it.

"Dale, Pincer's accountant's brother, tried to get into the house and he's being attacked by wasps! And they're still not home."

"Oh boy," Arlo said.

After what seemed a very long time, but probably only a minute, Dale came back on the line.

"Are you there?" he mumbled.

"I'm here, are you okay?"

"They were on my face too. God! It's okay, boy, I'm okay. Kwee-coats came running, like he's worried about me."

"What are you going to do?"

"Penny, I have to call you back, I'm in agony."

"Should I call an ambulance? Are you going into anaphylactic shock?"

"No! Don't call an ambulance!"

"Okay, I won't. I'm sorry!"

I still felt responsible for things that happened to people as a result of Pincer. I hoped Dale knew what to do for his stings. Where were Pincer and Burt?

Arlo and I drove around Mount Isa then, removing the posters that he had been funding for the past five years, up and down streets wide and narrow, through neighborhoods, through shopping centers, finding them on windows and the sides of buildings and on poles along the Barkly Highway. In between Arlo phoned Jocelyn Reese and told her to call it off—everything. The posters, the bush-tracking. He thanked her for her services but said enough was enough. He reached Doris too:

"Doris, stop shouting. I can hear you. . . .

"Doris, you wanted me out. What's the problem here? . . .

"What do you think I'm doing? I am seeing my family and paying my respects to my daughter. . . .

"Doris, stop shouting. . . .

"Stop blaming me for everything and try to enjoy your life. So long!"

Dale called about an hour later, by which time we'd found twenty-three of the missing persons flyers.

"Are you okay?" I asked.

"That's debatable. I'm inside the house now."

"Which part?"

"Where? I'm sitting on a chair in the living room. I've taken the liberty of rummaging in your grandmother's bathroom. I found some twenty-year-old calamine lotion that was mostly crust, but a little liquid poured out so I applied that to my arms. I also found some ancient Benadryl, so I took some of those. And there were a few frozen items in the freezer and I'm using those on my face."

"Dale, I'm so sorry, the place is cursed."

"What I'm trying to decide now is how worried I should be. I'm wavering between despair and detachment."

"Have you found anything in the house?"

"Nothing that tells me where they are," Dale said. "Burt appears to have unloaded some boxes from his office and they're in the garage, and so are his hose and ironing board and bike and suitcases."

Arlo was rifling through the pile of posters on his lap, pausing to examine the ones that had been defaced.

"No futon?"

"I didn't see a futon."

"So it sounds like he made space for sleeping in the van," I said. "Maybe they went camping?" This comment was neither shrewd nor funny.

Dale said, "I don't really want to spend any more time here. I've called Burt probably twenty times today. That's what concerns me most. Anyway, I'm going to blockade the door by the fireplace, then I'll let myself out the front door making sure it's locked, is that all right?"

"Sure, that's fine."

"Maybe I'll rest a little first. Feeling a little strange right now. Kweecoats won't leave my side. He keeps licking my arm! I didn't realize he liked me so much."

"Dogs are so great that way. I mean, I'm sure he likes you specifically, but—you know what I mean! I really hope you feel better."

"Thanks, Penny. Goodbye."

After I put down my phone, flooded with regret at having implied Kweecoats's affection for Dale was generic, simply a trait of his species, Arlo said, "I think you like the accountant's brother."

"I think you like Catherine Janssen," I rejoined.

"Very funny. I'm a married man."

"Well, Dale is a married man too." Then I added: "And I'm still married, by the way."

"Marriage is a funny business," Arlo said.

I had to put Dale, Burt, and Pincer out of mind for the moment, because Arlo and I had not come all this way to be thinking about them. Though Arlo was through with the services of Jocelyn Reese, he still wanted to see the topography of the scrublands that had interested my mother and Hugh and brought them here. We'd studied the map and decided to take the Camooweal Urandangi Road that skirted the Wiliyan-ngurru National Park near the border of the

Northern Territory. The terrain there was known as the Barkly karst—an underground formation of brittle limestone and dolomites riddled with caves and sinkholes, much like the topography and formations that my mother had noted in *Voss*. It took us about two hours to reach Camooweal, but in so doing we managed to escape the path of the dust storm and see the sky clear.

Once we were off the main highway, the road was unsealed, made of dirt as red and fine as chili powder. The land in all directions was flat, dotted with stunted eucalyptus trees. Arlo said, "Go that way."

"Off the road?"

"This thing's like my old jeep, made for it," he said.

So I turned off the road, heading west.

"Watch out for holes," Arlo said. "But keep going."

"Okay."

He had something in mind, so I drove on, kicking up rocks into the undercarriage, stirring up clouds of dust behind us.

"Farther?" I asked.

"I'll tell you when to stop."

Ahead, green parrots exploded from one of the scrubby trees into a sky that to the west was the brightest blue I'd ever seen. For a split second I wished Sherman could see it; in the past I'd always wished he could see things I saw when he wasn't with me—would that circuit ever break? Occasionally the tires of the Land Cruiser struck larger rocks and sent us bouncing, but Arlo was right, it was made for this. We saw kangaroos and wallabies bounding at a distance. No water bores, no pumps, no windmills, not even a fence. No doubt due to the ongoing drought, the ground was fractured with fissures.

"Are we there yet?" I asked.

"Not yet," Arlo said.

On we went until Arlo said, "Stop there." He was pointing ahead at a small rise, on which sat a cluster of boulders.

When we reached the spot I parked on a cracked, claylike surface. Arlo had practiced getting out of the car and had a certain exact way of doing it. He'd open the door, swivel his hips, extend his legs, then kind of ooze down holding on to the handle above the door until his feet reached the ground. Then he'd stay in that position for a few seconds before straightening to a full stance. This time, once his feet hit the ground, he turned and gathered the pile of posters and moved toward the rocks, which were arranged in something of a circle. I followed, close behind, as he placed the posters at the center and sat.

"Penny, do you have a match?"

We had them in our supplies. "Just a minute," I said, and I rummaged in the box in the back of the car until I found them.

Arlo said, "Sit down. I want to say a few words about Ardie and Hugh." And then he lit the pile of posters on fire.

The flame moved slowly at first, curling the edges, gradually spreading from one sheet to the next, turning the paper brown, then black, and I watched as the descriptions and images of my mother and Hugh were consumed in the flames.

"Ardie, you were born in Chicago on a cold winter night. I made it back in time to be there. You were the cutest thing I'd ever seen. Your mother was hard on you and I'm sorry I wasn't around more when you were growing up, but I always looked forward to seeing you more than anything when I came home. You were smart as a whip and you turned into a beauty. I didn't understand Gaspard, but when you had Penny that was one of the greatest things that ever happened to our family. Then you found Hugh, and Hugh was a keeper, and then you brought Margaret into the world, the other great thing that happened to our family. I never thought I'd see the day when I'd say goodbye to you this way."

His voice caught. The bonfire of the posters flared. Tears were running down my face.

"But I think you've found your place, so I'm going to try to accept it and tell you that you were the best daughter a father could have. Hugh, you were a good man and Ardie couldn't have done better."

With that, Arlo removed some photographs from his breast pocket. He had brought one of my mother as a young girl holding a straw basket in a field of tulips, and one of my mother and Hugh the day they got married, and he set them on one of the boulders.

"Hand me that rock, would you?"

I gave him the oblong stone he was pointing to, and he dusted it off and placed it on the photos to anchor them.

"Do you want to say anything, Penny?" he asked.

My chest was tight; my voice had died out.

"I liked what you said," I finally uttered.

"Let's sit quiet a few minutes," he said, and closed his eyes.

20

I closed my eyes too. I was heartbroken and full of love. For Arlo, for them. Emotions were pulsating through me to an almost unbearable degree. And yet this was what Margaret had advocated for when she said she hoped the trip would be cathartic, and what had alarmed me. Mostly, I'd thought I would never "heal" from losing our parents, unless I found a way to compartmentalize the loss in such a way that was beyond my comprehension. I realized I did not come along on this trip to finalize things.

The heat of the sun was baking me into the rock. Bright orange squiggles danced on the inside of my eyelids, while flies made their motorized sounds in orbit of my head. I thought of Dale, hot and swollen with wasp stings, multiple jabs of venom coursing through his flesh. Then I thought of Kweecoats tending to him, and my obtuse comment about the indiscriminate quality of dog love, which had dampened the conversation, I was sure. It was worrisome that Burt and Pincer hadn't shown up all weekend, and I knew I should have been in town to manage the situation. But here I was, on a large chunk of dolomite on an ancient seabed with my grandfather, pledging a truce with the unknown.

The fire had reduced the posters to ghostly ash, a few last puffs of smoke drifting past. I sensed the presence of an ant on my hand, a wayfaring scout who would now be sent flying through the air for no reason it would likely understand. I couldn't hold on to my thoughts on their absence, it was too painful. But I was harboring an almost overwhelming desire to know what my mother and Hugh would think of the situation with Pincer and Burt and even Dale. We would've had so much to talk about. I remembered my last conversation with my mother on the eve of their grand trip. We spent much of it discussing Sherman, who was at that time still working on his dissertation, "Phenomenological Disunity in Heterodoxical and Ontological Texts of the Post-Bubonic Mongol Khanate." By then his fellowship had run out, his adviser had suffered a stroke, and we had been relying on my job to support us. She urged me to help him stay on track while still straining to understand what I was doing with myself. She thought I should apply to grad school myself or try to find a job at a publication or bookstore, something in line with my interests. She was afraid that if Sherman didn't complete his PhD soon, he'd ruin his chances for a position in academia. I didn't mind; I already knew he believed his department to be swarming with vipers who ridiculed undergraduates behind their backs, who had political motives for everything they did, who stabbed people in the back and slept their way into advantageous positions, who would soon give up their research to become power-intoxicated administrators, and that he was generally through with that scene forever, but knew how disappointed she'd be so had yet to break it to her. I'd been ready to defend his knife-sharpening business, it's a noble and ancient profession! So I had a strong hunch that my life wasn't going to look anything like she might have wanted it to. All the complexities, hassles, and joys of being her child, how I missed them!

But for now, for Arlo, I tried to quiet my thoughts and listen. I could hear nothing—or maybe something if I tried. At last there was a whispering sound, perhaps as sand slid across sand, catching on rocks and dry grass. And the humming of flies, and the distant cries of birds. And a crackling sound back by the Land Cruiser, probably the engine cooling off. I strained to hear more, to extract the most from the moment, as if something mystical could happen if I believed in it enough. Of course they had not been whisked into another dimension, but just say they had, why couldn't they reach out now? I imagined my mother and Hugh trying to make themselves known to us, pounding on the boundary of the other dimension to get our attention. I heard more creaking and crumbling sounds from the direction of the car, and happened to look back just as the ground beneath it gave way and swallowed it whole.

Arlo and I emitted croaks of wonder. Rocks and raw earth continued to crumble onto the roof of the car, until at last, all was quiet again except for the whispering of the sand.

Wherein:

A new Toyota Land Cruiser, albeit recently pitted and nicked, has plunged at least ten feet into what looks like a sinkhole,

it's hot, and the satellite phone is in the Land Cruiser in the sinkhole, neither one of us, oddly, feels this is a calamity; rather, we're astonished and giddy instead,

the Land Cruiser is now tightly wedged in the pit, the opening of any of its doors impossible, so our only choice is to pelt the sunroof with sharp stones until it cracks,

the sunroof fails to crack, so I tell Arlo I'm going to climb down the exposed sides of the sinkhole, which I then do, scraping my fingers and arms, sneezing, noting the openings in the exposed rock face that reveal dark subterranean chambers of all depths and dimensions, and think: *Classic karst!*,

Arlo voices the possibility that the sinkhole may be deeper than we think and tells me to be careful,

I start to stomp the sunroof but hear some creaking sounds around the car so I wrest a large jagged rock from the stratum and pound the glass until it shatters and Arlo says, *Thatta girl!*,

upon clearing the tempered shards I lower myself through the opening and gather my purse, the satellite phone, and a couple bottles of water that I toss out of the pit and then climb my way out, jabbing the toes of my shoes anywhere that won't crumble under my weight, now covered in orange grit, sneezing, glad Arlo is wearing his wide-brimmed hat under the carnelian sun,

I call 112 because Margaret has previously made me memorize the number in case of emergency,

a voice asks what kind of emergency it is, and I say I'm with a ninety-three-year-old man and it's hot and we are unable to return to civilization because our car is in a sinkhole,

the voice takes our GPS coordinates,

the voice says to remain still, not to wander, they will send a car from Mount Isa, the voice says they've changed their minds due to Arlo's age and are sending a helicopter,

I return to the sinkhole while we wait, climbing back through the open sunroof to fish out our stuff, only noticing the blood running down my good leg as I'm climbing out,

the slice in my shin resembles a crack in a carrot, and it starts to sting,

Arlo is sitting on one of the rocks drinking water, shooing flies, breaking out in sudden bursts of laughter,

we hear it coming, blades chopping the sky,

the large yellow RACQ helicopter touches down about twenty yards away, stirring up a dust storm,

three male medics in flight suits jump out with a gurney and attend to Arlo, who says he doesn't need a gurney but they respectfully say it's the easiest way to get him in,

one of them notices my bleeding leg and removes gauze and tape from his kit, wrapping it up and saying, *That's a bloody big gash!*,

Arlo is carried aboard and his vital signs are good and once I'm in we're given special helmets that cover our ears and it's the first time I've ever been in a helicopter,

the rotor spins, we achieve lift and bolt across the sky, Arlo's eyes fastened on the controls in the cockpit,

we come in over Mount Isa, tin roofs glinting through the orange haze, landing on a helipad in the hospital parking lot,

I call Margaret but when she doesn't answer opt not to leave a message,

Arlo is further examined in the hospital and found in satisfactory condition, while I'm cleaned up and given a shot of lidocaine and receive stitches on my shin,

I try again to call Margaret, leaving no message,

we're visited at the hospital by a member of the Mount Isa police and give our account, provoking a congenial reaction by dropping the name of Detective Roger Kwabble and laying claim to the missing Fieldings,

I call the rental car agency advising them of a slight mishap with the car,

we take a taxi to the airport for a five-thirty flight to Brisbane,

we're waiting at the gate when I finally reach Margaret and tell her what's happened,

Margaret screams.

Part 3

21

I woke the next morning on the inflatable bed in the well-organized confines of my sister's home office. It was Sunday and the house was quiet. Collecting what could be called my wits, I became aware that I could barely move, but whether it was from the night on this slowly deflating loaf or the athletic feats I'd performed the day before, I couldn't be sure. I shifted my stabbed and septic leg, pleased to see it moving at the end of the bed. The leg with the fresh stitches moved too, but with greater effort. It had been so hot and dry around Mount Isa that my lips were as cracked as the desert floor, and were now slathered with some kind of balm from my sister's medicine cabinet. I had failed to open the window the night before and the room was stuffy, the parley of the kookaburras muted. As the room came into focus, I spotted the faithful gecko sitting on the blade of the fan, gazing down at me, while sun poured through the window from the east, spotlighting some of the framed family photos on the shelves.

I did not yet know this would be my last day in Brisbane.

I closed my eyes, hoping to slip back into a languid, semiconscious state. For some reason, rising from the ground in the helicopter, I'd found myself possessed of the fiercest longings I'd experienced in some time, all focused on an unavailable man whom I had once judged to look like a hedgehog. Waves of desire surged through me as we lifted up and away, and using this as a salve I put all thoughts of my parents aside.

Now, as I tried to replace the object of my amatory daydreams with the helicopter pilot named Lachlan who had commanded his craft like an ace, my phone, charging on a cord under the desk, began to shudder. I rolled onto my side to reach for it. I didn't recognize the number.

A hearty male voice addressed me. "Hello, Penny, this is Tom Beaudry, from Tyler, Texas. Remember me?"

Tom Beaudry, the real estate agent who resembled LBJ. The distant cousin. "I do."

"We had quite a time a few years back, didn't we? Listen, I just wanted to check in with you about your grandmother. She serious this time?"

I sat up with a start.

"Serious about what?"

"Selling her place. I'm still at the office, going over there soon. To tell you the truth, I'm quaking in my boots. Hoped you'd be with her."

My grandmother had gone to Tyler? With Burt?

I said, "Yes, I would've come, but I'm actually in Australia right now visiting my sister. So, she sounded okay when you talked to her?"

"Charming as can be. Course, after what happened last time I have my guard up."

"I understand completely. I definitely hope this time will be different," I said, as if I'd known all about it.

"Me too. Well, she's older now, probably lost some of the fight in her."

"I'll keep my fingers crossed."

"Whatever happens, I won't take it personally. You just can't do that with the demented."

"True," I said. "Listen, can you do me a favor? She doesn't have a cell phone and I'd like to talk to her. Could you call me when you get there?"

"I don't know about that. How could I explain that we've talked? I seem to recall that set her off big-time. Remember, she thought we were ganging up on her?"

"You're totally right. Then could you call me back right after you see her? I'm trying to find out if her accountant Burt Lampey traveled there with her. Could you see if he's there?"

"That I can do. That I can do," Tom said, clearly relieved. "What's he look like?"

"He's tall, bald, late fifties."

"All right," Tom said. "I'll look for him."

"Thanks for calling," I said.

"You bet."

What a relief. She wouldn't have gone alone, she must have coerced Burt. The crafty old bag had struck again!

I was engulfed then by recollections of my time in that house a few years back—the poignant tokens of Pincer's life, the garish over-sized rooms, sleeping on the carpet, how she called the police, the whole horrible thing. She was supposed to be taking care of Burt—he must have gone along.

The boys were up, quietly watching TV in the little den off the living room. Due to her late shift at the hospital, Marga-ret would not be up for hours. I didn't know where Wilhelmus was. I wondered what they would think if I made my coffee and came in and joined them on the couch. I had very little experience around children and suspected them of being prickly and judgmental. In the kitchen I used the fancy Nespresso coffee maker with one of the pods, whipped up some warm milk in the frother, and, sensing the boys were deeply involved in their show, decided to join the guinea pigs instead. From the shelter within the cage, four copper-colored eyes peered out in sheer terror and one of them wheezed. So I decided to move outside onto the veranda, to the side of the house beside a tall gum shedding meter-long shards of bark. The air was pleasantly humid. Insects trilled and lorikeets shrieked. The cacophony put me in mind of an enormous processing plant, life and decay at full vol-ume all around.

I was reasonably sure Burt had been found and I looked forward to having a new reason to call Dale, though I might again say some-thing unnatural and perplexing. Further, Burt's presence in Tyler would give us new things to worry about—what would happen if she turned on him like she'd once turned on me? And if she did, how would Burt handle it? I assumed they'd flown there. Would he re-turn without her? How was he feeling, anyway?

I returned inside to take a seat in the den. The boys were wearing matching red pajamas, intently watching *Fireman Sam*. Moments after I joined them, a tour bus full of happy cartoon characters anticipating a lovely day at the beach plunged off a cliff into the ocean. I screamed in exaggerated fright and the boys looked at me with surprise and laughed. When the incoming tide slapped the bus, I gasped and covered my eyes and kicked my feet, and they laughed more.

At last my phone rang, and I bolted from the room to take the call.

"I've just spent a pleasant time with your grandmother and I think this time she's ready to make a deal," Tom said.

"Great! Is Burt there?"

"You know what, I can't tell you. I thought I heard the motor of the Jacuzzi but was afraid to stray off-topic. Anyway, she says she's serious and I'm coming back tomorrow with the paperwork, so maybe I'll see him then."

My disappointment was intense. "Tom, that's great, but Burt's been missing for a few days and nobody can reach him and we think he came along with her on this trip but we really need to know."

"Well, I suspect somebody's in the tub."

"Could you go back in an hour or so and pretend you need to ask something?"

"No, can't do that. We're having dinner with my wife's mother, I'm grill master."

"Wow." I didn't feel like waiting until tomorrow. "I really hate to ask, but is there any way you could see if it's Burt, like look in the window?"

He didn't speak for a moment. "You're asking me to go back there and spy in the bathroom window?"

"Just a quick look to find out."

"What if he sees me looking at him? I'll have to go shoot myself."

"I know it's a lot to ask, but a lot of people are worried."

"What if he's not in the tub, what if he's on the john?"

"Look, Tom, Burt had heart surgery a week ago and he also had a perforated ulcer, so he was in really bad shape. My grandmother's supposed to be making sure he takes his medicine and watching out for him. It's really important to know if he's there." My voice quavered with emotion.

Tom sighed heavily. "I can just see it. I'll be 'Peeping Tom' Beaudry for the rest of my days."

"You could say you're taking notes to get ready for the sale!"

"You say he's in his fifties, big guy, hairless?"

"His body's not hairless," I said for some reason. ·

"I hope I don't have to see his body," Tom said.

"Sure, I understand. Thank you so much. It's important."

A squelching sound could be heard, as if he were unhappily pressing his eyeballs into the far reaches of their sockets. "Heck. All right, I'm only a few blocks away. I'll do it right now and call you back."

I waited expectantly, imagining him clambering through the bushes approaching the window. I seemed to recall the master bathroom had high windows over the tub. A few minutes later he called.

"All right," he said, breathing heavily. "Deed is done. I saw the top of somebody's head and figured that was plenty."

"What kind of head?"

"Kind of pinkish with a few scabs on it. That your man?"

"Pinkish with a few scabs? It's not definitive, but probably."

"All right. The tri-tip is calling. Don't say I never did anything for you."

"I won't, Tom. I really appreciate it."

"One last thing. Does he drive a terrible-looking old Econoline? Because there's one parked in back."

"Oh my god. They drove there! Yes, that's his."

"You sure he's legit? Not some gigolo?"

"Do gigolos go after eighty-five-year-olds?"

"Of course they do!" Tom said, like an expert. "That's their specialty!"

I said I didn't believe Burt was a gigolo and thanked him again, and we said goodbye.

I decided to phone Dale at once. I imagined he would find this news adequately reassuring. But it rang until his voice mail kicked in, leaving me lots of room to imagine the indescribable riches his life in San Francisco was no doubt keeping him busy with. I wanted to say something snappy and clever, but my mind went blank, so I hung up. In that moment, the prospect of coming up with a snappy, clever message had raised my cortisol levels to new heights, and my heart was racing. This fixation on my rapport with Dale, if you could call it that, was out of control. All I had to do was say that it was likely Burt was with my grandmother in Tyler. What could be simpler than that?

I tried to imagine Pincer and Burt driving to Texas together. Had Burt done all the driving? Did they stay in motels, or did they sleep together in the back of the van? And if so, what did that look like? I didn't really want to know. Had Burt really wanted to go or had Pincer browbeaten him? Why hadn't Pincer told me she was ready to go back and sell the house, did she mistrust me still? Had the intrusion of Adult Protective Services in Santa Barbara put her in mind of an alternate residence?

I called again. "Hi Dale," I said to his voice mail. "Some good news, I think, Burt is in Texas with my grandmother. She has a house there and that's where they're staying. So I think everything's okay for now. I'll keep you posted. Hope you're doing well and say hi to Kweecoats." And with that I hung up, reasonably satisfied with what had come out of my mouth, though more apprehensive about the situation than I'd let on.

As I was leaving the message I noticed a brush turkey strutting about in the undergrowth near the house. It was scratching at the ground and flinging up debris. It had a head that was bright red and featherless, a ruffle of yellow skin at the neck that resembled an ascot, and an ear hole so large I could see it at a distance of twenty feet. These brush turkeys liked to tear people's gardens apart, so weren't well-liked, but nobody was allowed to kill them, so they ravaged at will.

In fact, at that very moment it advanced into the plot beside the house where Margaret had a small herb garden and went into a frenzy, as if carrying out a precision attack. Greens were flying. Within seconds, all of Margaret's basil, parsley, oregano, sage, and dill had been flung or flattened, and I had done nothing to stop it. Curiously, the turkey cocked its head and stared up at me then, as if daring me to approve of its crusade to preserve the natural order despite casualties.

And still the day progressed without undue hardship: Arlo enjoyed a visit from Catherine Janssen early in the day and had much to tell her. She brought him a large glass tumbler etched with biplanes she'd found at a church rummage sale, and which he proclaimed the size he'd always dreamed of for martinis. I received a curt, analysis-defying text from Dale: Appreciate the information. Thx. We had a wheezing guinea pig on our hands who required a trip to the vet once Margaret was up. He had a chest cold! And then we paid a visit to our parents' house, during which I gathered a few things I wanted, especially from the file cabinets and bookshelves. Margaret and I jumped from topic to topic driving around town, as if somehow we already knew our time together was limited: yes, we'd rent the house until the seven-year period elapsed; no, we wouldn't "swear death" and she wouldn't use the horrible Viola Mitchell; yes, she'd take care of the Australian paperwork and when the time came I'd take care of the American.

In a spare moment I'd tracked down the couple I'd followed into the op shop in Dalby, Harold and Ann Farrar. They lived on Jilba Street in Indooroopilly; a quick look online showed me that Harold Farrar was a professor of climate science at the University of Queensland, and Ann Farrar the director of a child-care center in Mount Gravatt. On our errands I asked Margaret to drive past their house, a request she found puzzling, even after I explained they were the doubles of our parents from the backside. But it seemed her curiosity was piqued and Indooroopilly wasn't too far out of the way, so she entered the address in her GPS. The house faced away from the road, into a thick belt of vegetation growing by the river. There was nothing to see but a fence and a mailbox. Did I want to knock on the door? No, it didn't really make sense. Driving on, turning the corner, Margaret drew in her breath.

Ahead were the replicas, walking away from us down the road, the man now in shorts, the woman in a sand-colored tunic, resembling our parents no less than before. Margaret pulled over and wept.

"Oh, Margaret!" I hugged her, felt her tremble. I had not seen her cry since she was a child.

But she regained control of herself quickly, and began to crawl down the road. I said, "Be prepared, there's no resemblance from the front." And panicked and slid down in the seat. She leaned out her window as we approached. "Pardon me. What's the best route to Fig Tree Pocket?"

I could hear shoes scraping gravel on the road, and all at once the face of Harold Farrar was at the window. Not a bit like Hugh. Nothing like him. As he explained the way to Fig Tree Pocket, he happened to notice the figure crouched in the passenger seat.

I sat up and revealed myself. For the next half hour, standing in the shade of a poinciana tree, Margaret and I chatted with the Farrars. They remembered the incident in Dalby, and I confessed that we'd stalked them and came clean about why. They did not appear to feel harassed and were actually quite understanding about it. They offered to let us photograph their backsides! And we did! Margaret knew some people at the university that Harold knew, and she also had friends whose kids went to Ann's preschool. The Farrars knew some of Margaret's colleagues at the hospital. I was never in this situation of knowing anybody through my profession, so I felt proud of Margaret's accomplishments in her adopted country. In truth, I felt validated by it. *My sister is a surgeon with an important position at a university hospital, so that means I'm okay too.*

"And I take it you know full well the way to Fig Tree Pocket," concluded Ann Farrar.

Margaret reminded them this was my idea, that she was merely following instructions.

"It wasn't a bad idea at all," said Harold Farrar. He gave Margaret his card and suggested we stay in touch.

As we drove back to Paddington, Margaret suddenly said, "Harold and Ann Farrar. Do you realize they have the same initials as Mom and Dad?"

I had noticed this already, but thought Margaret would ridicule me if I pointed it out. Cosmic coincidences were not her thing. "Wow. Bizarre and defying explanation!"

"Very much so."

We somehow got onto the topic of the Palms and the deteriorating situation with Doris. Margaret wondered how long Arlo's funds would hold out. "It's too bad he moved in right before you came here. He's paying a lot of money and he's not even there."

I said, "But moving out was the catalyst. He couldn't think straight before. Doris was on his case every minute." We went over unpleasant episodes involving Doris from the past and tried to formulate theories on why Arlo had married her.

"She wore those really short shorts for tennis," Margaret recalled.

"She must have seemed better than Pincer, at least at first," I said.

"But I'd say it's possible she's worse," Margaret said, not having seen Pincer recently.

"I'd say it might be a tie."

We then talked about Pincer in Texas with Burt. And Pincer's tax delinquency. We wondered if that was why she'd decided to sell the house in Tyler now, and agreed there was nothing much to be done but sit back and watch.

Once we returned, I spent the afternoon resting on a lounge on the veranda looking through the materials I'd taken from the house. Of particular interest was a folder marked "River Trips."

Our mother kept diaries on those trips in small spiral-bound notebooks, and I leafed through them randomly. I saw things like:

Could it be that man was meant to deal with physical problems of the wilderness rather than social awkwardness? How beautiful the air, the sand, the grit, the living and the dead tufts of grass. Never mind there's a rock behind my head with reptilian potential, my bed is here tonight and my soul will absorb every ounce of beauty from this place. My God, what force that rapid! This dune and the curtain of willow. A private world.

And:

The canyon narrowed toward noon. We ate lunch on the boats, a can of beans apiece, excellent with hot peppers. Then a downpour, the rain horizontal entering the canyon. In well-bedded formations by afternoon. Saw a beautiful stag on the right bank who followed us for a good half mile. Amazed by his sure-footedness. The canyon narrowed later and the current grew swifter. We followed the topo sheets carefully that afternoon as we didn't wish to miss the junction of the Colorado. Spanish Bottom was our destination. A half mile down the Colorado a true and ferocious desert cloudburst struck. Progress next to impossible. Turned to hail briefly. But the storm soon ceased and in the dry Utah air we were dry by the time we reached Spanish Bottom. After the wind died the water was glassy smooth. There we made camp in a thicket of willows. I noted boulders of fossiliferous Hermosa, also found crinoids (three bags of stems), pelecepods, bracks, corals replaced with jasper. A magnificent view of the Paradox gypsum plug.

And:

We rode some tough rapids and stopped to bail out and try to film the others as they came through. Otto and I watched as Ellen was swept out of the boat when it lurched sideways. Then we approached Rapid 8, got through, only to be followed by Wayne's boat, coursing past us upside down. We rushed over enormous talus boulders to a point where we could aid in the rescue. Everybody came out all right but we lost some food and spread out the remaining supplies to dry. Then came the long lining, maybe only 100 yards but climbing over boulders the size of rooms. Phil's raft flipped again immediately. This really broke the morale of the group. By now it was dark and everyone extremely fatigued. The Steeleys decided not to go on against all logical arguments and there were many hushed discussions.

Ellen Miller was also in a very bad state. Rick, Wayne, and I talked until the logs died. I had no doubt we would get out safely—for a while I went berserk and wished it would never end.

That line really got to me. In what way did my mother go berserk? Laughing until it hurt? Making out with Rick or Wayne or both? Maybe she only meant that she was in high spirits, the highest of spirits. I was glad my mother had gone berserk and wished something would never end.

I called out for Margaret, who responded promptly. I told her I wanted to read her something and she took a nearby wicker chair. The passages seemed to affect her as well, rendering her without instruction or summation, without any of her habitual tools.

"So what really happened out there?" she asked, at last.

A staghorn fern on the trunk of a eucalyptus shuddered as a large bird settled on its crown. It was a tawny frogmouth! Not often seen in daylight. Our mother used to love screaming out that name when she saw them, almost as much as she loved screaming out, *Pheasant coucal!* when she saw one of those. Almost as if articulating the name meant more than the bird itself.

I told her about Arlo wanting to gather and burn the posters and how I'd followed his instructions driving off the road after turning south from Camooweal. How he'd told me where to stop, like he'd seen the spot in his mind's eye. About his tribute to our mother and Hugh, how he'd asked for the moment of silence.

"And right then the car disappeared into the ground?"

I said yes.

We sat there without speaking. The tawny frogmouth took off into the sky, and I felt the air it displaced on my cheek.

"Like they were reaching out from another dimension," Margaret allowed, to my astonishment.

They gave their lives to pierce the secret of the Inland.

For a brief time that evening I felt whole, even good. Life was going on around me. Wilhelmus was home early, kicking a ball on the grass with the boys. Arlo enjoyed a martini in his new glass, and I chose a frosty can of Foster's. An ailing guinea pig was on the mend. For dinner Margaret made noodle pork and bean cakes from a local Vietnamese cookbook she especially liked, *Green Papaya*. And with this insanely fancy Thermomix machine she has, she whipped up a delicious dessert with mangoes and ice.

After dinner we played an old board game called Squatter. The aim of the game is to have the most successful station with the greatest number of healthy sheep. Upon taking your turn and moving around the board you might be told to vaccinate your flock for pulpy kidney or drench for liver fluke, that your bore had dried up, that you had to pay for fencing repairs or flood damage. Alternately, you could land a windfall at a wool sale or pick up a prized stud ram. I had Emu Plains Station, Arlo had Coolibah Creek, Wilhelmus was at Wanbanalong, Margaret at Mount Mitchell, Bram at Coorumbene, and Boaz at Warramboo. Boaz kept hitting all the disasters and couldn't improve his paddocks. Bram won a Soil Conservation Trophy. Arlo received a bonus for sale of his Fat Lambs, and Wilhelmus, by careful management, eradicated foot rot. Quite unfairly, at least karmically, Margaret was injured by a tractor and missed two turns.

And then it was bedtime and I had taken lots of ibuprofen, my legs were free from pain, and I slept soundly until my phone began to ring and I lunged for it in the dark. A quick glance at the screen told me it was Burt calling and that it was four a.m.

"Oh my god, Burt!"

"Penny." There was a lot of noise in the background. "You down under?"

"I am," I said, finding my voice. "Are you in Texas?"

"How'd you know? Sorry I haven't called sooner. I just listened to all the messages. Dale's probably pissed as hell. My phone wasn't charging, lint in the port, I guess. Got it taken care of. Man, things are a mess, though." His voice sounded weak.

"What's happened?"

"Let's see. Where to begin? I guess I was feeling pretty low after that hospital crap. She convinced me this trip would be good for both of us. Hitting the road with the Dog and a cause. I'm a sucker for such things. We had a good time driving down. Amazing food in Albuquerque. Gorgeous weather, thunderclouds on the horizon, I was feeling good. She talked the whole way. The woman's fascinated by the physical characteristics of Europeans. Skull shapes and stuff like that. Apparently I'm *dolichocephalic* and definitely a Neanderthal."

"I despise it when she brings up that subject."

"I can see why. Anyway, we made it and she got in touch with a cousin, a real estate guy, and this morning we went out to get some light bulbs and all of a sudden she's freaking out and calling me a traitor and saying I stole her something-or-other. No idea what she was talking about. She's pointing at the floor under my seat and I see this silver thing. Kind of looks like an ancient blow dryer. Penny, I told her I didn't know why it was there and that I had no interest in it, but it was too late, she'd totally snapped. Full Jekyll and Hyde.

She told me to take her back to the house and scram. She grabs the thing and it's tangled up in this ratty-looking wad of cloth and she gives me the weirdest look and disappears into the house."

"Oh no. I'm sorry. I was afraid of this!"

"Yeah, but I'm not done. I want you to hear this from me, okay? I don't want any confusion."

"Okay."

"So I'm still parked in back trying to figure out what I'm going to do next, and suddenly I hear her calling for me in that sugary voice she uses when she wants something. I look at the back door and she's standing there wearing this ancient negligee. I couldn't take it, Penny. I took off and didn't look back."

"Good god," was all I could say.

"What should I do?"

"This is my fault! I wrapped the thing up in that old nightgown and hid it under your seat the day you went to the hospital. And then forgot about it."

"What the hell is it?"

"It's called a Scintillator and it's for detecting radiation. I think she used it in her medical work. Remember how we thought she had a gun?"

"Sort of. Seems like a long time ago."

"It does. How are you feeling these days? Do you have your medications with you?"

"I just ate a couple pounds of ribs and I'm not feeling that great, to be honest."

"Oh wow. Maybe you should be careful, with your stomach problem?"

"I don't know, Penny. I eat when I'm nervous."

"Where are you now?"

"It's a barbecue stand called Babe's, saw it on the way into town."

Just then I heard a woman yell, "*Number fifty-eight!*"

And Burt saying, "That's me, put it here, thanks." Then, "I went back and ordered a turkey leg and an okra basket too." There was a lot of ambient noise, cars, people talking, and then Burt said, "They have great lemonade here. It's hot. I'm sweating bullets."

"Burt, you sound a little tired. Can you check into a motel and rest?"

"I can always rest in the Dog. But what about her? I can't leave her here."

"Yes, you can, if you need to. Think about yourself right now. Maybe save the turkey leg and okra basket for later?"

"Yeah, maybe. Ribs aren't settling too well."

There was a long silence.

"Burt? Burt, are you okay?"

"I'm sorry, Penny, could you excuse me a second?"

Before I could reply, he was gone.

22

I called and called and kept calling until a voice answered, but it wasn't Burt.

"I'm with Smith County Emergency Medical Services. We're bringing a Caucasian male into the ER at UT Health right now and we found this phone on his person."

I must have let out a terrible cry, because I heard somebody jump out of bed and shake the floor.

"Is it Burt Lampey?"

"Correct. We checked his wallet."

"What's wrong with him?"

"Ma'am, I'm going to leave that to the doctors, but his heartbeat's racing and his temperature's high and that's all I can tell you at the moment. Excuse me now, we're going inside. Call UT Health in a few hours."

The call ended just as Margaret opened the door, in silhouette against the light from the hall. "What is it?"

"Burt passed out at a barbecue place and he's being admitted to the hospital in Tyler."

I reminded her of Burt's recent medical history and told her he'd just gorged on ribs.

"It could be another bleed-out," Margaret said grimly.

From that moment, I was up. There was no question in my mind that I had to leave at once. Some people had jobs and/or children; I had Pincer and Burt.

"Wait, are you sure? How can you help?" Margaret said.

"Leave Pincer alone and Burt in the hospital?"

"Can't his brother go?"

"Even if he can, we can't expect him to deal with Pincer."

"But what about Arlo?"

Though it was only a little before five a.m., I went and knocked on the door to the guest room and let myself in. "Well, good morning," Arlo said calmly from the bed, as if he'd been expecting me.

I sat by his feet and described the circumstances, concluding with: "Do you want to come with me, or stay here?"

"I'll come if you need me," he said.

"I'd better deal with Pincer without you," I said.

"Can I stay, then?"

Margaret was right behind me. "Of course you can. You don't have to go back now."

"That suits me," Arlo said. "As long as you don't need me, Penny."

"I'm glad you can stay here," I said.

I was on the phone with the airlines next. I found a flight from

Brisbane that left in a few hours and would get me to Sydney in time to catch the flight to L.A. Seats were available. Margaret let me charge it on her credit card.

Then I realized it was necessary to call Dale, and, at the same time, that I was trembling.

"Penny!" he answered, with some possible pleasure.

It was harder to deliver the news than I'd anticipated. I could barely get the words out.

"Penny?"

"I'm here," I finally managed. "So. It's true what I told you, that Burt is in Texas. But it hasn't worked out as well as I'd hoped. Basically, I left my grandmother's radiation-detecting device under the seat of the van, which she discovered and accused Burt of stealing, but then she changed her mind and tried to seduce him. Burt took off and ate too much because he was nervous. And now he's in the hospital."

"*What?*"

"I'm very sorry this is happening," I said.

"I'm trying to absorb this," Dale said. "What's his condition?"

"He's at a hospital in Tyler called UT Health. They said to call back in a few hours to find out."

"I see. I'd better get moving, then."

I told him I was on my way too, though it would take me a little longer.

"You're coming back from Australia for this?"

"Of course. My grandmother needs a chaperone, and I care about Burt, believe it or not."

"I believe it. Why wouldn't I believe it?"

"I wasn't sure you did, that's all."

"Let it be established that I believe you care about Burt. It seems our paths may cross again."

He didn't sound very happy about it, but why would he?

We said goodbye.

Then I had to book the flights from L.A. through Dallas–Fort Worth to Tyler. I was able to find one departing four hours after I'd arrive in L.A. I'd make it to Tyler in a little over twenty-four hours.

I also thought I'd better let Tom Beaudry know that Pincer was now on her own and potentially a danger to herself or others. So I called and left a message explaining that her escort had been taken to the hospital and that her mood was labile and to be prepared for anything.

It was terrible following Margaret into the boys' room and waking them to say goodbye. Perhaps they were disoriented by the sudden wake-up and it had nothing to do with me, but they both burst into tears. I hugged them and felt their wet faces press into my neck. I told them I'd be back soon, and I meant it.

Wilhelmus stumbled out of their bedroom and said, "I don't understand. This is monstrous!" I wasn't sure what he meant by that, but we hugged goodbye.

And then Margaret drove me to the airport.

23

I don't think it's a loss to skip over the flights that brought me back to California. They were uneventful relative to the trip over. It's true that I didn't sleep the whole duration, that each leg was in pain in its own unique way, that on the long hop there was an annoying man next to me who drank one cocktail after another until he nodded off and began jolting and spasming in his seat, occasionally lashing me with an arm or leg, and that upon landing at LAX I removed my canvas carry-on from the overhead bin only to discover that it had been sitting in a pool of some kind of chili oil, which then dripped on me. Who didn't tighten the lid on their chili oil, who didn't transport it double-bagged? I cast accusatory glances at the tired, disheveled humans gathering their belongings around me.

But no amount of vigilance could have prepared me for what was next. As I waited in line to get through immigration, I activated my phone, whereupon I was confronted by the following messages:

> Penny, Arlo here. Gaspard called me as he does every once in a while. I told him we'd come to Australia together but that you'd just left. I think he might be planning to meet you at the airport.

I gasped.

And another message, from Margaret:

> Arlo regrets telling Gaspard you're flying in. Feels terrible about it. So sorry! Just what you need!

And another:

> Let us know what happens. You only have a few hours there anyway, right?

And another:

> Didn't mean to jump to conclusions about the undesirability of seeing Gaspard. Maybe it's good, right?

I closed my eyes so long that the woman behind me told me to keep moving. Was I now about to run into Gaspard when I came out of customs? I didn't want to see Gaspard now. I needed to get to Burt. To put it bluntly, Burt had been nicer to me in a handful of encounters than Gaspard had my whole life. My head was pounding. I needed some coffee. I smelled like chili oil.

Passport stamped, I progressed into the baggage area and grabbed my suitcase off the carousel. Herds of people were pushing carts of their personal effects toward the customs lines. I took the bag to an open space by a wall and unzipped it. Margaret had given me some of her old clothes, including a long, leopard-patterned scarf. I don't know why I'd accepted it, but she'd given me some good stuff too. I wrapped the scarf around my head multiple times until my hair was fully tucked beneath it. Nobody could possibly recognize me wearing such a thing. I moved through customs without a hitch and slipped on my dark glasses just before passing through the automatic doors.

A semicircle of expectant friends and relatives surrounded the exit and I attempted to scan the crowd without being obvious about it. Sure enough, leaning against one of those heavy pillars frequently seen in airports was Gaspard.

I kept my head down and pushed forward, pulling my bag along at a brisk hobble. However, I soon heard Gaspard calling: "Hey! Quack Quack! Slow down, kid!"

I sped up, stumbling into the first women's restroom I came upon.

The community of women in a restroom had never looked as reassuring. In and out they moved, all shapes and sizes, young and old, using the stalls, washing up, brushing out hair matted on their journeys. I saw each and every one as an ally who would swarm and bash Gaspard over the head with their bags should he try to invade. I washed my hands and took off the scarf and brushed my hair, mildly shocked by the horrible sight in the mirror. My eyes were puffy and bloodshot, I appeared to have developed jowls, and even my nose looked swollen. Quack Quack! Like I'd come to that call? Gaspard had always been fixated on the way I walked.

I entered a stall and changed out of my shirt and pants, rolling them up to contain the chili oil and then stuffing them into my bag.

I still had a few hours before the flight to Texas. Every move I made triggered the toilet. I tried to sit perfectly still on my suitcase. In the echo chamber of flushing toilets and roaring hand dryers, the past caught up to me. I was a ten-year-old again, sitting across a desk from Dr. Fountain-Goose.

"So," he was saying, leaning over the desk on his elbows. "I'm ready anytime you are. Please, start from the beginning."

"Well, but I'm not sure where the beginning is," I said, at that time very literal-minded.

"All right, then," he said. "Why don't you start with the problem?"

Dr. Fountain-Goose then had black, oily hair severely parted on the side and combed flat, a pale face, and chapped lips. He wore a white lab coat as always. I'd been having checkups and shots with him most of my life, he'd tapped my knees with his little rubber hammer, he'd looked down my throat with a Popsicle stick, he'd stuck a plastic cone in my ears, he'd placed a cold disk on my chest and listened, he'd confirmed I'd had mumps and chicken pox, but as far as I could remember, I'd never really talked to him. He was right, there was a problem, but there was more than one problem, so I was struggling to zero in.

He cleared his throat and said, "This is what I know. Your mother tells me you have trouble when you visit your father, and that you come home very unhappy, even unable to speak. She wants to see if I can be of help. Do you think I can be of help?"

Yes, it was all trouble! But at the same time, I had no under-standing of any of it.

"Penny? Help me out here. How old are you?"

"Ten," I said. That much I knew. Though I was the kind of ten that missed being nine. I liked every year of my life so far. I didn't like things to change.

"Just starting fourth grade?"

I nodded.

"Happy at school?"

"I like school," I said.

"Good. Do you have trouble making friends?"

"No," I said, "I have friends."

"Very good. And how are your grades?"

"Pretty good. I get As and Bs."

"Okay. And your home life here, are you happy with that?"

I nodded.

"No comment?"

"I'm happy," I said. "Everything's fine."

"Your stepfather, do you get along?"

I nodded. "Yeah, very much." Then, as an afterthought, I said, "But I really really really hate the word *stepfather*."

"You hate it? Why is that?"

I didn't then know how to explain how lonely and desolate that word made me feel whenever it was used to introduce him. But I could tell Dr. Fountain-Goose was taking it the opposite of how I meant it, so I said, "Because I love him so much and that word makes it sound like he's fake."

"You'd rather just call him your father."

"Sure, like my sister does. Also, I feel bad when people find out

I have a different last name." My voice trailed off, since there was no reason to mention this either. But I'd never really had a chance to complain about stuff like this before, or even put it into words.

"Why is that?"

"I guess, because, maybe it makes me feel like I'm tagging along, not really part of the family." Just saying it made my throat catch.

"But you very clearly are part of the family, are you not?"

"Yeah. I know it shouldn't bother me."

Dr. Fountain-Goose looked satisfied, as if he'd finally achieved something.

"All right. So what went on in San Diego?"

I took a few deep breaths, like I was preparing to leap over a trench. "Okay, it's—it's when I go to San Diego, to see him, well, it's not a good situation."

"Why not?" He leaned in farther over his desk.

"It's not good because . . . it seems like he's not happy I'm there," I finally managed.

"What makes you think he's not happy you're there?"

Was it possible he didn't believe me? Maybe he thought I was spoiled and expected too much.

"I guess because he seems mad right from the beginning. He seems mad when he comes to the airport to get me. He makes fun of my clothes—*Slip out of the straitjacket, kid. Where does mother think you're going—a job interview?* That's what he said."

"My goodness. What kind of clothes are you wearing when you arrive?"

"Uh—well, this year I was wearing a matching skirt and jacket. It's sort of blue corduroy. He made me change in the backseat of his car before we even left the parking lot. And while I was changing, he kept making fun of me for worrying that people were looking."

"Hmm," he said.

"Well, then he asked me a few questions about my year since I last saw him, but when I answer, he'll start imitating me in this high squeaky horrible voice. Like he thinks the way I talk sounds stupid, or that what I'm saying is stupid, it's hard to tell which."

"Would you be able to remember any examples?"

"Sure. I told him my teacher liked a poem I wrote and I won a prize, a book of poems by Ogden Nash. So in this horrible high voice he said: '*Oooh, I'm a poetry genius, I won a prize, I won a priiiiiiiiiiiiiize!*'"

My rendition was so repulsive, Dr. Fountain-Goose grimaced. "Okay. Then what did you say?"

"I didn't know what to say. I was confused. I was trying to figure out what was going on."

"Is that the main thing, that he makes fun of what you say?"

"Oh no, that's not the main thing at all. That's just one thing. Then there's how I walk. As soon as he sees me in the airport! He imitates me and keeps nagging at me to stop walking like a duck. He even quacks at me!"

"Right there at the airport?"

"Yep. He said I looked like a duck in a straitjacket."

"Is it possible he's just trying to be funny?"

Remembering this now, I could feel pressure building in my chest and stomach.

"Describe your father," Dr. Fountain-Goose had said.

"What he looks like?"

"Yes, please."

I could see him then, as I had now, waiting for me at the airport— about five-foot-ten and two hundred pounds, bald. His heavy arms were crossed, but the forearm with the jade-colored scar was in full view. His badge of indecision. The remnant of an anchor, his former tattoo. Big nostrils packed with hair that looked like straw. A few gold teeth. Light blue eyes like ice. He could add a stack of numbers in seconds and had the face of a boxer to back it up. He could cut to the chase and see the flaw in anything, especially me.

"I'm getting the sense, Penny, that your father makes you unduly nervous. Would that be a fair assessment?"

"Very fair," I said. Even then, I was sweating all over.

"Is there anything else you wanted to mention about your visit there?"

"Okay. If I'm reading, he'll call me a bookworm and tell me to go outside and play. This summer he even grabbed my book and ripped it up!"

"Literally ripped it up?"

"Yes. It was *Call of the Wild*. It was brand-new! He tore it in half down the spine and then started shredding the pages. I started crying, then he started imitating me crying, rubbing his eyes and going, *'Boo hoo hooo! Boo hoo hoooooooooooo!'* So then I went outside to play, and later he got mad I was talking to this kid down the block who happens to be a little younger than me even though he's nice and he's fun. He says only chumps play with younger kids."

"Hmm. Do you have any idea why he might think that?"

"Maybe if I was playing with a toddler it would be weird. But Winchell's only like six months younger."

"I see," Dr. Fountain-Goose said. "Where does your father work?"

"He sells insurance to marines and he has a used car lot and a vacuum shop. Sometimes he takes me with him, but mostly not. He has a friend who works at the San Diego Zoo, and whenever they're doing an animal autopsy we have to go over there."

"That could be interesting, I imagine?"

"This summer we saw a dead walrus. There was a lot of blubber and guts and stuff."

"Maybe your father hopes you'll become a doctor?"

"I don't think so. He just wants the meat," I said bitterly.

My doctor frowned. "What meat?"

"The walrus meat. He calls it meat for the mutt. He gives it to a lady a few houses away who has a giant schnauzer."

"He gives it to a lady who has a giant schnauzer," Fountain-Goose said, writing for a while on his pad. For the first time, he looked concerned. "What exactly is the home situation at your father's?"

"You mean, like who lives there?"

"Yes, that, the neighborhood, that sort of thing."

I remembered describing Mission Beach—the narrow spit between the beach and the bay, crowded with huts and cottages and makeshift summer places, no yards, no grass, because the waterfront was all around us. People ate on their front steps, on the bricks beside the narrow courts that divided the rows of houses in place of streets. Damp and sandy towels tossed over fences, swimsuits flapping like flags on clotheslines. Everybody sunburned, feral, barefoot. Empty wine bottles out on the picnic table. The bikers over the garage.

"Bikers over the garage, can you elaborate on that?"

"Well, there's an apartment there. And these guys who are in a motorcycle gang called the Pallbearers rent it. I think three of them, but lots of their friends hang out and work on their motorcycles all day."

"Do you feel comfortable around these bikers?"

"Not at first, but then I got to know Roar, and he gives me candy bars and he taught me how to throw an axe."

"I see," he said. "So, Penny, tell me what it was like when you couldn't talk."

This had been the heart of the matter, but it was also the hardest part to figure out. "So this summer he started getting mad that I wasn't calling him Dad. I didn't even *realize* I wasn't calling him Dad, I wasn't doing it on purpose. But after he started waiting and watching for it, I couldn't say it at all! Then almost every day he'd start screaming at me about it. And every day it became harder to say. It became hard to say anything! After about a week I couldn't talk at all," I said quietly.

"Very interesting. I think we've uncovered a lot already. It sounds like we have some things here we could work on right away. Why don't you pretend I'm your father and start a conversation with me?"

"I don't think it's going to work," I said.

"Let's give it a try," Fountain-Goose said.

I shrugged. "Hi, Dad. How's it going, Dad? Good to see you, *Dad. Dad*, wow, great to be here."

"There you go!" he said, looking very pleased with himself.

"No, you don't understand. You're not him, so it's totally different! You're not staring at me with your beady little eyes."

"Beady little eyes," he said, writing that down. "Well. I think you can work that through."

"I can't work it through!" I said, feeling the start of a sob. "I tried. My voice goes away. No matter how much I yell at myself to say it, nothing comes out."

"And this isn't something you regularly do to people?"

"Do? You mean not call them by name?"

"Yes, that's what I mean."

"It's never happened with anybody in my life, besides him."

"I see," said the doctor. He scribbled furiously on his pad.

At last he sat back, tapping his chin.

"Has your father . . . how shall I put this? Has he ever done anything you thought inappropriate?"

"Yeah, everything I've been telling you about," I said.

"Of course. But beyond that . . . any inappropriate . . . touching?"

I shook my head.

"No fondling, caressing, stroking?"

"No way! He never touches me. He doesn't hug or anything like that. Anyway, I'm not his type."

"What do you mean, what is his type?"

"Well, my mother is his type. Or his new wife, Dana. He thinks I'm dumpy and look like a duck."

"Do you think you look like a duck? And that you're dumpy?"

"Sure, I guess so. Why else would he say it?"

"So you're not happy with your appearance, I take it," Dr. Fountain-Goose said.

I said, "I don't think I'm majorly ugly, like a freak at a freak show, or someone people would stare at walking down the street. But I know I'm not pretty like my mother. He always talks about how stunning she was and how she'd walk into a room and everybody would stare, then he'll say something like, *Where'd you go the day they handed out the looks?*"

"I see. Are you jealous of your mother?"

"No, I'm proud of her, she's very smart."

"I see. Anything else?"

"Well." Even then, there were still so many weird moments to choose from.

"Okay, well, this summer I had to go wash my hands while he was taking a shower, I think Dana told me to because she wanted me to set the table, and while I was washing my hands he pulled back the shower curtain."

"And?"

"Well, that's what he did."

"Did he know you were there?"

"Yeah, for sure, I'd just knocked and asked if I could come in and wash my hands and he said yes."

"So he revealed himself to you."

"Yeah. And it was worse than just being naked."

"Worse? You mean he was more than naked?"

"Yeah." I hoped he understood.

"I'm sorry, but what is more than naked?"

"Oh," I said. "Well, it was . . ." What was the word, what was it?

"It?" he said, sitting forward in his seat.

I nodded.

"He was playing with it?"

I grimaced. "What do you mean?"

He cleared his throat. "He was touching his penis?"

I shook my head violently. "No, but it has to do with that."

"To do with touching?"

I shook my head again. "With, with . . ."

"With his penis."

"Yeah."

"Something to do with his penis but he wasn't touching it."

I nodded.

"He was washing it?"

"No."

"He was looking at his penis?"

"No."

"He *wasn't* looking at it or washing it."

"Right."

"There was something wrong with his penis?"

"Maybe."

"I see. Can you explain what was maybe wrong with it?"

I nodded and gulped.

"It was . . ."

"Tumescent?"

"What is that?"

"Tumescent means that the penis was swollen."

I nodded.

"The penis was swollen. Was it erect, then?"

"You mean sticking out?"

"Yes."

I nodded.

Dr. Fountain-Goose pushed away from the desk. "I see. You came into the bathroom, your father was taking a shower, he pulled back the curtain. And stood there, with an enlarged, erect penis."

Now that he was putting words to it, I wished I hadn't mentioned it.

"What did you do?" he asked.

"I ran out of the bathroom really fast."

"I see. He didn't say anything, he didn't reach for you, he didn't touch you, he simply stood there on display."

"Yep," I said.

"Then I don't need to report this. But did that make you uncomfortable?"

"Yep, it sure did."

"Was that when you found yourself unable to speak?" he asked.

"No, it was already happening."

I would have preferred it if I could've forgotten about the month of July completely. But my mother had been worried about me when I got home, seemingly cowed and listless. I had been trying so hard to hold it all in and act normal! Except I couldn't sleep, causing my mother to obtain some gross green sleeping syrup from Dr. Fountain-Goose. It made me retch, so it was useless. Finally, she received a letter from Gaspard leaving a lot of things out but making sure to say he thought I had mental problems and needed to be seen by a doctor as soon as possible.

Dr. Fountain-Goose chewed on the skin of his chapped lips, then abruptly stood and removed an encyclopedic volume from his bookcase. The clock on the wall ticked on. "Penny," Dr. Fountain-Goose said, "is nudity a problem for you?"

"What do you mean, a problem? I'm not used to hanging around with naked people, if that's what you mean."

"Do you regularly see your mother or stepfather nude?"

"No! Hardly ever. Maybe once or twice by mistake."

"Is it possible that your father is comfortable with nudity and simply wanted to be natural with you?"

"Sure, I guess. Let's stop talking about it."

"I'm perfectly happy to stop talking about it. We're trying to figure out what went wrong and how to make your court-appointed visits with your father a little easier for you in the future. And I think the solution must be found in you calling him Dad. You'll just have to make yourself do it next time. You're his only child, are you not?"

As far as I knew, I was.

"Think how the man must feel. You're perfectly happy here. You have replaced him with your stepfather. He sees you one month a year. I think it's obvious he just wants reassurance that he matters to you."

Could I make him feel better next time? I wasn't sure I was capable of it, but I had a year to think about it.

"A duck in a straitjacket," I said. "I guess that's pretty funny."

So there I was, picturing a duck in a straitjacket, holding very still on my suitcase in the stall so as not to activate the highly responsive toilet, when Margaret called.

"Hi! I made it, I'm in L.A.!"

"I know. Gaspard just called Arlo again and says you're hiding in the bathroom."

I was so tired! "It's true," I said.

"Are you okay?"

"Yeah. I just don't feel like talking to him right now."

"Don't you have to catch a flight?"

"I do. Did Arlo tell him where I was going?"

"I don't think so."

"Thank god. Could Arlo tell him we can talk some other time and that I'm attending to an emergency? He respects Arlo. Maybe he'll listen."

"I'll ask Arlo to call him and say that."

"That would be good."

"I miss you already!" Margaret kindly said.

"Same here."

I checked the time and did my best to consolidate my inner resources. I did some stretching exercises, triggered the flushing mechanism about ten more times, and finally came out. Peering from the entrance, I could see Gaspard across the corridor, sitting in a seat talking on his phone.

This could be my best chance. I steeled myself and bolted. I ran right past him, and gave him perhaps the only thing he'd ever wanted. I said, "Hi, Dad."

Then put everything I had into my legs.

24

I didn't look back, but the sound of winded lungs and jingling change shadowed me for a stretch. At one point I heard: "Your suitcase is old and ugly, kid!" And then: "With that bag you look like a criminal!" I ran through the crowd on the sidewalk outside the terminal, crossed the road to the island where a shuttle was just about to leave, and jumped on. Squeezing my way to a seat, I could see him looking up and down the passenger loading zone, having lost sight of me. Even with two gimpy legs I'd outrun him as I had as a child on the beach. Maybe he had bad legs too, for all I knew. Or other ailments. I decided that I'd write him a note when things settled down.

I debarked at the next terminal, checked my so-called old and ugly suitcase, scanned the perimeter for Gaspard while I waited in line through security, and eventually found my gate. I'd take American to Dallas and an American Eagle regional jet to Tyler. I had some time to spare and took a seat with a view of the tarmac and the baggage trolleys and all else that goes on when planes come in to dock.

There were some new missed calls and messages on my phone. Margaret had called again. Tom Beaudry had called. Detective Storke had called too—why?

And Dale had sent a text:

> I have a car and can pick you up at the airport. If you change your plans let me know.

Nothing about Burt. That put me at some ease. How nice of Dale to offer to pick me up!

I called Margaret first and told her I was on schedule for my next flight and that I'd managed to evade Gaspard. She already knew, because he'd called Arlo, huffing and puffing.

"What does Arlo think?" I asked.

"He said you must have your reasons."

She made me vow to let her know what was happening in Tyler at my earliest opportunity and wished me well.

Next call, Tom Beaudry, who answered.

"Hello, Penny. Where you be?"

"Just flew to L.A. from Australia. I'll get to Tyler this afternoon."

"Good to hear. Your grandmother could likely use your help."

"What's happening?" I seemed to be saying that a lot lately.

"So I came by yesterday with the paperwork for the house. She didn't mention anything about her friend, so I asked if she knew anything about the van that had been parked in back the day before. She told me she'd had a handyman out. I didn't press my luck. I didn't want to poke a bear with a stick, if you see what I mean."

Amazing. Totally insane. "Did she sign?"

"She did. Treated me like her best friend. Something unexpected happened, though. She asked if I had a guest room and could she stay with us. Said the house was empty and not fit for staying in, and she's right. Lily said it was okay, so we had her at our place last night."

"Very kind of you," I said with a heavy heart.

"So this male escort of hers is in the hospital?"

I explained that he'd had some health problems lately, so it wasn't entirely sudden. I told him I'd call when I got to town and that I'd likely bring her back to Santa Barbara as soon as I could. Tom sounded relieved.

Last, I phoned Storke; he picked right up.

"It's Penny Rush returning your call," I said.

"I know who you are," he said. "I've been out to see your grandmother and she's not there. I wonder if you can tell me where I might find her."

"It's so nice of you to check up on her," I foolishly gushed. "She's out of town now, actually. She went to Tyler, Texas, where she has a house."

"I'm afraid my reason for checking up on her isn't all that nice," he said.

"What do you mean?"

He cleared his throat and said, "It would be best if you could just tell me where she is."

What was going on? "You can't tell me why?"

"Where is she?" pressed Storke, now jettisoning all attempts to be lovable.

"She's at Tom Beaudry's house in Tyler," I said. "I'm at the airport in L.A. and I'm flying there this afternoon. Why do you need her? Was the house burglarized?"

"Who is Tom Beaudry?"

I explained. "Do you want his number?"

"I can find it," Storke said. "I need to take care of something. You'll be hearing from me."

"Okay," I said. "Hope you're doing well."

"What?"

"I said I hope you're doing well."

He said well enough and hung up.

Now what? I settled on thinking there had been a break-in at the house, possible vandalism, maybe even a fire. Rats pouring onto the road!

Shortly it was time to board.

Flying time to Dallas, three hours. Nothing compared to crossing the Pacific, but it felt like the longest flight of all. I stared at the back of the seat in front of me, wondering how long Burt would have to stay in the hospital, dreading dealing with Pincer, and thinking about how I'd be seeing Dale that very day. It was clear that Dale was a perfect distraction for keeping distress at bay, given my impulse to embroider our every interaction.

Instead of thinking about my disturbing encounter with Gaspard, I could think about an idealized version of Dale. Same with Pincer's problems or worrying about Burt or my parents or Sherman or especially myself and all the ineffectual things I'd done over the past handful of years. But this mechanism wasn't really fair to the real Dale. Seeing him in person was bound to be a letdown, considering how much work he was doing in my head.

More to the point, I knew what lows one could get to with another person! I never wanted to be in that situation again.

All went well changing planes in Dallas. I even had time for a snack—a big soft pretzel covered with jalapeños. It came with a little cup of hot fake cheese, which I chose to discard. The last was a very short flight, only half the distance to Shreveport. We came in over the crowns of loblolly pines; in the clearings between them I spotted a few petroleum pumpjacks bobbing in the manner of giant mantids.

In Tyler the twin-engine turboprop was met by a rolling staircase and we passengers ambled down the aluminum steps as warm autumn gusts mussed us up. I tried to walk gracefully, holding in my stomach, feet pointing straight in case Dale was watching out the window. Getting my suitcase at such a small airport was quick and easy, but no Dale at baggage claim. So I went out front and checked my phone. I realized I was looking for the red sports car he'd had in Santa Barbara; that's why it took me a while to see him hovering in the loading zone in a charcoal-gray sedan. But when he opened his door and stepped out, I barely recognized him. His expression was entirely unnatural. A jet took off and a taxi honked. The late afternoon glare was bouncing off mirrors and glass from all sides and my legs started to shake. Somebody was speaking loudly into a phone. An older woman was having trouble with a large pink suitcase that had spilled onto its side. Dale was almost upon me. There could be no doubt he was about to tell me something terrible. And he did.

25

I said I didn't believe it, that I'd spoken to Burt yesterday and that he was completely and fully alive. Dale said that didn't make sense because people are always alive the day before they die. I stupidly kept saying it was impossible and Dale said he understood Burt meant a lot to me. I said it was nice of him to say that, but that Burt was his brother and there could be no comparison. I asked did he think it was my fault and he said of course not and I asked did he think it was my grandmother's fault and Dale said it was Burt's decision to come here so it was nobody's fault and to stop saying that.

A traffic officer blew a whistle and spanked the hood of the sedan.

My recollections of that afternoon are both foggy and precise. Driving out of the airport, Dale said that he had to go by the mortuary and make arrangements and did I mind. I may have asked if he was sure there hadn't been some kind of mistake, but Dale said there was no mistake because he'd been with Burt when he died. At that point, heading into the heart of Tyler, I sobbed.

In a register that sounded far away but was right beside me, Dale explained that the omental patch used to fix Burt's perforated ulcer had apparently been sewn in too tightly. It had become gangrenous and leaky before giving way. That Burt had not complained sooner showed he'd had too high a threshold for discomfort, and his final act, of ingesting an exceptionally large meal, had been fatal. Toxins had poured into his abdominal cavity. He'd gone into shock and rapidly had multiple organ failure. Time of death, 10:11 a.m.

I was likely in a stupor trying to take this in. Meanwhile, Dale found the place and parked beneath a large old catalpa tree thick with dangling pods. He asked if I'd consider coming in to help make some decisions, and though this surprised me, of course I said yes.

It was a typical mortuary as far as I could tell, though I'd never been to one before. Inside a brick building with Grecian columns in front, the lobby was a salesroom of various types of coffins and urns. To the side was a sitting area with a box of tissues placed prominently on a glossy table, with a lugubrious portrait of the founder looming over the scarlet velvet settee. The temperature of the place was practically arctic. A small man with a number of warts on each cheek came out and introduced himself as Ewell Spach. He had been expecting Dale.

"Our sincere condolences, Mr. Lampey," he said, shaking Dale's hand, at which time I noticed warts on his wrist as well. "Mrs. Lampey," he said, taking mine.

"This isn't Mrs. Lampey," Dale said, rather gruffly, I thought.

Burt wanted to be cremated, Dale said. They'd discussed these matters when Burt was in the hospital in Santa Barbara. Ewell Spach said they did all their cremating on Saturday. Dale asked if there was any way it could take place sooner, since he'd be returning to San Francisco in the morning. "Afraid not," Spach said, with a pleasant smile. Dale said perhaps if he paid an extra fee, as it would mean a lot to him to take Burt's ashes with him. Spach said this wasn't California and that they did things differently down here. Dale said he knew this wasn't California, he was just wondering. Spach said they would be happy to send Burt's ashes following postal guidelines, so Dale relented.

He picked a simple wooden box, and I nodded my approval, paving the way for Spach to say: "That style is usually for folks without loved ones."

Dale said, "My brother had plenty of loved ones and two of them are standing right here."

"To my eye those look like the choice of someone without loved ones but of course it's up to you."

Dale said, "Frankly, those fake urns look like the choice of someone without loved ones, if you ask me."

"We only carry the finest urns available and they certainly aren't fake."

"The receptacle is immaterial because Burt wishes his ashes to be scattered, so there's no reason to keep talking about this."

"As you wish, Mr. Lampey."

Then Dale had to complete some paperwork while I sat under the founder's portrait feeling chilled. After a few minutes of shivering, I said I'd wait outside.

I started picking up the pods beneath the catalpa tree. Some were green like string beans, others had browned, and many had cracked open, revealing the seeds clinging inside. In my childhood I collected natural freebies like these with the intention, supposedly, of crafting something with them, but I think I mostly liked amassing collections of like objects. I also recalled reading a story in a college class featuring catalpas. The professor had suggested these elongated pods, dangling outside the window of the story's spinster, were of obvious phallic significance. As I considered them in the palm of my hand, Dale emerged from the building.

"All right. That's done," he said. "What now?"

I threw the pods back where they came from. "The problem with you picking me up is that now I need to check out my grandmother, and it doesn't seem fair you'd have to be involved in that."

"I'd rather have something to do than sit around," Dale said, looking distinctly peaked.

"So you don't mind taking me over there?"

"Let's do it," he said.

Tom didn't answer when I tried his phone, so I entered his address into my maps and discovered we weren't far from his house at all.

It was a neighborhood of restored Queen Annes and handsome gardens at the end of their summer runs. Leaves turning yellow to red. A few late-blooming rhododendrons and roses. Rounding the corner onto Tom's street, we were confronted by the sight of three police cars parked around his beautiful house. There was a colloquy happening on the lawn. At the center of several uniformed officers was my grandmother wearing a yellow velour sweat suit, Tom at her side. She was hunched over, leaning hard on a cane, as if she'd aged cartoonishly over the past two weeks.

"Oh my god," I said.

"What's your best guess on what we're seeing here?" Dale said, finding a place to park.

"She's probably accusing Tom of trying to steal her property or something horrible like that." I wished we could drive on, but Tom had spotted me and was waving frantically. "I don't think I can take this."

Dale said, "It's not exactly what we need right now, but let's deal with it."

The man had just lost his brother and wanted to help? "I don't know what to say. Thank you."

My grandmother was holding forth. Neighbors up and down the block were watching from their porches and lawns. Tom separated from the group and met us on the street. The successful and energetic realtor looked drained of his life force. "Penny, this isn't my bailiwick. I'm glad you made it."

I introduced Dale as the brother of Pincer's friend Burt, who had passed away that morning in the hospital.

"Good lord," Tom said, and without a moment's hesitation he grasped Dale in a bear hug. "What befell the poor man?"

I said, "He had a perforated ulcer, but it was worsened by a lunch at Babe's Barbecue."

Tom released Dale, who coughed. "Why, that's the best place for ribs anywhere around," he said.

"Well, it wasn't good for Burt," Dale said.

"My sincere condolences. Food poisoning?"

"No, he just ate too much," I volunteered.

"My god. I understand. I always eat too much at Babe's Barbecue."

Dale said, "We're not laying fault at the feet of Babe's Barbecue. My brother had impulse control problems. Let's leave it at that."

I almost shouted at Dale. "Don't say that! He was stressed out. Everybody eats too much sometimes!"

Then I felt terrible and put my hand on Dale's arm.

Tom said, "I hardly know what to say, knowing you're both bereaved. But these officers have come here to arrest your grandmother."

I said, "I beg your pardon?"

"I got a call a couple hours ago from a detective in Santa Barbara giving me the heads-up. They're saying she's a fugitive from justice and must be extradited to California. They've got an arrest warrant! But you know her, she doesn't cooperate with anyone."

Before we could ask Tom anything further, a shout could be heard from the cluster of officers surrounding Pincer. It seemed she had just poked one of them with her cane.

Now she was in trouble. The cane was seized. I ran to her side.

"Penny!" she yelled. "What took you so long? Get me out of here!"

"I'll try to help," I mumbled.

"Tell them to get their hands off me. Is this any way to treat an old woman who's nearly crippled with rheumatoid arthritis?"

"Sorry, ma'am, but we gave you the opportunity to come peacefully," said one of the officers.

Should I tell her about Burt? Now didn't seem to be the time.

"What's this all about?" I said.

"Don't listen to their nonsense!" yelled Pincer.

Dale stepped forward and announced he would serve as Pincer's legal adviser.

"Who the hell are you?" she barked.

"It's not helping anybody to have you yelling and behaving this way!" I yelled, though I tried to put my arm around her. She batted me away.

"Et tu, Brute?" she said viciously.

I could not, at that moment, distinguish between this and a hellscape. My brain was overheating.

"Would you mind repeating the charges?" Dale asked calmly.

"Glad to," said another of the officers. "She's wanted in California, in the county of Santa Barbara, for questioning regarding human remains found on her residential property."

"*More* human remains?" I sputtered.

"I can't tell you that, ma'am," said the officer.

26

I needed to lie down. I was about to expire. I sat on the curb with my head on my knees.

Dale came over and asked if there was anything he could do. Upon receiving a curt no, he presented a plan nonetheless. "I'm assuming Burt's van is still at the barbecue place and we should move it. I have the key, it's in the bag of Burt's things they gave me at the hospital. How about if I drop you there and I'll find out what's going on with your grandmother at the station?"

"Okay."

I felt neither grateful nor ungrateful. Only bleak and empty. While Pincer shouted at the officers coaxing her into the back of a patrol car, I followed Dale to the sedan. I noticed he was wearing some nice suede desert boots but didn't care. I don't think we spoke more than a few words before we reached the shack known as Babe's Barbecue. It sat on a large asphalt lot alongside three locomotive-sized grills upon which a number of meats were smoking. The Dog was parked next to a dumpster under the shade of an old walnut starting to shed its leaves.

"Burt liked parking next to dumpsters," I noted.

"Penny, are you all right?"

"I've been better."

"Are you thinking it's a bad idea that I have anything to do with your grandmother?"

"I don't know. You tell me."

"It's probably not a good idea, but hopefully I can help sort things out for now."

"For no reason at all, she thinks I've betrayed her."

"She's cornered and lashing out. Don't take it personally."

"I shouldn't even care. She didn't take care of Burt!"

"Burt didn't take care of Burt."

I flinched and thought of something else. "Kweecoats!"

"Yes, Kweecoats."

"He's yours now."

"Yes, it looks like he is."

"Will you keep him?"

"I imagine so."

"Have you grown fond of him?" I insisted on knowing.

"I never imagined having that kind of dog. Growing up we had a Lab."

Kweecoats wasn't me; why was I taking this personally? "Well, do you like him or not?" I said sharply.

"Of course I do," he said.

"Okay, well, here we are." Tears were streaming down my face. Dale's too, I realized.

"Don't forget, that hot rod is all yours now."

"That doesn't make sense. Why should I get it?"

"Burt wanted you to have it, for some reason. But obviously you don't have to accept it. I advise you to drive it straight to the nearest junkyard."

"Don't insult Burt's van," I said crossly.

"Oh! Hands off the Chore Cow?"

"Forget Chore Cow. Chore Cow has nothing to do with Burt!"

"All right. I'd better get to the station," Dale murmured.

I grabbed my bag from the back and hobbled toward the van. The opening of the rear door ushered forth a small tuft of orange fur.

For about an hour I lay on the futon in the back of the Dog, paralyzed with dread. I was having trouble putting my thoughts together, so gave up trying. I fastened my attention on the rusty rivets across the ceiling and the amenities Burt had installed for this trip. Using double-sided tape, he'd attached a box of tissues to one wall, and slapped up a few hooks on which hung a Dodgers cap and a wide-brimmed straw hat. A piece of fabric with little pouches sewn onto it, embroidered with seahorses, had been tied onto the back of the passenger seat. In these pouches were a variety of odds and ends, such as a half-eaten roll of Tums, several pairs of reading glasses, loose batteries, a package of toothpicks, and, to my surprise, a box of condoms. I refused to believe those had anything to do with Pincer! Otherwise, all that remained in the back of the Econoline, besides the futon and a couple of pillows and the same sleeping bag I'd used in Burt's office, was a green plastic garbage bag stuffed with Burt's clothes, a red ice chest holding a few inches of water, the tire, and the dusty old piñata, now standing aslant because one of the front legs was buckling. I wondered what the piñata had meant to him, and grasped that it was one of the many irreducible things about Burt that I'd probably never find out. Why hadn't I asked him before? Think of all the other things I hadn't asked him!

While it felt beneficial to stretch out, I was soon aroused by some very aromatic scents. I wasn't hungry but needed to take some pain-killers and thought it best if I avoided doing so on an empty stomach.

I hauled myself out and joined the line in front of Babe's. Some Van Morrison was being piped in through a sound system, lending a mellow vibe. Picnic tables ringed the place and I tried to imagine which one Burt had been sitting at when he called me. It seemed gro-tesque and perverse that I was about to order food at the place that had killed Burt, but, in fact, I recognized it as a tribute.

"What can I get you?" said the woman at the ordering window.

"I'll take a rack of ribs, macaroni and cheese on the side, a peach cobbler, and a large lemonade," I said before I could stop myself. She gave me the number 35 on a greasy metal spike.

I found one of the last unoccupied tables, likely rejected by oth-ers because half of it was splattered with bird droppings. Perfect. I didn't want anybody to sit with me anyway. There were enough people around as it was—I was hemmed in on all sides by rowdy fam-ilies with many screaming children, a crew of burly highway mainte-nance workers at the end of their shift, and solitary gluttons alike.

Shortly a voice bellowed out, "Number 35"—it was surely the same voice I'd heard when Burt was here. I couldn't believe it. I blinked back tears and waved the metal prong until I received my tray.

It was hard to dive in under the circumstances. I wanted to eat

this food to thank Burt for entering my life and in appreciation of
the short time I'd known him, and I lowered my head to observe a moment of silence. There was something about Burt that had touched
me deeply. Why did he have to die now? Having moved toward an
acceptance that my parents may have been ingested by the earth, I
needed him now more than ever. Not that bringing me enjoyment
or comfort was his life's purpose, but why now, right when I was getting to know him? I didn't automatically like everybody I met the way
I'd liked Burt. Burt was a once-in-a-lifetime special person!

Cursing the loneliness and self-pity welling up inside me, I jabbed
my plastic fork into some rib meat. There was no denying it, these
ribs were something special. So, even, was the macaroni and cheese.
The lemonade, as Burt had testified, was fresh, perfectly sweet and
tart. The peach cobbler like homemade. How much he must have
enjoyed his last meal!

Twenty minutes later I'd left the place and was walk-
ing around sipping the remains of my lemonade. Both of my legs were
sore and stiff and I wanted to stretch them out before hitting the sack.
Within a block of Babe's Barbecue were any number of medical offices and clinics, low-lying brick buildings with unobtrusive signs
slightly sinister in their modesty. The streets in this area were paved
with brick as well. The air was crisp and the sounds of insects faint.
Dry leaves scuttled along the brick surfaces.

First I wanted to give Margaret a call, and was very grateful that
I caught her. I groaned for sympathy.

"What's wrong?" she cried.

I unloaded it all—Burt's death and Pincer's arrest. She was aghast. She said she'd come right away if I needed her, and I said thank you but maybe it wasn't necessary. As if it would cheer me up, she also told me Arlo was doing really well and they loved having him there. She even said maybe we should think about canceling his room at the Palms.

I'd assumed I'd be watching over Arlo at the Palms sometime soon when he returned. The idea that he wouldn't come back disturbed me, as if Australia were siphoning off yet another loved one. I said I couldn't think about it now. When we ended the call I felt somewhat worse than I had before.

I then called Storke. It was early evening in Tyler but only a little after five there.

"Ms. Rush," he said.

"Hello," I said sullenly.

"I'm aware that your grandmother's been taken into custody," Storke said.

"Yes. Would you mind telling me why?"

"I can tell you the facts of the case as we know them at present," he said.

"Please do."

As best as I can piece together, since I was unusually fatigued at the time, Storke's narrative went something like this:

A call had come in from a woman whose daughter's dog had returned from a walk around the neighborhood clutching a large bone in its jaws. ("That could be Casper!" I interrupted. "Casper it was," Storke replied.) Upon questioning, the girl admitted having taken recently to wandering around the yard of "the hermit," as Pincer was evidently known. For the past several days Casper had gone straight to a spot on the hillside at the back of the property and commenced to dig. Today he'd unearthed the bone, which to her untrained eye looked distinctly human. Possibly a femur.

Storke took the information from the intake desk and when he noted the address his hair stood on end. He drove over at once and determined that Pincer had not been home for a while, based on the accumulated mail in her box. The girl and her mother met him there and guided him to the small pit, where more bones were visible peeking through the soil.

Storke, I concluded, felt betrayed. He'd been taking pity on Pincer and helping her out since the last body was discovered. She'd left town without saying a word. Further, for a few days he had been sitting on a disturbing piece of information. When Pincer had given him the materials that she claimed proved that Dr. Matsumoto had donated his body to science, he'd sent them to a translator for verification. The translation had only just come back, and apparently one of the documents was in fact instructions for the use and care of an electric blanket. Another document was indeed an anatomical bequest, but the donor was not Dr. Matsumoto. It was someone named Hisato Nagata. Storke said he couldn't really begin to imagine what this meant, and had since requested a search warrant and a forensic anthropologist.

By the time he'd finished telling me this, I had returned to the van and was contemplating a drive over to Pincer's mostly empty house to wash up. I still had a key from the last time we were there, on a ring with my keys to the Santa Barbara house. "So now what?" I said.

Storke said he had a proposal. He wanted to bring her back to California himself. He was fascinated by sociopaths, he said, and had developed a rapport with her and thought she would accompany him willingly. Plus, he said, he could drop in on an aging uncle in Dallas before collecting her.

Storke no longer sounded in need. He was a man with a mission who had been waiting for his moment to shine. That he would take Pincer off my hands this way was the best news I'd heard in some time.

"I'll be very grateful if you can make that work," I said, and we agreed to be in touch, just as a call from Dale was coming in.

"Penny?"

"Hello."

"I've left the station. Your grandmother's been released and has agreed to return to Santa Barbara voluntarily. She'll be escorted by a detective from Santa Barbara."

"I was just talking to him. Why such favorable terms? Why isn't she being held in jail?"

"I thought you'd be relieved."

"I don't know what she's done. How can I be relieved?" When Dale didn't reply, I said, "Where is she now?"

"Tom Beaudry has taken her back to his place and he'll keep her there until the detective arrives."

"Did she say anything about the bones?"

"She did not, and I advised her not to. She'll need to find representation once she returns to Santa Barbara."

"What about Burt? Did you tell her?"

"I did. I'd prefer not to repeat her response."

"Oh, Dale! And you were there helping her!"

"Such as it was. So, how about joining me for dinner?"

Dinner? What was he thinking? That we were going to have a nice evening talking about current events? In addition, I didn't want him to know I'd eaten at Babe's Barbecue, he might find it ghoulish. And I couldn't eat a second dinner even if I wanted to.

"Penny?" he said again. "Are you interested in having dinner together?"

"You know, I would really like to, but I'm not sure I can stay awake. I haven't slept since I left Australia."

"Where are you staying?"

"I thought I'd stay in my grandmother's empty house."

"No! You should get a room. The hotel I'm staying at is reasonable."

"I'm probably going to fall asleep immediately, so it really doesn't matter."

Dale exhaled conspicuously. "Sure. I'd forgotten how tired you must be."

"You fly back tomorrow?" I mumbled.

"I don't know that there's anything more I can do here," Dale said. "What about you?"

"I'm going to drive back in Burt's van," I said, for I'd just decided it.

"No! Seriously?"

"Yes."

"You can't really want that thing!"

"If it's really mine, I do."

"We don't even know if it will make it."

"I'll find out soon enough," I said.

"Well, I don't know what to say. What if it breaks down in the middle of nowhere?"

"It probably will break down," I said impatiently. I was tired of Dale going on about it. "You don't have to feel responsible for this. Go back to San Francisco and enjoy your life there!"

After a pause, Dale said, "Good night, then."

"Good night. I'm tired."

"Get some rest."

"I will."

"Goodbye."

"Goodbye!"

Babe's Barbecue was now closed, and the woman who'd delivered my order was hurling some trash bags into the dumpster only feet away. She glanced at me suspiciously. I then made my final call of the evening, to Tom Beaudry. "Can I drop by?" I asked. "I know it's getting late, but I need to talk to my grandmother."

Tom murmured, "Penny, things are a little strained here at the moment. My wife's not too happy about the arrangements."

"I understand, and I really appreciate what you're doing. Could I talk to her on the phone?"

Tom said, "All right. She's sitting in the den drinking some sherry. I'll bring you in there."

I heard him announcing my call and Pincer saying: "It's about time!"

After the handoff, she said, "Cousin Tom is a most courteous gentleman. Good thing you called. I have a list of things I need you to do. Ready?"

"But why are there bones in your yard?" I simply asked.

"Why should they be anywhere else? In some commercial grave site surrounded by strangers?"

"Who are they?"

"Keep your hat on. I have a very good friend who's going to help me through this, so you need not get involved."

"But who is Hisato Nagata?"

"Hisato was Hiroshi's friend. He came to me only after Hiroshi was gone. There's no crime in it."

"What are you saying, that he had radiation sickness too?"

"I've been advised not to say anything to anybody."

"So there's no killing involved, is that what you're saying?"

"No killing? I am an American. We murdered over two hundred thousand men, women, and children in Hiroshima and Nagasaki. Not to mention the one hundred thousand dead in the firebombing of Tokyo. Who can claim innocence in respect to that? If you could see what the bomb did to these people, not the ones incinerated on the spot, but the ones who survived and were poisoned, you would be deeply ashamed."

She actually said more than this, a lot more, really. She told me she'd originally swiped the Scintillator from Arlo because he'd bought it for staking uranium claims in Nevada. The world didn't need more uranium, she said, and after the divorce she re-upped her connections in Japan, traveling there for conferences and serving for some time as a host for *hibakusha* who came to the States to share their stories. Those were lonely, desperate years, she said, after my mother shivved her in the back by siding with Arlo in the divorce, and her work gave her life meaning. All I knew was that my mother had found her unbearable and had made life-changing decisions simply to get away from her, including a youthful and hasty marriage to Gaspard and later a move to another continent. It was all pretty sad.

"I know what I'm doing, Penny," she was saying. "Law enforcement picked over my carcass tonight. Please not you too. Ron wants me to stay put until he gets here, and that's exactly what I'm going to do."

"Ron?" I then realized she was referring to Storke. "Okay, then," I finally said. "I guess I'll see you back in Santa Barbara sometime."

"Now that you're through with Sherman, maybe you'd like to live with me."

"We'll see," I said, and shuddered.

. . .

An hour later I was soaking in the Jacuzzi in Pincer's bathroom. One leg had turned yellow and the other bore a four-inch gash with black threads coming out of it. My feet looked strange to me too, not having seen them for a few days. They were covered with uniform indentations, like meat that had been pounded into schnitzel with a mallet. Only two nights before, Burt had luxuriated in this bathtub, blissfully unaware that Tom was peeping in the window at him, blissfully unaware that his body was about to shut down.

Not much had changed since I'd been in the house three years ago. The partially unpacked dishes were out on the counter in the kitchen. The cardboard wardrobes full of her clothes still stood in the master bedroom. Luckily a few of the overhead bulbs still worked and Tom had paid the utilities! There was a chill in the air, so I adjusted the thermostat, but when a stale, burnt smell began to issue from the vents, I closed it down.

I'd brought in my bag from the van and discovered that the smell of chili oil had permeated everything I had with me. The place had a washing machine and dryer, so I threw my clothes into the washer with some dish soap I found by the kitchen sink and hoped for the best. Maybe Pincer had something I could wear in the meantime. Luckily I did not come across the old negligee, even though I was looking for something soft and light. But it seemed like all she'd brought along for her fantasy life in Tyler were scratchy party dresses and a number of furs in garment bags.

The bath was bubbling fiercely all around me, giving me the opportunity to set my sights a little higher. Why should I return to California at all? I could go anywhere! Pincer would have to sell this house to pay the debts she'd racked up. Probably the other house too. Arlo would soon have a better life at Margaret's. Doris would hopefully be out of our lives forever. Sherman was holed up with Bebe Sinatra on her Christmas tree farm. It was time to make a plan of my own!

I dried off with a dish towel I'd found in the kitchen and then transferred my washed clothes to the dryer. Just as I was preparing to find something to keep me warm in the meantime, someone began to knock on the front door. I raced across the carpet to peer through the peephole. It was Dale.

"Just a minute!" I shouted.

In the bedroom I grabbed the first dress I saw, tearing it from its hanger. It was made of cantaloupe-colored chiffon and smelled like mildew. Next I unzipped one of the garment bags, revealing a full-length fur of some kind, maybe sable, maybe mink. The horizontal sectioning made it look like a coat for the Michelin Man. But it smelled all right, so I shook it out a few times and slipped it on, returning to the door to open it.

Dale appeared surprised.

"I'm washing my clothes," I explained.

"Naturally one wears a fur coat at such a time."

"This is my grandmother's."

"I assumed so. Can I come in for a minute?"

Moths were flying in, so I said okay.

Then he said, "I'd like to drive back with you in the van."

For a moment I was speechless. What was he doing to me? "Why?" I finally said.

"Because . . . I feel Burt would want to make sure you got back safely."

"Don't you have to get back to work?" I said irritably.

"I can manage a few days off. Google says it's a twenty-four-hour drive. We could try it in two days, trading off."

"I don't even know that I'm going back there," I said.

"Oh. Where are you going?"

"I haven't decided. And who says I want to hurry? I'd want to stop at Carlsbad Caverns."

"That's fine, I have nothing against Carlsbad Caverns."

Standing unclothed in the heavy fur coat, I was being driven to distraction by unfamiliar tactile stimuli. I hoped Dale would leave.

"Well, I don't know. I need to think about it."

"Of course, but is there some reason you don't like the idea?"

Perhaps the prickling sensations caused by the coat pushed me to a frankness I would have been incapable of otherwise. "Yes, actually. I don't understand. What does your *significant other* think?"

Dale raised his eyebrows and laughed. "I don't know what he thinks. He probably would think it's great."

"He?"

"What are you talking about?"

"Nothing, I didn't realize you were married to a man. Which is great, of course."

"I'm not married to a man," Dale said.

"Then who's *he*?"

"Kweecoats! Who do you think I mean?"

"That's your significant other?"

"You're the one who called him that!"

"I meant your wife."

"What wife? I'm not married."

"You said you were married. The first night we met!"

"I did not! I said I was *not* married. I made a point of saying that!"

I pulled the coat around me and shuddered. Dale stepped back and uttered a noise of frustration or contempt, I was unable to tell the difference. The coat had been a terrible choice. I felt as if I were modeling a bear costume. "Dale, I'm too tired right now to react to this, so I think you should go and we can talk in the morning."

Dale said, "Let me get this straight. All this time you thought I was married."

"I guess I misheard."

"Either that or you've been willfully obtuse," he said, reaching for the door. "I think I'll go." And with that, he let himself out.

Willfully obtuse?

"Dale, wait," I called out.

He slowed.

"Dale, I'm sorry if I've been willfully obtuse. That's a startling observation."

Now he stopped and turned. "It's been a very long day for both of us."

"I know," I said. "I don't know why I misheard you. I need to think about it."

"That sounds like a useful step."

"Who's taking care of Kweecoats?"

"I have a nice neighbor with a pug."

"I was annoyed that you were married," I blurted out.

"Annoyed?"

"I thought you had a wonderful life in San Francisco and it repulsed me."

Dale moved into the glow of the porch light. "I do have a good life in San Francisco in many respects. I'm sorry that's repulsive to you."

"Great. I'm glad you do. It's just that somehow over the past few years I developed an aversion to people with sensible lives."

"No wonder you liked Burt so much," he said.

"There's no reason to wonder why I liked Burt," I yelled.

"Of course not, and I appreciate that." His face went slack. "I lost my brother today and I can't help feeling it could have been avoided!"

"It's terrible," I said, choking up.

"Yes, it's terrible."

An autumnal breeze rattled the dry leaves falling on the street. I wanted to hug Dale, but didn't feel dressed for it.

"By the way, my feelings for Burt weren't romantic," I said for some reason.

"I didn't think they were. I take it you haven't been on the dating scene in a while."

"As you know, I was married. Actually, I still am."

"It's all online these days," Dale said. "I've always felt it's better to meet somebody by chance."

I shrugged.

"Well, my offer still stands. I'll go if you'd like some company. You can let me know in the morning."

I was sure thousands of mites were migrating from the coat onto my skin, and if I didn't remove it soon, I might panic.

"Okay," I managed to say.

"Good night. Again," Dale said.

I ran inside and hurled the fur onto the floor, rinsing off in the shower with urgency. A quick toweling with the damp dishcloth led me to feel grateful that my clothes were now tumbled hot and dry.

What turned me against staying the night inside was not the lack of a bed, but the waxy, tail-twitching scorpion that came crawling across the carpet as I sat there brushing my hair.

I slept in the Dog. In Burt's bag. I wouldn't sleep in Pincer's house, this one or the other, for anything.

27

The morning sun was behind me as I motored west through the greater metropolitan area of Dallas–Fort Worth, casting a foreshortened shadow of the Dog onto the highway that I was continually overtaking. From Tyler it was 583 miles to Carlsbad Caverns, my destination for the night. Considering the distance I'd covered with Arlo in Queensland, this was nothing more than a normal day behind the wheel.

I wasn't checking my phone. I'd already seen there were messages from Dale, but I was ignoring them. Every mile that I put between myself and Tyler filled me with a sense of accomplishment and relief.

It was my feeling that if Dale were to experience the toll of mile upon mile of captivity, he'd have regretted his offer. Feeling his impatience to get back would not be good for me. I'd imagined a soulful journey at my own pace. Likely he'd find the ride especially uncomfortable and make negative comments about the van. I didn't want to hear those comments. I knew the Dog needed some work

but didn't want my decision to keep it to become a topic of conversation for fifteen hundred miles. And he might continue to call it
the Chore Cow, as if that were some great bond we shared. And
think of the effort of conversing all those hours! I was tired out!
Further, I felt that I was not adequate to the grief he must be expe-
riencing, and it would be better if he got back to his surroundings
in San Francisco, where he could lean on his true friends. I had grief
of my own, and very selfishly didn't want to have to defer to his
right to a greater grief.

There was also the chance he would insist on driving even though
I was capable and in the mood to drive, that he might wish to stop
when I wanted to keep on, that he might wish to listen to music that
annoyed me, and that he might not like listening to the news, which I
liked to do. Also, knowing he believed I was *willfully obtuse*, I would
be on guard the whole way, worrying that my willful obtuseness was
on display, and that I was being sized up and found wanting.

If anything went wrong with the van, he'd likely say I told you so
and I'd be to blame. He'd probably want to stay in a motel or two
along the way, whereas I couldn't afford it. (He wouldn't understand
that at all.) He might take over and try to boss me around. Alternately, I might ask him about his case with the mother who'd strangled her baby and put him on the defensive. I might ask questions
about Burt's life that would tire him. Old resentments toward Burt
might continue to bubble up, and a primal reckoning could ensue.
New resentment toward Pincer and likewise toward me might surface as well.

At dawn I'd left a note on the windshield of his rented sedan in
the parking lot of his hotel. I'd also left a note on Tom's front porch.
To Dale, I'd said he didn't need to feel responsible for getting me
home when he had his own issues to deal with. To Tom, I'd expressed

my thanks for all he was doing and said I had to get back to prepare for Pincer's return.

As for money, I still had three hundred and twenty-five dollars thanks to Margaret. In case I needed more, I had five furs in the back that I could sell at stops whenever I needed some cash. I knew they weren't fashionable anymore but surely I could get twenty or thirty dollars apiece for them just for the novelty. Pincer never wore them anyway, and the idea of peddling them at rest stops gave me some well-needed, albeit warped, satisfaction.

I spent the day listening to the radio and the miles crawled by. Heading west the terrain grew dryer and dustier, the glare of the open sky fierce. I heard a story on NPR about scientists in Australia growing primitive human kidneys in a petri dish. Good for the Australians! This was amazing—the primitive kidneys were called "organoids." I wondered if Margaret knew about it. I also thought about how the suffix *oid* made any word it was attached to sound scary, and spent a long time thinking of examples. *Humanoid. Arachnoid. Factoid.* In other news, Jeb Bush was failing to hold on to his presumed front-runner status. There was a running discussion on the efficacy of his Jeb! logo, as if a bad font choice (Baskerville) might have ruined everything for him. Texas executed its eleventh inmate of the year by lethal injection. Things were a mess in Syria, and there had been some historic flooding in South Carolina due to a catastrophic storm complex.

At one point "These Boots Are Made for Walkin'" came on and I blasted it and sang along as if sending Sherman a deferred threat; that it was being performed by someone named Sinatra was not lost on me, and probably gave me more of an edge. I needed it because Texas had a way of going on and on. In Abilene I refueled and bought a Coke and a large bag of Fritos and threw down a few ibuprofen to take the edge off the stiffness in my legs. It seemed an extra-large horsefly decided to jump aboard at that stop, only to wait a few miles down the road to start pestering me. All at once it rocketed forth, flying into my hair with a gusto that could only be described as nasty and intentional. The buzz, near my ear, went straight to my brain and nearly cost me a meltdown, and it was lucky there wasn't much traffic at that moment, because I engaged in some combat and swerving. I never saw the fly's corpse but after that it left me alone, and on I proceeded through Sweetwater, Colorado City, Big Spring, Andrews, and finally by dusk across the state line into New Mexico, stopping at a wide spot in the road just outside the national park.

I had dinner in a little café—a couple of tacos stuffed with that pre-chopped, brown-fringed lettuce sold in plastic bags, mixed with the pre-grated, desiccated cheddar also sold in plastic bags, along with a Pacifico to relax. A reasonably nice-looking man in a Stetson across the room tipped his hat at me, like a cowboy in a movie! Despite my disinclination to flirt with people when out on my own, the gesture made me feel included in the human race. There was no camping in the park, I learned from my waitress, but she said there was an RV park across the road. That wasn't necessary. It would be too expensive and I didn't need hookups. Instead, I parked down the road next to a clump of ocotillos and moved into the back, taking full advantage of the space Burt had left me.

Though I slept well that night in the Dog, I woke the following morning at the climax of a frightful dream. In it I'd been exploring some caves and had come upon a dark shaft that went deep into the earth. Just as I became aware of the danger, somebody knocked into me and pushed me over the edge. I managed to grab hold of some rocks jutting out around the opening, but they began to crumble almost instantly. I knew I was about to fall into an eternal abyss, and that's when I came to.

I bolted up, breathing hard, suddenly shocked by my ostensible plan. Yes, Carlsbad Caverns was a place where I'd always wanted to go, but I had failed to consider that it would entail descending into the ground in a karst formation much like my mother and Hugh may have done in their final moments, and that there was inherent trauma in that, and why would I be pursuing such an experience, especially after recently contending with a sinkhole myself? Carlsbad Caverns had been nothing more than an abstraction to me. It was as if I'd rushed to visit an aquarium just after my parents had been eaten by sharks, or to an Indy 500 after they'd perished in a fiery crash.

And yet—I'd gone straight to Babe's Barbecue. There was precedent for this behavior. I seemed to be trapped in a continual reckoning between present and past. Was visiting caves a righteous activity despite my personal associations with brittle limestone formations? Was it a tribute, like the ribs? I think what shocked me most was that I hadn't thought of the connection until now, as if my psyche were hopelessly compartmentalized, and in anything I did, I would never achieve any kind of harmony.

It was in this state of flux that I exited from the back of the Dog to purchase some coffee at the café and use the restroom. Imagine my surprise when I noticed a dark gray sedan parked behind me; in the driver's seat, reclining, was Dale! Asleep!

I rapped on the window with a full view of his startle mechanisms— the spasming of the limbs, the whiplash of the neck, the blinking eyes. "What are you doing here?" I yelled through the windshield.

With that, he fumbled with the door and soon stood before me. "Hello, Penny."

"What is going on? Why are you here?"

"Great to see you too."

"Why aren't you flying back?"

"Can we get some coffee first?" he asked, rubbing his eyes.

So we went into the café and picked up some tall cups to go. Then we brought them outside into the morning light and sat under a wind chime. Braids of red chilies festooned the building, and whirligigs in the shapes of roadrunners and cardinals were spinning their wings in planters filled with lavender. The air was cool and carried the faint fragrance of sagebrush and piñon, and our breath came out in plumes. As we sat there sipping our coffees, Dale explained that he'd decided to drive to Carlsbad Caverns after receiving my note. He couldn't get over feeling the van might leave me in a bad situation and said he couldn't pretend it didn't worry him. He said that it wasn't an entirely unselfish decision; he hadn't been ready to return to work, and thought the drive would give him some time to come to terms with what had happened to Burt. When he pulled into this town last night he spotted the van right away.

"I'd been leaving you messages all day. Apparently you never listened to them."

"Why didn't you knock when you got here?" I wondered.

"At close to midnight? You would have been terrified. You would have screamed."

I shrugged. Maybe this was true. "Okay, but why did you sleep in the front seat?" I asked. "Why not the backseat?"

Dale squinted and stared. "Do you actually care where I sleep?"

"It's just, I can't sleep sitting up," I said, keeping my hands on the warm cup.

"Not a problem for me," Dale said. "Is there anything else you want to know?"

I asked what he thought of the drive yesterday.

"Long."

"Did you listen to the radio?"

"Briefly."

"Did you hear the story about primitive kidneys?"

"Primitive kidneys? I don't think so."

"They're growing them in petri dishes in Australia."

"I did not hear that. Did you see primitive kidneys when you were in Australia?"

"No!" I said. "It's not like they're just all over the place."

"No, they wouldn't be, would they? I was listening to a wild-card game, Cubs and Pirates. The Giants didn't make it to the playoffs, but Burt's team did. They're up against the Mets tomorrow."

"The Dodgers?"

"Yes. I'm trying to decide what to do."

"You mean, whether or not to root for them?"

"It would be very difficult for me. But I feel strongly moved to give it a try. Should we drive into the park together?"

He wished to prolong this? The reunion was exhausting my meager resources. My equilibrium, fragile to begin with, was being rocked.

"Dale, when I woke up this morning I came to the realization that I might not wish to descend into any caves right now."

"Oh? Why?"

I hadn't had the chance to tell him anything about the trip to Mount Isa and Camooweal with Arlo, so I embarked on that now. He listened attentively and seemed impressed by the grand finale of the account featuring the ceremonial burning of the posters and the

Land Cruiser falling into the pit and the helicopter ride over the desert.

"Wow," was exactly what he said. Just to make sure he understood, I explained that the Permian Basin, on which we currently stood, and the Cretaceous seabeds of Queensland, had both been filled with exoskeletons and other organic debris that had formed reefs and then been buried by the sands of time, but were permeable and easily hollowed.

"Interesting."

"I didn't use to pay attention to geology when my mother was around, but now that she's gone I've started stepping up."

"I understand," Dale said with feeling, as if assessing what voids had now to be filled in his own life. "So. Did you want to see the caves, or skip it?"

Before proceeding, I felt the need to tell him about my conversation with Pincer the night before, indicating she had continued to act on her impulse to care for radiation victims, including a willingness to provide burial services. Like Storke, Dale seemed stumped by the legal technicalities of the case, saying that there was clearly a lot more to learn.

"I should also mention that I had a nightmare about falling into a shaft in a cave just before I woke up this morning. Somebody bumped into me."

"If we go, I'll do my best not to bump into you," Dale said.

I surrendered to the original plan, and we decided to take the van together into the park. The cavern entrance was near

the visitors' center. We had, thanks to Dale's foresight, two tickets
for a self-guided tour of the Big Room, and we took our place in
line. It was heartening, somehow, to see how many random people
had gathered to see a geological wonder. I hoped I would not freak
out as had Adela Quested in the Marabar Caves in *A Passage to India*,
yet another tragedy of colonial arrogance, and accuse Dale of attacking me. Of course I would not do that! Though the disorienta-
tion wasn't Adela's alone; her companion, Mrs. Moore, had freaked
out as well. She'd hit her head, she'd panicked, and she'd heard an
echo that was so ghastly it revealed to her the meaningless hollow
at the center of all the universe.

Unfortunately, I started to feel slightly wobbly as we stood in line
in the sun. There were so many people around us talking to each
other. Not only were a bunch of simultaneous conversations hard for
me to decode, but strangers seemed to be communicating effortlessly,
which made me feel envious of their ability to strike up connections
like that. Even Dale was at it. To distract myself, I opened the map
of the caves and began to read the names of some of the formations
we were soon to see. There was Baby Hippo. And Rock of Ages and
Fairyland and Santa Claus and Hall of the Giants and Temple of
the Sun, and finally: Bottomless Pit. I decided to keep my distance
from that one, and eventually we went in, and I survived. The formations were spectacular, better than expected. I even said to Dale,
"Is it better than you expected?" "Much better," he said. When we
came out into the light again we made a plan; we'd drive in tandem
to Tucson. He could return his car at the airport there, and we could
go the rest of the way in the van.

That is what happened. That night he sprang for a room at a
desert resort in the foothills of the Santa Catalina Mountains surrounded by saguaros. We had dinner at a fancy restaurant in Tuc-

son and my feelings for him started to come on again, but this drive was dedicated to Burt and that meant staying with the Dog the whole way, not conjuring up a night in someone's room even if such an invitation were to be extended, which it may or may not have been, seeing as my skills at detecting such things were rusty. The next day we talked the whole way back to Santa Barbara and it wasn't as exhausting as I'd feared. He said he wasn't sure what he'd do with Burt's ashes once they came, and I suggested taking them to the San Juan Islands, and Dale thought that was a great idea, and we ended up planning to do that together. He didn't complain about the van once. At one point that day he offered to drive and by that time my legs were tired and I was glad to take him up on it. He bought the gas and I didn't have to sell any minks. He never mentioned the Chore Cow again.

The future looked a little more exciting as we neared Santa Barbara, where Pincer would soon return with all of her problems, where Doris would continue to storm the streets with her FOR SALE signs, and where I'd soon have to remove Arlo's belongings from the Palms and figure out what to do with them. But by exciting, I mean that though I still had many unpleasant tasks facing me, it felt safe to say I had a new friend in Dale, who invited me to visit him, and Kweecoats, of course, up north at my earliest opportunity. He said if I came on a Friday we could go to a fondue place called the Matterhorn and then go see a great improv group called BATS. They performed at Fort Mason, he said. I liked how he didn't try to rush me into anything.

Acknowledgments

I would like to thank Jory Post for his generosity and friendship, to be forever missed. My deepest gratitude to my friends who were willing to read this novel in progress, and who provided great insight and support, including Kathleen Founds, Karen Joy Fowler, Liza Monroy, Micah Perks, Melissa Sanders-Self, Susan Sherman, Tatjana Soli, Peggy Townsend, Meg Waite Clayton, Jill Wolfson, Patricia Stacey, Catherine Segurson, Wallace Baine, Jessica Breheny, John Chandler, Clifford Henderson, Richard Huffman, Richard M. Lange, Dan White, Farnaz Fatemi, and Paul Skenazy. I am very grateful to Emily Forland for her enthusiasm and skills too numerous to name, and to Virginia Smith for shepherding this novel into print with her perceptive suggestions and optimistic take on its earliest pages, along with Caroline Sydney and the other great people at Penguin Press. I am indebted to Donka Farkas, whose companionship and keenness to discuss anything and everything on our loops is nonpareil; to merrymakers Deborah Hansen, Terry Miller, Diana and Kellogg Fleming, Syed Afzal Haider, and Roberta Montgomery; to Pal, the greatest dog that ever was; to my sons Nick and Stuart and my sister, Emily, with love; and finally to Steve, for everything.

The Portable Veblen

A Novel

The Portable Veblen is a dazzlingly original novel that's as bighearted as it is laugh-out-loud funny. Set in and around Palo Alto, amid the culture clash of new money and old (antiestablishment) values, the story follows the charming and free-spirited Veblen and her fiancé, Paul, a brilliant neurologist whose invention launches him into a new social status. Throughout, Elizabeth McKenzie asks: Where do our families end and we begin? How do we stay true to our ideals? And what is that squirrel *really* thinking?

"A story that, beneath an entertaining, clever surface, is deep and wise and complicated . . . *The Portable Veblen* has the feel of an instant, unlikely classic."
—Jeff VanderMeer, *The Los Angeles Times*

 PENGUIN BOOKS